bannas
11/99

A LADY'S CHALLENGE

"If you are so taken with me, Cosmo, then perhaps you had better kiss me."

"Only a rogue would refuse to comply with such a suggestion." Lowering his head, Cosmo pressed his lips to hers. He drew Lucinda more tightly ___inst him, deepening his kiss, tasting the sweetne___ ___ ___ lips.

He had never wanted a woman___

And Lucinda Partridge, twi___ ___ ___essed of no little experience ___ ___ght back. . . .

BOOK YOUR PLACE ON OUR WEBSITE AND MAKE THE READING CONNECTION!

We've created a customized website just for our very special readers, where you can get the inside scoop on everything that's going on with Zebra, Pinnacle and Kensington books.

When you come online, you'll have the exciting opportunity to:

- View covers of upcoming books
- Read sample chapters
- Learn about our future publishing schedule (listed by publication month *and author*)
- Find out when your favorite authors will be visiting a city near you
- Search for and order backlist books from our online catalog
- Check out author bios and background information
- Send e-mail to your favorite authors
- Meet the Kensington staff online
- Join us in weekly chats with authors, readers and other guests
- Get writing guidelines
- AND MUCH MORE!

**Visit our website at
http://www.zebrabooks.com**

THE HUSBAND HUNT

Bess Willingham

Zebra Books
Kensington Publishing Corp.
http://www.zebrabooks.com

ZEBRA BOOKS are published by

Kensington Publishing Corp.
850 Third Avenue
New York, NY 10022

First Printing: November, 1999
10 9 8 7 6 5 4 3 2 1

Printed in the United States of America

To my favorite husband
Frank Bennett Williams II

Prologue

In his five-year absence from London, Sir Cosmo Fairchild had forgotten how suffocating the Orange Street Opera House could be during a packed performance. Even in the dead of winter, the theater's hothouse climate made his linen cravat feel like a noose. His nose prickled, too. The stale scent of too many fashionably dressed bodies in close proximity wafted through his box on a breeze stirred only by ladies' ivory fans.

Hundreds of candles studding magnificent chandeliers washed both audience and performers in unnaturally bright light. Peering down, Sir Cosmo watched with mild amusement as an orange vendor dickered with a stingy fop in a pea green, wasp-waisted, chest-padded coat. This was certainly not the King's Theater or even the larger Haymarket Theater where Prinny and the Carlton House Set heard Madame Catalani perform Mozart's greatest operas in perfect Italian.

On the contrary, the Orange Street Opera House catered to a more egalitarian audience who preferred their entertainment be sung in English, *thank you very much.* The librettos inevitably suffered in translation, but Sir Cosmo preferred the Orange Street Opera House for one reason: it boasted Mrs. Lucinda Partridge as its shining star.

The din below was distracting. Men took snuff and

drank from silver flasks while women gossiped, flirted and quizzed one another with their opera glasses. Cosmo estimated half the audience cared not a fig about the happenings on the stage. He wondered why they bothered attending the opera. Indeed, the only time the entire congregation showed proper reverence was when Mrs. Lucinda Partridge sang.

Undoubtedly, she had a loyal claque. There were those in the audience who leaned forward each time Mrs. Partridge warbled a note. They gasped when she hit her high C. Like Cosmo, their gazes were riveted to her shapely ankles and bare shoulders.

Cast as Julius Caesar, Lucinda Partridge wore a shapeless Roman toga and gold sandals. But her femininity was clearly evident. With her pale skin and golden hair, she was the most lovely female Cosmo had ever seen. He vowed to see Julius Caesar every night that he was in London—as long as Mrs. Partridge sang the title role.

A gentleman seated in the front row, just behind the orchestra, caught Cosmo's attention. He was a hefty, barrel-chested man with a balding pate fringed by thinning, russet-colored hair. As Mrs. Partridge moved across the stage, the man adjusted an incongruously delicate pair of pince-nez spectacles on his bulbous nose.

Cosmo watched. The man tracked the soprano with a hungry stare. He mouthed the words to the aria Mrs. Partridge sang in the second act. To Cosmo's ears, the English lyrics were a murderous rendition of the Italian libretto. But the man in the front row seemed not to notice, or to care. He was fixated on the golden-haired performer.

But, then, so was the gentleman in the box opposite Sir Cosmo's. An impeccably dressed man, this obvious nabob sniffed the fetid air with disdain, though the intensity of his fascination with the soprano rivaled the fat man's. Of all the men in the audience that night, the nob and the fat man watched the soprano with more proprietary interest than anyone.

Eventually, Sir Cosmo returned his attention to Lucinda Partridge. Her soprano voice was mature and agile, sweet and fully nuanced. Her final aria, climaxing the reunion of Caesar and Cleopatra, was sung with such vigor that Cosmo's nape tingled.

Eyes closed, he drank in the sound of her voice. At last, the boisterous underlings were becalmed. As Mrs. Partridge clasped her hands to her bosom and sang the last note of the aria, not a single chuckle or whisper was uttered. Awestruck silence spun out. Then the fat man below blew his nose in a pocket kerchief, and the gentleman in the opposite box shouted, "Brava." After a beat, the audience erupted in a deafening round of applause.

As always, Cosmo's heart grew heavy as the opera drew to a close. The fantasy of the stage, the bright lights, the somewhat absurd costumes, created an atmosphere of otherworldliness that salved his invisible wounds. For a short time, he could forget who he was, a wounded war veteran turned spy, an unlovable man whose heart was scarred and whose leg was shattered by cannon shot, a man whose every attempt at doing something noble and selfless resulted in disaster.

Standing, Cosmo stretched his weary muscles. With a grimace, he tested his right leg, carefully shifting his weight as he reached for his gold-handled walking stick. He glanced at the stage, a scene of pandemonium now that the opera was ended. Stage workers raced to and fro while performers yanked off their wigs and mingled with the audience. Mrs. Partridge disappeared behind a falling curtain.

The thought of visiting her dressing room popped into Cosmo's head. He studied the fat man, who was still daubing tears from his ruddy face. Then he looked at the gentleman in the opposite box, who was already collecting his matronly companion and ushering her toward the corridor. No doubt they would approach the object of their fascination, perhaps offering to take the beautiful singer to dinner, or out for a coffee. It was well known that such liaisons were often formed in the theater and opera world. Mrs. Partridge had probably been offered *carte blanche* by a dozen men.

She's the sort of woman duels are fought over. Exiting his box and descending the stairs, Cosmo supposed that there were many men vying for the affections of Mrs. Partridge. As compelling as her voice and looks were, there was also an indescribable quality about her that transcended skill, beauty, and even talent. There was something about the passion with which she performed, mingled with an almost alarming air of vulnerability, that made Sir Cosmo, and he guessed a hundred other men, want to possess her, protect her, cherish her.

Ah, such was the stuff of fantasies, he mused, pushing through the crowd toward the door that opened into the blistering cold night. He had no *real* intention of ever approaching Lucinda Partridge. Other than to satisfy his physical needs, he had no intention of approaching *any* woman. He simply could not bear a repeat of the heartbreak he had suffered at the hands of Monique Lafleur.

The biting chill instantly penetrated his bones, stiffening his right leg so that Cosmo leaned on his cane more heavily than usual. Ordinarily, his limp was indiscernible. But after sitting still for over two hours, then emerging to an arctic blast, his leg ached, and his gait was crimped.

Carriages clogged the street, and noisy theatergoers crowded the walkways. Tugging the brim of his beaver cap, Cosmo leaned into the cold. A hot toddy awaited at the tavern down the street. Then he would return to his rented quarters in Sutton Row, near Soho Square, not far from the theater, and toss himself into bed.

Suddenly, his spirits plummeted. Whether it was from the cold, or from the memories his aching leg invoked, Cosmo wasn't certain. Perhaps it was the thought of Monique. But that was silly; this melancholy seemed to spring from nowhere. The opera had been satisfying. And being alone wasn't so awful as long as he had his opera, his toddy and an occasional bottle of contraband Bordeaux.

The endless prospect of *sleeping alone,* however, gnawed at Cosmo's soul. The lack of female companionship, warmth and affection—bloody hell, the absence of physical pleasure!—was inconsolably painful. Some nights were worse than others. Cosmo had an inkling this night was going to be a bad one.

A pistol shot cracked the icy air. Instinctively, Cosmo halted, tensed, and scanned his surroundings. The night went eerily silent as pedestrians pricked their ears and searched for the source of the report.

After a moment, the bustle of traffic resumed. But Sir Cosmo remained frozen in his tracks at the corner of the opera house, just where the alley ran behind it. The ground beneath his feet vibrated. Then a horse's hooves sounded on his left. Gripping his cane in his right hand, Cosmo leapt out of harm's way as a horse and rider bolted from the dark alley and galloped west, toward Haymarket Street.

The horse's hooves missed trampling him by a hairs-breadth. Scrambling to his feet, Cosmo muttered a curse and stared after the mysterious figure who had almost killed him. The black-caped horseman disappeared into the night, scattering frightened pedestrians, and eliciting blood-curdling threats from drivers and passengers alike. Cosmo knew he wouldn't recognize the man even if he met him face-to-face.

Brushing off his clothes, Cosmo breathed a sigh of relief. A miss was as good as a mile, he told himself. Slowly, he turned and headed toward a familiar tavern.

A feeble entreaty sounded from the dark alley.

Cosmo stopped, and peered into the darkness.

"Help me . . . help me, please! For God's sake, I'm dying!"

Without hesitation, Cosmo left the well-lit street and walked into the alley, toward the voice. The narrow lane was slippery, wet from melted snow, debris and all manner of foul-smelling things, the origins of which were better left unsaid.

His boots slid along the treacherous cobblestones. "Where are you, man? I can't see a bloody thing!"

"Here, sir, to your left. Here, below you! You're almost stepping on my hand."

A quick scrape sounded. Then a tiny flicker of light materialized, giving scant illumination to the scene. A man, slumped against the back of the opera house, sat at Cosmo's feet. He held a flickering match between his fingers, his legs were splayed out before him, and his shirtfront was covered with blood.

"What happened?" Cosmo took the match and stared into the face of a dying man.

"Did you see his face?" the man whispered.

"The man on the horse? No, I could not identify him if he shook my hand, I fear. Who was he? Tell me, and I will see to it that justice is done."

The man drew a strangled breath. His lips moved, but the only sound he made was a horrible gurgle. Then he was silent, with his gaze fixed straight ahead.

"Tell me, man! You must!" Cosmo cried, gently shaking him.

But it was too late. Cosmo could do nothing save close his eyes and bid him good night. He started to stand, then hesitated. His training wouldn't allow him to leave without performing at least a cursory inspection of the crime scene.

Reaching into the man's waist-coat pocket, Cosmo extracted a ticket stub for the opera, a folded paper filled with snuff, and a few coins. Nothing odd there. On instinct, he opened the man's cape and inspected the lining, quickly finding a hidden breast pocket expertly sewn into the fine black satin.

Inside the pocket was tucked a sheet of paper. In the quickly dwindling match light, Cosmo recognized it as a page from the libretto to *Julius Caesar.* There *was* something very odd about that. Stuffing the libretto and the dead man's other possessions into his own pocket, Cosmo rose to full height. His curiosity was piqued.

But, he reminded himself, a civilian's death—probably the result of a gambling debt unpaid, or the price of having dallied with the wife of a jealous man—was hardly his business.

His business was spying, pure and simple. And this man's murder had nothing to do with Sir Cosmo Fairchild's clandestine activities as an agent for the British Home Office. Besides, he was between assignments at present, enjoying a little rest and recreation after having been in Paris for five years. He wasn't looking for trouble any more than he was looking for women.

Cosmo simply wanted to attend the opera, watch Mrs. Lucinda Partridge play Julius Caesar, drink some very fine wine, and keep a *very low* profile. God knew, he needed a respite from his career as well as from his private life. As he emerged into the hustle and bustle of Orange Street, he inhaled deeply. A hot toddy awaited. That was some consolation.

Then it was off to bed. *Alone.* But it wasn't his singularity that bothered him. It was *loneliness* that made his heart ache and his fists clench with anger.

One

Two Weeks Later

The curtain slowly descended, and the applause died, only to be replaced by the raucous din of a full house scrambling to exit the theater. Behind the velvet screen, as stage workers scurried about and exhausted singers retired to their dressing rooms, Mrs. Lucinda Partridge stood for a moment, exhausted yet somewhat saddened by this inevitable return to reality.

She should be used to it by now. The make-believe ended when the curtain fell; then real life resumed.

Bending to scoop up a handful of flowers thrown at her gilt sandals by admirers, she winced. Playing Julius Caesar required the wearing of painfully restrictive undergarments. She could scarcely draw a deep breath in the bindings that flattened her ample bustline. That she could belt out the lyrics of an aria written for a castrato, with her lungs squeezed into a corset too small for a pair of figs, was an unparalleled achievement in positive thinking and determination.

Straightening, she took strength from the thought that she had been able to pull off this role night after night for the past year. Not another soprano in London could have done it.

With an armload of wilted flowers draped over her

elbow, Lucinda exited the stage, then pushed through the throng of musicians, actors and singers clogging the narrow passageways that wound around a warren of small dressing rooms. Her own room was a tiny compartment filled with racks of gowns, headdresses, Egyptian costumes and elaborate unmentionables. Inside, Lucinda closed the door and pressed her back to it. Eyes shut tightly, she recalled with disturbing clarity the bad news she had received just before going on stage.

"Mrs. Partridge?" A man's voice, low and throaty, intruded like a thief.

Gasping, Lucinda opened her eyes. A man with the thickest, shiniest, shaggiest grey hair she had ever seen sat in a chair on the opposite side of the room. He stood, filling the room with his imposing, broad-shouldered, lean-legged figure. Wearing a dark blue coat and skin-tight buff breeches, he was a breathtakingly handsome man. Instinctively, Lucinda reached behind her, grasping the doorknob.

"I didn't mean to frighten you." The stranger took a step forward, then hesitated, as if uncertain whether his advance would further alarm her. "Please forgive me. 'Twas a mistake to visit you unannounced. I will go, and return another time if you'll allow me."

He nodded, dipping his head in gentlemanly deference, but his eyes, Lucinda noticed, roved the length of her figure. Well, it was hardly appealing, corseted as it was to restrain the fullness of her breasts and the swell of her hips. She thought the Roman toga completely obscured her feminine form.

"Who are you?" Lucinda found herself staring into the stranger's gaze. His eyes, dark, deep-set and heavy-lidded, set her heart to thudding.

"Sir Cosmo Fairchild, ma'am. My deepest apologies for having frightened you." He crossed the room, reaching for the knob that was pressed against the small of Lucinda's back.

She didn't move, and for a moment, the two stood awkwardly, the gentleman unwilling to offend her by wrenching open the door, Lucinda unwilling to step aside allowing him free passage.

"What did you want, sir?" Lucinda's voice was more hoarse than usual after a performance. Strangely, she was reluctant to let Sir Cosmo Fairchild go.

Stepping back, he pinned her to the door with his inscrutable gaze. "I wanted to speak with you. About the opera. About your career. You see, I am a great admirer of yours." The creases bracketing his eyes deepened. "I have followed your career for years."

"For years? Good heavens, you make me feel ancient!" Lucinda laughed girlishly, then flushed, embarrassed by her lack of polish. She was rarely at a loss for words, but this man had an odd effect on her.

His silver hair, shot through with strands of black, fell across his forehead in a most unfashionable manner. Thick black brows accentuated his compelling gaze. "I am hardly a spring chicken myself, dear lady, but I am not as old as this snowy hair would indicate."

She could see that. Lucinda noted the broad span of Sir Cosmo's shoulders, the flat plane of his belly, and the taut muscularity of his legs. His body looked a good decade younger than his face. Aware that she had been caught staring, Lucinda forced a trembling smile to her lips.

When he smiled back, her heart skipped a beat.

"You appear quite healthy to me, sir," she stammered.

"I suspect that your costume belies your youthful figure, as well," he drawled. "Forgive me for being forward, but you are the most voluptuous Julius Caesar I have ever seen."

Releasing a breath, Lucinda moved across the tiny

room, brushing Sir Cosmo's shoulder as she passed. At her dressing table, she sat and studied his reflection in the mirror. Alternately gazing at him and herself, she removed her garland wreath and began to uncoil the tight braids pinned to the top of her head.

" 'Tis the role that was offered me, sir. Paying jobs are few and far between these days, so I must take what I can get. Serious opera is out of vogue, you know, and I don't care for that comic stuff produced across the street."

"You are to be commended, Mrs. Partridge. One has to travel to Italy, it seems, to hear good opera. Your voice, however, makes living in London bearable."

"Have you been to Italy, sir?"

He hesitated. "It has been many years since I have been abroad. Nowadays, one is safer staying at home, what with Boney trampling the Continent."

His gaze followed the movement of her fingers. When Lucinda let her long braids fall down her back, his expression tightened. She knew then that he admired more than her voice.

"And what do you do, sir?" Her curiosity was now fully aroused.

"I am a writer. Which is why I am here in your dressing room. I would like to write a book about a diva's life. I'm afraid, dear lady, that I have chosen you as my subject."

Lucinda let out a hearty laugh. "And to whom do you think you will sell such a book? My patrons don't even have the patience to listen to opera in Italian!"

"Are you suggesting that writing about you is a waste of my time?" Cosmo's dark eyes twinkled.

"No. I understand what it is to pursue one's *calling.*" As she locked gazes with him, a shiver of awareness rippled over Lucinda's bare shoulders.

"You would rather sing than do anything on earth. Well, I would rather write."

"I understand," Lucinda said, in barely a whisper.

He took a step nearer, so that his body was palpably close. Lucinda breathed in the scent of him, slightly briny, thoroughly masculine. Her senses came alive, and her limbs tingled with irrepressible desire. *How foolish,* she thought. Countless men—handsome ones, rich ones, powerful ones—had come through her dressing room, and she had never experienced this sort of arousal before.

Certainly, she had never felt anything like this in the first five minutes she met a man. This was the sort of feeling she usually developed after months of knowing a man, after learning his small habits and predilections, and, most importantly, after ascertaining that his pockets weren't as flat as hotcakes.

Her mind flashed on the figure Ivan Pavlov had scribbled on a piece of paper and pressed in her hand just moments before she went on stage. It was a shockingly low number, representing the balance of Lucinda's accounts. Her contract at the opera house would expire in one month, and Pavlov had not been able to secure a renewal. He had been so embarrassed and hurt for her, he could hardly talk.

Suddenly, Lucinda's precarious predicament flooded her with dread. And to think she was sitting at her dressing table, entertaining erotic thoughts about a total stranger—*a penniless one, no doubt*—while her future hung in the balance.

Drawing one braid over her shoulder, Lucinda unthreaded the golden skeins. "Sir, what precisely can I do for you?" Her voice was far more brusque than she had intended.

"I should like to interview you for my book, use you as research material, as it were. If my book is published, a likelihood you seem to doubt, you will be even more famous than you are now. Your fame may even spread to the Continent, and you would never have to worry about money again."

"I don't care about fame." But Lucinda did care about money, and perhaps the fame would generate some.

"You would be doing me a great favor."

"And in return? My time is very valuable, sir."

"I am afraid I cannot pay you, not much, anyway."

Lucinda brushed through the tail end of her braid. "Then, I am not interested."

Cosmo's gaze flickered. Abruptly, he straightened, his features taking on a harsher cast. The dark eyes, deep-set and liquid, grew cold.

Lucinda's hands moved, but her spine was as rigid as steel. An icy wave of apprehension washed over her. Had she rebuffed Sir Cosmo so thoroughly that he would retreat and leave her in perfect solitude? Again, she felt foolish, this time for speaking so hastily, so abruptly. She didn't really want him to go away. If she had to agree to help him research his book, she would.

"I am sorry for having barged in on you."

As he turned his back, Lucinda's heart leapt. "Don't go."

Tension rippled off his shoulders. Slowly, he pivoted, meeting her gaze in the mirror.

She laid her brush on the table. "Twenty percent of your profits. That's what I want. And I will tell you everything I know about opera, the composers, the performers, even the scandalous gossip and goings-on behind scenes. If nothing else, that will make your book popular among the *ton*. They may not have a taste for opera, but they do love a good scandal."

Reaching out, Cosmo held one of her braids. His fingers tested the golden strands, manipulating them as he gazed in apparent fascination. "Thank you, Mrs. Partridge. We shall begin tomorrow."

She fought to control the emotion in her voice. "Be here at two o'clock, Sir Cosmo. You may escort me to nuncheon, and we will begin our interview."

He smiled a devastatingly handsome, crooked smile that thrilled Lucinda to her toes. Then, with a softly murmured, "Good night," he turned and left. As the door shut behind him, Lucinda realized she had been holding her breath. Exhaling, she nearly collapsed forward on her dressing table. Meeting her gaze in the mirror, she chuckled at her red cheeks and glistening skin. Her arousal had been as obvious as the nose on her face.

Lucinda Partridge would have to make a concerted effort to conceal her attraction toward Sir Cosmo Fairchild, because the last thing she needed to do was fall in love with a struggling writer who hadn't a penny to his name.

No, what Lucinda Partridge needed was something else entirely.

"I won't do it. I have changed my mind. Bloody hell, I should never have walked down that alley!" As he spoke, Sir Cosmo paced the length of a high-ceilinged room in the building that housed the British Home Office. *"And I should never have entered Lucinda Partridge's dressing room!"*

An elderly gentleman sat behind a huge mahogany partner's desk, his fingers steepled beneath his jowls. An expression of weary tolerance pulled the old man's lips into a fleshy pucker.

"But you did, boy, and it's a good thing, too. You inadvertently stumbled onto the single greatest tragedy this agency has ever suffered—the murder of one of our best agents!"

Sir Cosmo frowned.

"Morton Clappford was an experienced operative," the old man continued. "Careful. Savvy. Whoever killed him managed to remove one of our top men. A terrible blow to our intelligence operations, and at a dreadful moment, just when Morton was about to crack a very effective network of French spies. A network no doubt intimately connected to the opera house itself. Ingenious of the French, if I must say so myself!"

"You have not heard a word I said," countered Cosmo. "I won't be used like this, not again. I do not want this assignment."

"Your country needs you, Cosmo."

Suddenly, Sir Cosmo ceased his pacing and whirled. He faced his superior officer with a look of barely suppressed violence. "Christ on a raft! Haven't I sacrificed enough for good old England? Look at me, Sinclair! Five years ago, every hair on my head was black as jet. Now I look like an old man. And I feel like one, too!"

Sir Milburn Sinclair laid his palms on his desk, spreading his fingers and studying them for a moment as if they held great interest. At length, he sighed and lifted his gaze to Sir Cosmo's. "Sit down, and listen to me. You can't blame the Home Office for the fact you fell in love with that woman—"

"That woman has a name," inserted Cosmo, lowering himself into the wing chair opposite Sinclair's desk.

"Monique Lafleur." The older man said the name with a sneer. "Have you had any communication with her of late?"

Cosmo's blood ran hot as he imagined Monique's face. Through gritted teeth, he whispered, "You know I have not said a word to her since I left Paris. In disgrace, I might add."

"You received high marks from this office for your work. Don't be so hard on yourself, Cosmo."

"I was a fool."

"We did not know that Monique was a spy when we assigned you to her case. Not at first, anyway. Then, we made the decision not to tell you—you were too deeply in love with her, by then. It wasn't safe for you to know that."

"You mean it wasn't safe for you. It might have compromised my assignment. Or, perhaps you were testing me."

Sir Milburn nodded. "Don't forget, boy. You volunteered for this line of work. You knew it wouldn't be easy when you did. You must also have known it was no noble endeavor."

Raking a hand through his hair, Cosmo blinked back a hot, angry tear. He brought his emotions under firm control. When he met Sir Milburn's gaze head-on, he was dry-eyed and stone-faced.

"But I had no idea serving my country would destroy my principles so thoroughly. Or that I would feel like such a cad for betraying a woman whom I was foolish enough to fall in love with. Or, blast it all to hell, that I would suffer such disappointment in learning that *she* had played the game much *deeper* and more *skillfully* than I."

"Ah, boy! You have so much to learn. Don't let your experience with Monique sour you on women altogether."

Sir Cosmo gave a rueful grin. "I won't. That is why I am turning down this assignment. Spying on Mrs. Partridge will, I fear, be extremely unpleasant for me."

"Unpleasant?" The old man's voice was mildly chastising. "Do you think your own sensibilities and wounded emotions are taken into consideration when the Home Office taps you on the shoulder to ferret out the most egregious enemy agent in England?"

"I suppose not, but—"

"There is nothing more to say on that subject, sir. We are all aware of your unfortunate experience with Monique; but you succeeded in not blowing your cover, and therefore you are still of great value to our intelligence-gathering network."

"Choose someone else," suggested Sir Cosmo.

"You have all the necessary prerequisites, sir. You love opera, and if I may be blunt, women seem to be inordinately attracted to you. Care to tell me what your secret is?"

Cosmo gave a throaty chuckle. "I learned a few things from Monique that even the Home Office doesn't need to know."

"I envy you, Cosmo. This is a choice assignment."

"This is the very worst sort of deviltry. Spying on an attractive woman. Attempting to learn who her suitors are, and precisely what goes on between them."

"Our man in Moscow says it is a certainty that military secrets are being exchanged at the Orange Street Opera House. He captured a French agent who knew all about it. Interrogated him for nearly a week before he learned the man we're looking for is one of Mrs. Partridge's suitors."

"Why in God's name didn't he find out which one, then?"

"Bloody little French bugger died before he spit out the name."

"So, all we know is that one of the soprano's suitors is passing English military secrets to a French agent. Well, this is a disgusting assignment, isn't it? Insinuating myself into Mrs. Partridge's confidence so that I can learn what sort of pillow talk goes on between her and her lovers."

The old man was silent for a moment. "You have developed a *tendré* for her, then? Already?"

"Of course not." Standing, Cosmo shot his cuffs. A

band of uncomfortable warmth collared his neck. "I don't know her well enough to know what I think of her. But, she is attractive, I'll give her that. And she sings like a bird. You know I've a weakness for opera singers."

"No," drawled Sir Milburn. "I didn't know. But, then, I didn't know you had a weakness for big-bosomed, red-headed foreign agents who are married, either."

With a snort of disgust, Cosmo shook his head. "Monique cured me of that predilection, I assure you."

"Did she also teach you that falling in love with your target is a phenomenal display of poor judgment? I hope so, Cosmo, because I wouldn't want to see you hurt again. And though you were lucky with Monique—lucky in the sense that your very public case of lovesickness didn't get you killed, or worse, didn't jeopardize this office's mission—I wouldn't want to see your emotions get in the way of this assignment."

"Yes, yes, I understand."

Cosmo was eager to depart Sir Milburn's company. He had made the appointment hoping to reject the Home Office's order that he spy on Mrs. Lucinda Partridge, but Sir Milburn had made it abundantly clear that the assignment could not be refused.

"My experience with Monique cured me of many things, Sir Milburn," he said, reaching for the old man's gnarled hand. As he grasped it across the desk, he added, "She has certainly cured me of the ability to fall in love."

A watery twinkle shone in Sir Milburn's eyes. "You should be so lucky, boy. You should be so lucky."

Two

The contrast between his dark, liquid eyes and the silvery grey of his shaggy hair was striking. Lucinda Partridge couldn't stop staring at Sir Cosmo Fairchild over the rim of her teacup. It took all her years of theatrical training to maintain a look of cool composure and ladylike demeanor. Beneath her prim smile and neutral expression was a heart racing with excitement.

Pure physical excitement, to be sure. Mrs. Lucinda Partridge was past the age when she equated physical attraction with love. And she was far too intelligent to believe that just because a man was handsome, he was good-hearted as well. For all she knew, this man was as much a scoundrel as her dead husband. Given his charm, his wit and his incredibly handsome face, she had already concluded, in fact, that he was exactly the sort of man she should avoid.

The hotel restaurant Sir Cosmo chose for their first interview was nearly empty at three o'clock in the afternoon. Lucinda had polished off a hearty repast, then lingered over a dessert of fluffy meringue islands floating in a thick, sugary syrup. Now she sat sipping tea and staring across the small damask-topped table at the writer who proposed to make Mrs. Partridge as famous a name as Mrs. Siddons.

He looked up from the notes he was scribbling. "Are you all right, Mrs. Partridge?"

She started. Having drifted off into thoughts of her own—speculations concerning the texture of his hair, the imagined warmth of his lips against hers—she had failed to hear his last question. "Pardon me, sir. Last night was a difficult performance, and this late nuncheon has made me drowsy. What was that you asked me?"

"I was asking about your admirers. Whether there are men who become obsessed with you, either as an operatic character or as . . . a beautiful woman. You are quite attractive, you know. Surely, there are those men who frequent the theater and who, after watching you perform countless times, imagine that they actually know you."

Lucinda shuddered. "I know the type. 'Tis a form of mental illness, I'm afraid. Yes, there have been several men who have focused their attentions on me and deluded themselves into believing we were in love!"

"Tell me more."

"Presently, there are three men who court me assiduously. One is a wealthy gentryman who owns half the countryside and almost every cow grazing on it. The other is a fabulously well bred lordling. Oh, and, of course, there is always Ivan."

"Ivan?"

"Mr. Pavlov. I do believe he was a count or something in his old country, but in London, he's reduced to translating Italian opera into English. He provides the librettos for our operas, you see. Such as they are."

"Dreadful renditions of perfectly fine Italian opera, I must admit."

Lucinda chuckled, and her eyes met Cosmo's. An unspoken intimacy was exchanged, causing her pulse to leap.

"Have you ever been in love?"

Feigning indignation, Lucinda drew back. "Why, sir! What an impertinent question. What does that have to do with the book you are writing?"

His cheeks darkened. "I apologize if the question seems too personal. My interest in the men who pursue you is purely academic, I assure you."

"Nonsense. What can my private life have to do with your book?"

He frowned. "Everything. You see, there is a very important section of my book devoted to the theatergoers themselves."

Lucinda eyed the writer's earnest expression. His eyes were the very warmest color she had ever seen; it was nearly impossible to doubt him. Yet, experience had taught her that men were masters of deceit. "Why should I trust you? Perhaps you are a bounder yourself, perpetrating this fraud on me just to insinuate yourself into my company."

Sir Cosmo closed his leather journal, tying a ragged string around it to bind the loose pages. Leaning back in his chair, he crossed his long, booted legs in a languid fashion that emphasized his lean physique.

At length, he said quietly, "You may check my references. I should be pleased to furnish you my publisher's name and address. I am quite certain he will vouch for me and confirm my credentials. If you think I am a bounder, I strongly suggest that you do just that. For your own protection and peace of mind."

Lucinda felt like the very meanest sort of fool. "I didn't mean to insult you, sir."

He withdrew a small card from his vestcoat pocket and laid it on the table. "I insist. There is my publisher's name. Please make whatever inquiries you feel are necessary."

"No, truly, I didn't mean—"

"I insist," he repeated in a low, softly spoken tone.

Staring at Sir Cosmo, Lucinda felt her pulse quicken. Not for the first time, she wondered how old he was. His bracketed eyes and creased cheeks were those of a man who had endured much hardship, but his sleek, muscular frame bespoke virility and youth.

She wrapped her fingers around her teacup, not daring to lift the delicate china. Sir Cosmo stared at her mouth with such intensity that Lucinda felt her lips had been scorched. Confusion assailed her senses. Despite the mutual attraction between them, Cosmo seemed aloof and remote. The detachment in his expression was a strange and disturbing paradox to the liquid warmth his gaze produced.

Head ducked, she bit her lip to control her unbidden emotions.

His voice was a near whisper. "We shall continue this conversation at a later date, Mrs. Partridge. I see I have offended you. I apologize."

"No!" She looked at him. "I should like to proceed, Sir Cosmo. It is just that I am not accustomed to sharing such personal information with a stranger. To be frank, my private life is in quite a turmoil. I should think you will feel you are writing a romantic novel, rather than a book about opera, once you have heard it!"

Reaching across the table, he grasped her fingers and squeezed them. His eyes softened, and the corners of his lips quirked. "Now you have piqued my curiosity. I find it difficult to believe a young songbird such as yourself would not have a steady and faithful suitor, or—"

"Protector?"

"I did not mean to imply—"

"No, of course you didn't." Lucinda took a sip of tea and steeled her nerves. Her calm returned. And along with it surged a sense of indignation. "But that is what most people think, isn't it? That if a lady makes her living in the theater, she is a fast woman? Well, it isn't true, sir. I guard my virtue with as much vigor as the beefeaters guard the Crown Jewels."

"You have never been married, then?" Sir Cosmo shifted in his chair, leaning forward, but leaving his journal unopened.

"I am a widow."

"You have been married once, then."

Lucinda's cheeks burned, but she met the man's gaze straight on. "Twice, to be exact."

His bushy brows arched. "I presume the first one died—"

"In a duel. He was challenged by the father of a young woman who claimed he'd defiled her." With a shudder, Lucinda added, "Thank God, the other man was a crack shot. Luciano did not suffer; he never knew what hit him."

"Spared you both a lot of pain," murmured Sir Cosmo.

"I'm afraid not. Unfortunately, my sense of gratitude engulfed my better judgment. I was so thankful to the gentleman who shot Luciano that I married him."

"And how did that marriage end?"

"It is all so theatrical," Lucinda allowed. "I can hardly bear to tell it. But Paulo, in his haste to make me a respectable woman, failed to inform me that he was already married. It seems his wife was in Italy, keeping the home fires burning, so to speak."

"My stars! However did you obtain a license to marry this reprobate?"

Lucinda made a dismissive gesture. "We were married at Gretna Green, dear boy. At least, I thought we were. As it turned out, the marriage was a complete sham, in more ways than one."

"What is your legal status now, Mrs. Partridge?" The lines in Cosmo's face deepened.

"As there was no legally binding marriage in the first

place," Lucinda replied, "there was no need to obtain an annulment. As for my status, I should say the word *disgraced* pretty much sums it up."

"Poppycock," replied Cosmo. "I've never held with the notion that women should be held to a higher standard of virtue than men."

"Do you mean to say that you condone scandalous behavior for both the sexes?" Lucinda felt naughty, talking in such blunt terms with a man she hardly knew.

He laughed. "On the contrary, Mrs. Partridge. I fear I am as boring an individual as you are likely to meet. I don't drink excessively, though I do enjoy good wine, and a hot toddy before bedtime. I don't enjoy gambling above an occasional hand of cards at White's or a game of faro at Watier's. Dear me, I'm afraid my only true vice is opera. I love it."

She could only stare at him, amazed by the contradictions in his personality. Though rough-looking and weather-beaten, Cosmo apparently lived like a monk.

"What do you do to entertain your mind, Sir Cosmo? Surely, there is something—or someone—in your life, other than opera, that makes you truly happy, that makes your heart sing with pleasure?"

He shook his head tersely. "And you, Mrs. Partridge? Dare I ask what makes you happy? Other than singing, of course."

She closed her eyes. The answer was so easy, so simple, that it almost rolled off the tip of her tongue. But she refrained from telling the man about her crusade to help as many young wayward girls and women as she could. She didn't think Cosmo would understand her desire to build a London Women's Shelter where abused women could find sanctuary.

She wasn't certain she could explain it herself, especially in light of her present circumstances. If Lucinda didn't have such a passion for helping her less fortunate friends, she wouldn't be in such a financial pickle right now. She didn't want to admit to Cosmo that she was so desperate for money, she had agreed to allow an unknown scribbler to interview her. She sure didn't want to tell him that she was so eager to raise funds for her women's shelter that she had decided to marry a rich man.

She held her cup to her lips, only to discover she had already drunk the last drip of tea. "I think it is time to go now, sir. I must rest before this evening's performance."

"I have offended you."

"No. I am just tired, that is all. We will continue our discussions tomorrow, if you like." Pulling on her gloves, Lucinda stood.

Instantly, Cosmo was at her side, grasping her elbow, peering into her eyes. A wave of sadness washed over her. Why couldn't she marry a man she was attracted to, a man like this Cosmo? Why was it that the men who always pursued her were either unattractive, insensitive, pretentious or callow?

"Can we continue our discourse tonight?" he asked. "After the opera? I will take you to dinner someplace quiet, where the food is excellent and the wine is passable. Please, Mrs. Partridge. I have a deadline—"

"Oh, all right." She chuckled, surprised by her own reaction to this strange, mercurial man. She was glad he insisted on seeing her that night, even though it would mean an inevitable conflict between her suitors. "But I warn you, sir. I customarily dine with Mr. Pugh on Wednesday evenings, and he will undoubtedly call to collect me after the opera. What excuse shall I make to the gentleman?"

"Have you promised to dine with him?"

"No, but it is routine. He will expect me to be available."

"Is he a serious suitor?"

She nodded.

"Then, it will do him a world of good to find that he cannot take you for granted, Mrs. Partridge. Explain that you have other business to attend to. It wouldn't do to make Mr. Pugh overly jealous, but his ardor will benefit from the realization that someone else has won your attention, if only for professional reasons. He'll realize how much he values your company when he discovers he must spend the evening without you."

Lucinda threw back her head and laughed. Then she draped her arm through Sir Cosmo's and walked back to the opera house with him. They walked slowly, stepping carefully through the littered streets. He held her close, squeezing her arm, almost as if for support. She thought his cane an affectation; it was not uncommon, after all, for dandies to sport ornamental white-thorn canes or fancy golden-headed ones. Indeed, it was quite the fashion and all the crack.

Despite the cold day, Lucinda deemed the warmth of Sir Cosmo's company comforting—and disturbing, too.

There was very little chance of Cosmo's falling in love with Lucinda Partridge. That was what he told himself as he stood outside her dressing room door, awaiting her invitation to enter.

Thoughts of Monique Lafleur had troubled him throughout the afternoon. Unwanted memories of their shared passion had inflamed his emotions to the point he was brimming with pent-up anger. He knew he would never put his heart at risk like that again.

Not only had he been incredibly foolish in falling in love with a target—who had turned out to be an agent herself, no less—but he had behaved like a whipped dog when she dropped him. The humiliation of having been betrayed and rejected burned in his gut even now.

"Come in, darling!" Lucinda's speech was as melodious as her singing voice.

He turned the knob, slipped inside the small compartment and pressed his back to the door. His heart squeezed as he met Lucinda's gaze in her looking glass.

She wore a white dressing gown, cinched at the waist with a length of satin. Seated at her dressing table, her long blond hair falling in lustrous braids down her back, she stared at his reflected gaze in her mirror. Slowly, she unwound a plait and began brushing it out with a silver horsehair brush.

Mesmerized, Cosmo moved across the room, his cane tapping the floor lightly. He stood behind her, watching her expression in the cheval glass.

Her lips parted, and her hands froze at her shoulders. Cosmo longed to touch Lucinda, ached to plunge his fingers in her hair, to bend and press his nose in the crook of her neck. But he didn't dare. Instead, he leaned his cane against her vanity and reached for the brush, removing it from her unprotesting fingers. Then he lifted a strand of gold that hung down her back, and brushed it . . . slowly, lovingly. . . .

Outside the dressing room, the opera house bustled with activity. Feet pounded down the narrow corridor just beyond the door. But inside this tiny room filled with perfumed costumes, feathered wraps, wigs, racks of clothing and rows of slippers, shoes and boots, the world stood still. A heavily charged silence filled the air. And Cosmo was acutely aware of the burning need he felt in his loins as he stood behind Lucinda.

He brushed until the hair in his fingers gleamed a lustrous gold. Then he gently released the remaining braids piled atop Lucinda's head, unwinding the plaits and brushing them one by one.

His body thrummed with desire. The simple act of brushing Lucinda's hair was a greater intimacy than Cosmo had ever expected to share with this exquisite creature. He was pleased by her compliance, but unwilling to press her for more. This was enough, he told himself. This was more than he deserved.

Besides, he reminded himself ruefully, he had no intention of developing an affection for Mrs. Lucinda Partridge.

A knock at the door startled them. Lucinda jumped, and quickly snatched the brush from Cosmo's hand. Color flooded her cheeks as the dressing room door swung open.

Grabbing his cane, Cosmo turned. In the doorway stood the man who stared nightly at Lucinda from the front row. With his fleshy face, pink-rimmed eyes and beefy lips, the man looked as if his features were carved from a slab of uncooked meat. His clothes were impeccably tailored, however, and his gleaming boots, cuffed at the top to accommodate his huge calves, were undoubtedly well made and sturdy, though not extravagantly expensive. In sum, he appeared wealthy but conservative.

Lucinda rose, her shoulder brushing Cosmo's. "Permit me to introduce Mr. Lawrence Pugh. Lawrence, this is Sir Cosmo Fairchild."

Mr. Pugh crossed the room and gave Cosmo a bone-crushing handshake.

"Good evening, Mr. Pugh," Cosmo said. "Mrs. Partridge and I were just preparing to leave. I have invited her to join me for a light supper, and she has graciously assented."

"Oh, she has, has she?" Mr. Pugh frowned slightly. "You haven't forgotten our dinner date, have you, Lucy?"

Lucinda stood between the two men, her hands

clasped tightly at her waist. "I was not entirely certain you would come backstage tonight, Lawrence. Sometimes you don't, you know."

"But I usually do," he replied, without the least rancor.

"Usually isn't always," she said. "Really, Lawrence. You confound me. Last week, you came backstage and took me to dinner, but the week before that, you failed to show. I saw you in the front row that night, and I waited. Waited till I was very nearly famished, but you never came."

"Forgive me, Lucy. I had business to conduct, dearest. And you know that my business takes precedence over everything. It must. I have so many who depend upon me, you know."

With some sadness in her voice, Lucinda said, "Yes, I know that, Lawrence. But I have made other plans for this evening. If you wish, we can dine together next week. If you give me some advance notice, that is."

"What sort of plans have you made?" Mr. Pugh said, his gaze shifting to Sir Cosmo.

Cosmo's grip tightened on the handle of his cane. "We are going to discuss a book I am writing, Mr. Pugh. Mrs. Partridge has kindly agreed to assist me in my research for the project. It involves the London opera scene, you see, a subject on which there is no greater authority than Lu— I mean, Mrs. Partridge."

The fat man rubbed his cleft chin, then scratched his head reflectively. "I see."

"Don't let us keep you from your own dinner, Lawrence," interjected Lucinda. "I have an obligation to spend some time with this gentleman, as I have entered into a contractual agreement with him concerning the profits he will make from his book."

"He's paying you to tell him about the opera, then, is he?"

"It is all on the up-and-up," inserted Sir Cosmo.

"Well, if there is one thing I understand," said Mr. Pugh, pointing at his own chest with a thick finger, "it is the necessary nature of commerce. I wouldn't stand in the way of your earning a living, Lucinda. Are you quite certain this man is legitimate? Have you consulted a solicitor regarding the terms of your agreement with him? I wouldn't want to see you taken advantage of, my little dumpling."

This last term of endearment was uttered with a softening of Mr. Pugh's voice. Indeed, the rotund man's face colored even darker when Lucinda rose on her tiptoes and gave him a chaste peck on the cheek. The top of his head turned scarlet, and small beads of sweat appeared on his upper lip.

"Good night, Lawrence," Lucinda said, leading him toward the door.

In the threshold, he lingered awkwardly until the object of his affection gave him a squeeze on the arm and gently pushed him out the door.

Lucinda sighed heavily as she closed the door. Then she cast Sir Cosmo an inscrutable look as she disappeared behind a tole screen. Within seconds, the white dressing gown was flung over the top of the screen, igniting Cosmo's imagination. A flimsy sheath of muslin appeared next, draped over one of the tole panels, and finally two exquisite silken stockings, each still retaining the phantom shape of Lucinda's curvaceous leg. It was all Cosmo could do to resist crossing the room, grabbing the clothes off the top of the screen and absconding with them.

Clothes rustled and garters snapped behind the screen. Cosmo imagined Lucinda stepping into a linen rail, then struggling with the long row of buttons up the back of her gown.

"Need some help?" he croaked.

She chuckled. "I have learned to dress myself, Sir Cosmo, something every woman should know how to do, but few seem to manage it."

"I confess, I am at a loss as to how you can fasten buttons behind you."

She stepped from behind the screen, clad in an elegant dark brown walking gown with black cuffs and collar. "I am afraid I was unable to fasten all the buttons," she said, crossing the floor. "Would you lend me a hand?"

Pivoting, she presented her back to him, exposing a glimpse of alabaster skin and the most ephemeral slip of muslin he had ever seen.

He rested his cane against the back of a chair, then reached for the row of tiny fabric-covered buttons. His fingers burned at the touch of her skin, and he boldly allowed his touch to linger against her spine as he slowly fastened her into her gown. Lucinda turned her head to the side, and Cosmo leaned close to her, drawn by a force he couldn't quite comprehend, or resist.

Just when his lips were touching her earlobe, when he could smell the sweet perfume of her body mingled with lilac water, the door to Mrs. Lucinda Partridge's dressing room crashed open.

Three

In the threshold stood a tall, aristocratic man impeccably outfitted in the finest garb Sir Cosmo had ever seen.

"Who the devil are you, sir?" Withdrawing a pair of opera glasses from the inside of his bottle green waistcoat, the intruder quizzed Cosmo from head to toe.

"I might ask you the same," replied Cosmo, recognizing the individual who occupied the box opposite his each night. Nevertheless, he introduced himself, extending his right hand as the man stepped forward.

Nathaniel Upham, Lord Wynne-Ascott, intoned his name and title with great pride, slipped his glasses inside his coat, and extended an elegantly gloved hand.

Releasing the buttery kidskin grip, Cosmo reached for his cane. Lucinda distanced herself from him a step, obviously embarrassed to have been caught in a compromising act. Not that anything untoward had been going on. But had a few more seconds elapsed, Cosmo would have kissed her for certain. And judging from the deep color streaking her high cheekbones, he suspected she would have allowed him.

Lord Wynne-Ascott looked from Sir Cosmo to Lucinda with a distinctly unhappy cast to his patrician features. "I rapped on the door, Lucinda. I am not surprised you didn't hear me, however, with all the noise in the corridor. Not to mention that you were otherwise occupied. Perhaps, I should make my apologies and simply bid you good night."

"Oh, please do not go," Lucinda said. "I fear you misunderstand what you have seen."

"The man was standing so near to you, Lucinda, that he was quite literally breathing down your neck. Now, what am I supposed to make of that? Were I more firmly established in my affections toward you, I should call this gentleman out."

"Do you wish to?" challenged Sir Cosmo quietly. His blood ran hot with the prospect of running a sword through this dandy's belly.

But it was apparent that the aristocrat was equally loath to engage in swordplay or dueling of any sort. He blanched at the suggestion of taking his quarrel with Sir Cosmo to the dueling field. Yet, he tried in vain to preserve his dignity.

"I do not wish to make a scandal out of this, sir," he said. "I am certain it was all quite innocent."

"I could not reach my buttons," Lucinda said.

"It is just that, well . . . women such as Mrs. Partridge often do not appreciate the impropriety of certain acts. Having men in their dressing room without chaperones is often overlooked in this environ. Theater people, you know. They get comfortable with one another, and often ignore the mores of society."

"You never protested about the lack of a chaperone when you were alone with me, my lord."

Lord Wynne-Ascott smiled unctuously. "But, dear woman, you are absolutely safe with me. My reputation is beyond reproach—"

She drew in a quick breath, as if to dispute his assertion.

"Therefore you cannot be sullied by my visits to your dressing room," he continued. "Indeed, you have nothing to lose, and only fortunes in fame and wealth to gain, by associating yourself with me."

"Oh, good God!" Cosmo could hardly believe the arrogance with which this man spoke. "What blatant hypocrisy that is, not to mention bad manners, *and* the most convoluted logic I have ever witnessed!"

"It was just a joke, man! Surely, you did not believe that I was serious." Holding up his hands in mock protest, the tall sandy-haired gentleman laughed heartily at his own wit.

No one else joined in. Sir Cosmo simply stared at the man, convinced that the jolly lordling had been quite serious in his commentary, while Lucinda nervously twisted her fingers at her waist. Eventually, Lord Wynne-Ascott fell silent, and the men stared challengingly at each other for an uncomfortable moment.

"Well," Lucinda said at last. "Sir Cosmo and I were just about to leave. My lord, was there something you wished to discuss with me?"

He turned a quizzical expression toward her. "You are leaving? With this man? Tonight?"

She pursed her lips. "Yes. I don't care how improper you believe it is. As you pointed out, I am a creature of the theater world. Apparently, at least in your eyes, that puts me well below the salt. So, I suppose I have nothing to fear from breaking all the rules so rigorously followed by the fine ladies of the *ton.*"

"But, Lucinda, dear, you must observe proper decorum if you are to be my—" The lordling faltered.

"Your what?" Lucinda asked.

"Yes, what was that you said? Were you about to say the word *wife?*" Sir Cosmo queried.

Lord Wynne-Ascott shot him a withering gaze. "I should thank you not to put words in my mouth."

Cosmo, quite certain that *wife* was not the word Wynne-Ascott was thinking of, gestured toward the door.

"Come, Mrs. Partridge, we have reserved a table at a quiet little dining room down the street. You must be starving, so I suggest we make haste."

Lucinda hesitated, her gaze riveted on Lord Wynne-Ascott's stony face. She opened her mouth to say something, but changed her mind and clamped shut her lips. Then, shoulders squared, she swept past him and into the tiny corridor outside. Sir Cosmo followed, pausing in the threshold to turn and look at the startled aristocrat.

"I should think if you wish Mrs. Partridge to begin practicing the fine art of decorum, then you should adhere strictly to the rules yourself."

"How dare you speak to me in such an insubordinate tone!"

"I should start," continued Sir Cosmo, "by knocking on her door before entering her dressing room. I mean, *really knocking.* You might even consider sending a note beforehand to announce your intention of visiting. Which would, of course, allow her ample opportunity to arrange to have a chaperone present."

"I will not be chaperoned with my mistress, you impudent—"

"I am not your mistress," said Lucinda.

"I am afraid that the rules of this little game have now changed," Cosmo said. "You see, I have assumed the responsibility of protecting Mrs. Partridge from wolves such as you—"

"Wolves! Why, I should very much like to call you out!"

Sir Cosmo grinned. "You would very much be mistaken to do so. That is, unless you have a death wish. I am not as agile with the swordplay as I once was, as you can see by this cane; but I am a crack shot with pistols, and according to the rules of dueling, with which I am sure you are familiar, I would have my choice of weapons, given the circumstances."

"And just why have you assumed the role of Mrs. Partridge's protector?" seethed the lordling, his hands balled into leather-gloved fists at his sides. "Have you given her *carte blanche*, is that it? Stolen her from right beneath my nose?"

"So is she a chattel that can be stolen, bartered, bought, or traded?" Sir Cosmo suddenly hated this man, this human mass of tapioca who hadn't a shred of decency in his body.

"You are twisting my words again, you bloody jackanapes. Lucinda, you know very well that is not what I intended."

"He has not given me *carte blanche*, my lord," she replied, with unnerving calmness.

Sir Cosmo wondered why she tolerated the attentions of such a worm. He studied the man again, from the tips of his shiny leather boots to the top of his elaborately coiffed hairstyle. Everything in between—the immaculate buff breeches, white lawn shirt and stiff cravat, the bottle green waistcoat and matching jacket—was crafted from the finest materials in England. Yet, there was something about this man that was distinctly low class.

"Lord Wynne-Ascott," said Sir Cosmo. "I am a writer, and I am currently writing a book about Mrs. Partridge's career as a diva. She has agreed to assist me in my research. Obviously, her cooperation is invaluable to me. I couldn't write my book without her."

"And so you intend to occupy her free time while you are writing your book, sir? Without regard to the fact that I befriended her long before you appeared? Do you think it very fair to me, sir?"

"Have you asked Mrs. Partridge to marry you, my lord?"

"No."

And he never would, thought Cosmo. "Have you announced your intentions toward her?"

"No, I have not. But I have established, shall we say, a precedent. I always visit Mrs. Partridge on Tuesdays and Thursdays of each week."

Reminding the men that she was still a part of this conversation, Lucinda said, "Have you gotten your days mixed up, my lord? Today is Wednesday."

Lord Wynne-Ascott frowned. "I had thought we might add another day to our schedule. . . . I had thought—"

"Had an opening, did you?" asked Sir Cosmo. "A free night with nothing else to do, and you thought you might impose upon Mrs. Partridge to keep you company. Is that it?"

The handsome lord's face turned purple. He took a step forward, apparently so angry that he had forgotten his fear of provoking a duel with Sir Cosmo.

But Lucinda staved off any engagement between the two men. Reaching inside the room, she grasped Cosmo's elbow. "Come, that is quite enough. For my sake, the two of you, I demand that you cease this interminable squabbling. You are both behaving like children, and making me monstrously nervous. And have you forgotten, too, Cosmo, that I am hungry?"

Unclenching his fists, Cosmo looked at Lucinda. Hovering in the corridor, she appeared wan and unhappy. It occurred to him, then, that what had made him so angry about Lord Wynne-Ascott's incredibly selfish attitude must also have had an effect on her. A most unpleasant effect.

Backing out of the room, Sir Cosmo leveled a warning gaze at Lord Wynne-Ascott. If the arrogant lordling thought he could take advantage of Lucinda Partridge, he was mistaken. If he thought he could escape the attention of the Home Office while he passed vital information to French informants, he was dead wrong.

In Cosmo's mind, there was a very real possibility that Nathaniel, Lord Wynne-Ascott, was precisely the man he was looking for.

The dining room of Rule's, in Maiden Lane off Southampton Street, Covent Garden, was nearly deserted, and the scant candlelight emanating from the single taper on the table cast a romantic glow. Lucinda tucked into her meal with relish. She was always hungry after a performance, particularly if she felt she had rendered a good one.

Tonight had been a tremendous success; her final aria had brought the house down. Even the rowdy groundlings, ordinarily too consumed with their own revelry to pay attention to the action on stage, gave her an enthusiastic standing ovation.

"Why did you tell Lord Wynne-Ascott that I was under your protection, Sir Cosmo?"

He looked away for a moment. When he returned his gaze to hers, his dark eyes glistened in the candlelight. For a moment, Lucinda wondered if he would answer.

"Wishful thinking, perhaps," he said finally. "You appeared to be in need of protection at that moment. I apologize, Mrs. Partridge, for overstepping my bounds. 'Twas most inconsiderate of me."

She fell silent, content to savor her dinner in the elegant setting, replete with a violinist who wandered discreetly around the edges of the room. As she dined on roasted squab, perfectly accented with rosemary and thyme, her senses came alive while her inhibitions mellowed. Sipping the fine Bordeaux Sir Cosmo had selected, she closed her eyes with contentment.

His voice was as smooth and seductive as the wine.

"Well, Mrs. Partridge, you certainly don't eat like a bird."

"Birds actually eat quite a lot for their weight, sir. Scientifically speaking, my appetite does rather resemble that of the hummingbird species."

As the efficient waiter whisked Cosmo's plate from the table, Cosmo leaned forward. "Lucinda, your voice was wonderful tonight!"

Heat coursed through Lucinda's veins. Whether it was the delicious food, the wine, the ambience, or the handsome man who was staring at her, she didn't know. "How on earth does this restaurant obtain French wine nowadays?" she asked, unable to tear her gaze from Cosmo's.

A mischievous grin quirked at his lips. "I have a cache of wines that the establishment stores for me. This bottle is from my private collection. I am happy that you like it."

"Umm. You are a penniless writer, yet you keep a private stock of contraband Bordeaux at this exclusive little establishment." Lucinda allowed her gaze to sweep the front of his immaculate black coat. "My dear sir, you do not dress like a penniless writer, either. That coat you are wearing is one of the finest examples of tailoring I have ever seen."

"You have a discriminating eye," he said.

She sipped her wine. "You have chosen your clothes with much discretion so as not to draw attention to yourself. But I have had enough experience with men to recognize a bespoke suit, Sir Cosmo."

"Are we not on a first name basis yet? Lucinda?"

"All right, Cosmo." She felt her pulse accelerate. The gentleman's silver hair, shaggy and unfashionably long, sparkled like snowflakes. Lucinda longed to brush back the fringe that curtained his forehead, but she didn't dare reach across the table. And she prayed that her desire to touch Cosmo Fairchild wasn't as evident to him as she feared it was.

He tilted his head, never allowing his gaze to wander from hers. "I haven't always been poor, Lucinda. I had an allowance from my parents, but when I persisted in my ambition to be a writer, rather than manage the family's Kent estates, my family cut me off. Mother and Father are both dead now, may they rest in peace."

"Were you never close to them, then?"

"They did not understand my need for . . . creative expression. They considered me a ne'er-do-well, a lazy derelict, and they never passed up an opportunity to tell me so."

"So, you are a gentleman by birth and rank, but you have forsaken your family's patronage in favor of a more noble pursuit. Writing." Lucinda's lips quirked in a rueful smile.

His gaze snapped. "Do I detect a note of cynicism in your voice? Do you not believe me? Do you think that I am an aristocrat masquerading as a penniless scribbler?"

"Please don't be angry. I only smiled because your story is so sad . . . and so poignant a statement of the shallowness existing in today's society. Does that make sense?"

His lips softened. "Yes, I suppose it does if one is an artist. Besides, I would much rather see you smile than cry."

"The hardest thing to do on stage is cry," Lucinda said.

"Dear God, I should think it would break my heart to see you weep," Cosmo replied softly.

Lucinda didn't know what to make of this confession. For a long moment, she sat uncomfortably, staring at the handsome writer's mouth and his strong, slightly stubbled jaw. It was difficult to meet his gaze; each time she did, a small tremor of apprehension slithered through her veins.

At last, she found her voice and picked up the thread of their conversation. "To be sure, you look and talk and dress like a nobleman, Cosmo. And you have obviously spent considerable time in Italy, where you learned to love opera and know more about it than practically anyone in London, save the troupe at the opera house and Ivan Pavlov."

He sipped his wine. "Tell me about Ivan Pavlov."

"Why?"

"Idle curiosity. Conversation." He shrugged. "Research for my book."

"He is the theater manager, and he manages my career also. A brilliant man, really. 'Tis his responsibility to translate the librettos into English."

Cosmo shuddered. "And for that act of butchery, he is paid?"

"A pittance. But, as you have demonstrated, the pursuit of one's passion is worthy of much sacrifice. I don't suppose Ivan cares much about money. He inherited a fortune from his family in Russia."

"A nobleman's son pursuing an artistic life? Perhaps I would like Mr. Pavlov, after all!"

Lucinda laughed. "But, he is too serious by half! I have just about written him off my list . . ." She fell silent, having blundered badly. She supposed it was the wine loosening her tongue, but she certainly hadn't meant to speak so candidly in front of Sir Cosmo, a man likely to publish her thoughtless revelations for all the world to see.

As she expected, he caught her slip of the tongue, and refused to ignore it.

"Write Mr. Pavlov off your list? What sort of list are you keeping, Lucinda? Pray, tell. This sounds fascinating."

Lucinda considered lying, but a streak of defiance shot up her spine. She had been telling herself for days that she had no business nurturing an affection for Cosmo, anyway. A penniless upstart who hadn't even the sense to hang on to his family's largesse was hardly the sort of husband she was looking for.

She couldn't afford to fall in love with a writer! If she planned to survive now that her money had run out—if she planned to continue her work with her "girls," as she called them—she needed to marry a wealthy man. And quickly!

Well, there was one sure way to rid herself of Sir Cosmo. And that was to tell him the truth. There was nothing a man hated more than hearing a woman was on a husband hunt. If Lucinda had learned anything in her nearly three decades of living, she had learned that.

"My list of potential husbands," she replied, locking gazes with Cosmo.

Shadows appeared where a second earlier there had been none. Cosmo's face hardened. "List of potential husbands?" he repeated in a hoarse whisper. "So, you are looking for a husband, are you? And I suppose Mr. Pugh and Lord Wynne-Ascott are also on this list?"

"Indeed, they are, sir. You see, I am nearly thirty—"

"Egads!" he said, mocking her. "Pretty soon you'll be wearing false teeth and complaining of the gout."

Her jaw set. "You are making me angry, Cosmo. I hate it when men refuse to acknowledge the truth, that when women lose their youth, they lose their appeal to the opposite sex. You scoundrels are too shallow and silly to recognize that women mature and become wiser and more beautiful as they age. Yet, you pursue these skinny little greenies as if your own vitality depends on how many of them you can fleece before you wear out."

"Whoa! That is an awfully damning indictment—"

"Then, when women worry that they are growing old,

you call them vain. Or accuse them of being fortune hunters. I ask you, Sir Cosmo, how many women your own age have you ever been in love with?"

He raked his hand through his silver hair. Through clenched teeth, he said, "How old do you think I am, Mrs. Partridge?"

She wasn't certain, but she knew that when Cosmo's expression grew serious, or angry, his age showed. Not that it made him a bit less attractive to her. In fact, it galled her that he remained devilishly handsome even as he glared malevolently at her.

"I—I am uncertain as to your age."

"But you have judged me significantly older than yourself, have you not?"

Lucinda was suddenly weary of this topic. It seemed fraught with danger. Not the least of which was the prospect of revealing her own age. She had lied about it so often, she wasn't certain herself how old she was.

"It does not matter how old you are, Cosmo," she said gently. "You are a very handsome man. And you prove my point, you see. Men invariably grow more attractive as they age, as their experience is etched into their faces, as their eyes begin to reflect all that they have seen."

"And what does the reflection in my eyes tell you?" he asked, leaning forward, sliding his hand across the table to grip her fingers.

His touch sent a thrill through her body. Yet, his stare held such dark intensity, Lucinda shivered. What this man had seen, she didn't know. But, whatever it was, it frightened her.

Reluctantly, she pulled her fingers from his. "We came here to discuss the opera, sir. We have once again strayed far from our intended subject."

"Yes, and this conversation has become rather tedious," he said tersely. "I propose to take you home. Perhaps we can resume our interviews tomorrow."

Not wishing to commit herself, Lucinda merely lifted her brows in response. The carriage ride home with Sir Cosmo was as quiet as a tomb. They had little to say to one another. Lucinda was quite certain she had offended the handsome writer, not just by admitting she was looking for a husband, but by suggesting he was of an advanced age, as well. She might have tried to convince him how handsome he truly was, but to do so would have been contrary to her purposes.

After all, she had firmly concluded that Sir Cosmo Fairchild was not an appropriate prospective husband. He was too difficult to communicate with—they had had several interviews and hadn't even discussed her life as a diva. He was too mysterious by half—his dark gaze half scared her to death. And he was too poor to help her with her charities.

She barely afforded him a glance as she turned her key in the door and said good night. Cosmo Fairchild was the exact opposite of the sort of man Lucinda Partridge was looking for. She trudged up the two flights of stairs to her apartment with a troubled heart.

Lucinda had rented these quarters because they were near the Orange Street Opera House and unusually clean for the Haymarket theater district. Her rooms—a small sitting room and bedchamber—were drafty and lacked windows, but they were blessedly free of vermin and quite cozy after Lucinda decorated them with colorful quilts, plush cushions and delicate lace doilies.

What Lucinda prized most about her home, however, was the discretion of her neighbors. When Lucinda's homeless friends knocked on her door at all hours of the night, no one complained. When young girls wear-

ing entirely too much rouge, and not nearly enough
clothing, flitted up and down the stairwell, no one in
the building inquired whether Lucinda was running a
brothel. No one threatened to report her to the Bow
Street runners. Which made her tiny apartment a safe
haven, a retreat that Lucinda wouldn't have traded for
the Taj Mahal.

She unlocked the latch on her door and pushed it
open. Stepping inside, she stood still a moment, allowing
her eyes to adjust to the darkness. Slowly, the shapes of
her furniture, a rickety camelback sofa, and a second-
hand Empire chair, came into view. Pushing her door
closed, Lucinda leaned against it. She closed her eyes,
weary and overwhelmed with confusion. Sir Cosmo had
rattled every last one of her nerves, and she craved a
cup of tea.

Dropping her shawl and reticule on a settee, she
moved about in the blackness, lighting a taper, then
touching the flame to the wicks of a branch of candles
situated on her mantelpiece. Quickly, she made a small
fire in the hearth, heated a kettle of water, and brewed
a cup of weak tea. She drank the soothing liquid in her
sitting room, her bones slowly warming to the crackling
fire, her stomach settling as she unwound.

At last, she rose, stepped out of her slippers and
grabbed the candelabra perched on the mantelpiece. A
golden circle of light illuminated the bedchamber as she
padded across the threshold. She put down the heavy
silver object and quickly undressed herself, grinning wistfully as she deftly unbuttoned the row of buttons down
her back. As flexible as she was, she had never had any
trouble fastening or unfastening her clothes. Asking Sir
Cosmo to assist her in dressing had been a blatant ruse
to feel his touch on her skin.

What a fool I am! she thought, stepping out of her
gown and unlacing her undergarments. She grabbed the

flimsy night rail that was draped over the screen in her corner and threw it over her head. Then she flounced into bed, landing hard on what felt like a sack of potatoes.

Lucinda's voice caught in her throat as the object beneath her covers moved.

"Ooof!"

It grunted, too, and rolled beneath her while Lucinda lurched for the candelabra. She held the candles aloft, watching a mass of red curls froth on her pillow. As the body writhed and moaned, a freckled face, badly stained by bruises and dirt, appeared in the dim light.

"Clarissa, what are you doing here?" Lucinda sat on her heels in the bed, staring at her unfortunate friend.

The bloated face frowned; the puffy eyes squinted into the candlelight. When the young woman spoke, a mouthful of missing teeth was apparent. Yet for all the abuse this face had endured, an air of youthfulness survived. Lucinda's chest squeezed as she realized Clarissa had been beaten up—again.

"Sorry, Miz Partridge. But I used me key, just like ye tole me I could. If'n I was in trouble, that is. And I was. In trouble, I mean."

"Yes, I can see that. Care to tell me what happened this time?"

"Nothin' out of the ordinary, luv. Same thin' as always. Me companion wants to be a sharpster and take his pleasure widdout payin'. A girl what works for a livin' like me can't afford such as that—even if the man was a good-looking bit 'a blood . . . know what I mean? I ain't in the charity business, not like ye."

While Clarissa spoke, Lucinda placed the candles on the nightstand, then gathered a washbasin and facecloth. It was difficult to discern the dirt from the bruises that decorated the girl's face and neck. Complicating the matter was the fact that some of the bruises were obviously new, while others were old and fading. Clarissa was no stranger to violence.

"I'm not certain I know what you mean," replied Lucinda at length. "Was the man without blunt to pay you, then; is that what you're saying? Or did he simply misunderstand the nature of the transaction?"

"Coulda misunderstood, I suppose. He seemed a bit shocked when I named me price." Clarissa winced as Lucinda applied a bit of salve to her split upper lip.

"Can you describe the man's appearance, Clarissa?"

The girl rolled her gaze to the ceiling. " 'Twas dark in the alley, and I don't know if I got a good look at 'im. But, he had whiskers, that much I knew. They chafed me—"

"All right, then, he had whiskers. Was he tall, short, thin, fat?"

"No," answered Clarissa. "Medium-sized, I'd say. In all regards, if ye know what I mean."

"Yes, I'm quite certain I do," Lucinda said with an involuntary shudder. "Well, you'd better start concentrating on providing a better description of the man to the authorities, Clarissa. They'll want to know what he looked like, and any other distinguishing characteristics you can provide."

"The authorities? Are ye out of yer mind, Miz Partridge? I can't go to the Bow Street runners, not with a complaint such as this."

"Why not? You're a citizen just like everybody else—"

"Oh, I am, am I? Fergive me fer soundin' rude, missus, but have ye forgotten what I do fer a livin'? Just like everybody else, ye say? Well, damme, if that's the case, what am I doin' with a split lip and a handful of hair pulled outta the back of me head? Ye don't think the other girls at Almack's will laugh at me, do ye, when they see the bruises on me neck and shoulders? Oh, la! I couldn't bear it!"

"No need for sarcasm, Clarissa." Lucinda put away her washcloth, then reached for the other woman's hand. She held it in her own for a moment, staring at the difference between her pale skin and Clarissa's dirty fingers. Yes, there was a vast difference between the two women, and it was an injustice that pierced Lucinda to the core.

"Clarissa, you can stop, you know."

The prostitute made a derisive sound. "And who would feed me? Who would feed that lousy drunkard of a husband I got to keep care of?"

A surge of anger rose in Lucinda's breast. "You could get a job and feed yourself, damme! And as for that lousy husband of yours, he can just look after himself. It's high time you quit worrying about that man. He's been nothing but trouble to you since the day you met him. He's dragging you into the mire with him, and you're letting him do it. You are not powerless, Clarissa. There are people who can help you."

For a long moment, neither woman spoke. Clarissa turned her head on the pillow while a single tear rolled down her cheek. When she finally spoke, her voice was as rusty as an old saw.

"I don't know why ye bother with me, Miz Partridge. I'm no good, and never will be. Haven't got the courage to walk out on my old man, and haven't got the brains to get a skill so's that I can get a decent sort of job. This is all I'm cut out fer, really. If ye want me to leave here and never darken yer doorstep again, Missus Partridge, just say so."

"You're not going anywhere. At least for the night. In the morning, we'll figure out what to do next."

Four

From his private box, Cosmo watched the performance on the stage, the disdainful-looking aristocrat opposite him, *and* the fat man in the front row. Mr. Pugh and Lord Wynne-Ascott, it was clear, could not tear their gazes from Lucinda's bosom.

Cosmo sympathized. Despite the shapeless toga her role required, Lucinda's roundness could not be concealed. Even for a trained spy, it was nearly impossible to study Pugh and Wynne-Ascott when Mrs. Partridge was on stage.

But he was, he reminded himself, duty bound to crack the spy ring operating at the opera house. Thus, Cosmo's attentions invariably returned to Nathaniel Upham, Lord Wynne-Ascott. Interestingly, the nobleman had hardly watched a minute of tonight's performance. He had spent half the night chatting with his matronly companion, and the other half eyeing a particularly handsome woman in the third row down below.

Lucinda's applause was rousing, especially for a weeknight. And especially given that her voice lacked its usual volume and strength. Of course, Cosmo doubted that most of the patrons below could detect such a subtle thing as a few missed notes, a scratchy throat, or a shrill aria, but, after listening to Lucinda's voice for over two weeks, he could. Cosmo knew Lucinda's range as well as he knew the back of his hand. For him, it was painfully obvious that she was having an off night.

To the love-struck Mr. Pugh in the first row, however, Lucinda's performance was no different than it had been every other night—simply glorious. The fat man yelled, "Brava! Brava!" till his own voice wore out.

Cosmo wondered if the soprano was sick. Or whether she had failed to have a restful night. Or whether she was angry after their conversation the previous night. Lucinda must have sensed his disapprobation when she had said she was looking for a husband, and had narrowed her field of choices down to three men. She had surely sensed his anger when the subject of his age arose.

Perhaps he was too sensitive on the subject of his age. But his grey hair and his awkward gait made him extremely self-conscious. Truth be known, he hadn't felt *attractive* since Monique had cast him off.

Nor had he felt *worthy* of a woman's love. Hadn't Monique Lafleur told him, perhaps not in words, but certainly in her actions, that he simply wasn't good enough for her?

Not good enough. Those were the exact words used by Cosmo's mother when she announced that he was disowned. She had said he was unworthy of his birthright because he refused to follow in his father's footsteps. And because he refused to marry his second cousin, that horribly horsey-looking girl who lived in Kent and whose family was worth a fortune.

It was as vivid as yesterday. Cosmo had joined the military, got himself shot in Spain, then returned to London. The Home Office recruited him and dispatched him to France. There, he had been assigned to meet Monique Lafleur and wheedle whatever French military secrets he could from her. Considering that her husband was Masséna's most trusted confidant, that shouldn't have been difficult.

After his disgrace in Paris, he had returned to London to lick his wounds and await his next assignment. His career as a writer was a complete fabrication.

The lies Cosmo told Lucinda gave him a shiver. That he was insinuating his way into her life and possibly her heart made him feel like the worst rogue. Staring at the stage below him, Cosmo wondered what sort of man he really was. And then the answer came to him in the memory of his mother's voice. *He was unworthy.*

Rising, Cosmo muttered an oath. His leg hurt. His head hurt. Most of all, his heart hurt. But there was nothing for it. He had a job to do, and he would do it. For, despite his mother's constant insistence that he was good for nothing—or perhaps because of it—he was a man determined to finish what he started.

Nothing would have pleased Cosmo more than to tell Sir Milburn Sinclair to find someone else to ferret out the spy at the opera house. Someone else could fall in love with Lucinda Partridge, for all he cared. But it was Cosmo who had been given this assignment because he was the best man suited for it. It was Cosmo who had a way with the ladies, as Sir Milburn put it, and it was Cosmo who would seduce a woman just to hear her secrets. Never mind that he would get his heart broken in the bargain. He was a loyal Englishman, and he wouldn't shirk his patriotic duty.

Pushing his way through the crowded corridors, he steeled himself for his meeting with Lucinda. Singers and stage workers rushed past, their babble a prickly annoyance to his senses. Was he unhappy by nature? he wondered. Was there something terribly wrong with him for resenting other people's happiness? Why couldn't he be happy? Why couldn't he be in love?

He knocked on her door.

"Who is it?"

Cosmo's heart quickened. Touching the flimsy wood

frame of the door, he was shocked by his own reaction to the mere sound of Lucinda's voice.

" 'Tis I. Cosmo," he said, surprised by the throatiness of his reply.

A latch turned, and the door swung inward. "I have decided to be more careful about keeping my dressing room door locked. After last night, when both Lord Wynne-Ascott and Mr. Pugh came tumbling in unannounced—"

"I applaud your good thinking, madam," said Cosmo, stepping over the threshold and closing the door behind him. He turned the latch, insuring that there would be no more surprise visits from Lucinda's suitors. Which was absurd, given that it was her suitors he should be interested in.

"Please excuse me while I change from this costume," Lucinda said, disappearing behind the screen. She spoke while she undressed, casually draping her toga, her undergarments and small clothes over the screen.

A lacy garment, something that obviously cupped Lucinda's ample breasts, was flung over the edge of a tole panel. Cosmo's gaze fixed on it, and his throat constricted.

"What did you think of tonight's performance?" she asked.

He hardly knew where to look. At the screen? At the items of clothing being tossed over it? At the tiny cracks between the panels where he could spy disturbing glimpses of flesh and satin and lace?

"Cosmo? Are you there?"

"Yes! Tonight's performance? Well, dear . . . I mean, Mrs. Partridge, you were not in top form. But, you were spectacular nonetheless."

She chuckled. "You are kind, Cosmo. I sounded like a sick cat tonight."

"Are you feeling ill?" The concern in his voice was

evident. Cosmo cringed. He sounded like a lovesick schoolboy and he knew it.

"No, just tired. I confess I didn't get much sleep last night."

"Oh?" A single stocking, a sheer, nearly white diaphanous thing, floated over the side of the screen. Cosmo yanked at the suddenly suffocating collar of his shirt. His loins tingled with awareness as he anticipated the materialization of the stocking's mate.

It drifted through the air, settling over the edge of the screen like a dream.

"Something bad happened to a friend of mine, a young woman named . . . oh, well, it doesn't matter what her name is, does it?"

"On the contrary. Names matter very much. It is said that the sweetest sound on earth is the sound of one's own name being called."

"That is very true, Cosmo. And you are right. Clarissa's name is important, and so is she. How astute you are. Well, at any rate, Clarissa suffered an unfortunate accident last night, and I spent the remainder of the evening administering to her injuries."

"Good heavens, it was nearly two in the morning when I left you, Lucinda! Don't tell me you went out after that. Why, 'tis dangerous for a single female to roam about Town after dark . . . and to think I told that horrible bounder Wynne-Ascott that I was in charge of protecting you. I didn't do a very good job, did I, if I allowed you to play nursemaid in the middle of the night without an escort!"

"You don't understand, Cosmo, dear."

He could see her lift her arms, could see the tumble of white cotton as she pulled it over her head and tossed it toward the top of the screen. A slip of cotton, some sort of petticoat, only shorter, with dainty shoulder straps and satin lacing up the front of the bodice, hung over the tole panel.

Cosmo had nearly forgotten what Lucinda was talking about. "No, I don't understand. Why don't you explain it to me?" he whispered, moving slowly toward the screen.

He leaned heavily on his cane, inching his way toward that scrap of lace and muslin. He moved slowly, guiltily, as if drawn by an irresistible force. Standing before the screen, he transferred his cane to his left hand and reached with his right. His fingertips brushed the gauzy material, then clutched it, bunching it in a fist. The light airiness of it made him dizzy. The softness of it made his pulse leap.

It was still warm from Lucinda's body. Cosmo drew it over the edge of the screen and held it to his nose. The scent of lilac, mingled with an earthy undertone, tingled in his nostrils. He closed his eyes, inhaling deeply, drunk with the overwhelming sensation of physical awareness.

"Why, Cosmo! Whatever are you doing?"

His eyes flew open. Lucinda, fully dressed in a conservative dark-blue walking gown, stood with her hands on her hips and her head tilted. She stared at the chemise in his hands, then at him. Her question was quite rhetorical, of course, because it was obvious what he was doing.

No sense in trying to deny it, he reasoned. "It smells . . . quite wonderful."

She lifted her brows, but said nothing. Color flooded her cheeks as she reached for the crumpled undergarment.

Cosmo released it. "I do apologize, Mrs. Partridge. That was a boorish thing to do. And now I have abused your confidence. I would not be at all surprised if you refused me entrance in your dressing room from this moment forward."

Her lips made an O shape, and her lashes flickered against her pale cheeks. "I suppose there is no harm done . . ."

"I couldn't help myself."

"Couldn't you?" Her voice was soft and breathy. Clutching the chemise in her hands, she stepped closer to Cosmo, her chin tipped upward, her gaze searching his. "Were you that overcome by a scrap of muslin?"

"By a scrap of muslin that you had worn, dear." His heart galloped. Where to put his cane? He leaned it against the screen and opened his arms to her.

She stepped into his embrace, dropping the chemise as she pressed her body against his chest. "If you are so taken with me, Cosmo, then perhaps you had better kiss me."

"Only a rogue would refuse to comply with such a suggestion." Lowering his head, Cosmo pressed his lips to hers. He drew Lucinda more tightly next to him, deepening his kiss, tasting the sweetness of her lips.

He had never wanted a woman so badly.

And Lucinda Partridge, twice married, and possessed of no little experience with men, wanted him right back. Her insides melted as Cosmo's breathing grew more ragged, his kiss more urgent. She allowed herself to reach up and brush a few strands of silver hair from his brow, a brow she noticed was deeply furrowed. Then she pressed her palms against his rock-hard chest and took a step backward.

His eyes turned black, but his lips—so compellingly erotic that Lucinda had to suppress the urge to touch them—twisted in a bitter, unkind, smile. "I find myself constantly apologizing to you, Mrs. Partridge. I am not ordinarily so impulsive. Perhaps it is, as Lord Wynne-Ascott suggested, the theater atmosphere that causes a gentleman to forget his manners."

The cold edge in his voice sent a shiver up Lucinda's

spine. Was he suggesting that because she was an opera singer she was any less virtuous than the ladies who frequented Almack's, or poured tea in their parlors every afternoon at four o'clock?

She met Sir Cosmo's penetrating stare, but this time, instead of arousing her passions, his cold gaze merely steeled her nerves. She was right to put a halt to any further intimacies; this was a man quite unsuitable to be her husband. And she couldn't afford to dally with anyone who was not ready, willing and able to help her and, by extension, her little band of misfits. Clarissa needed her more than ever.

And there were hundreds of Clarissas in London who needed help, too. Organized help. A place to go when their husbands tossed them in the streets or their customers beat them. A haven where women—rich and poor alike—could turn for shelter when their men mistreated them.

But Lucinda couldn't build such a place without money. And since she had none of her own, she needed a wealthy husband who was generous enough to finance this shelter. If she fell in love with Sir Cosmo Fairchild, he might offer her a few moments of physical pleasure. Or a few *hours*, judging from the looks of him. But *her* pleasure was unimportant. What Lucinda needed was money to finance her dreams. And the way to get that money was to marry the right man.

In the meantime, Sir Cosmo, by offering her twenty percent of his royalties, might at least provide enough money to pay for a roof over her head, for Clarissa's medical expenses and for the food Lucinda regularly gave to the girls who depended upon her. Supporting a dozen or so fast women required quite a bit of capital. It was no wonder that huge fortunes had been squandered by dandies and bucks who routinely collected paramours and lovers. Supporting women was an expensive hobby, Lucinda had discovered.

"Shall we adjourn, sir?" Lucinda smiled sweetly, desperate to avoid alienating Sir Cosmo completely. For the first time in her life, now that she had determined to build a London Women's Shelter, every man she looked at seemed to have a price stamped on his forehead.

As she donned her ermine-lined cloak and black leather gloves, she glanced at the impecunious writer. Why couldn't he have got along with his parents? she wondered. Then, he would be rich and she could allow herself to fall in love with him.

Gripping his white-thorn cane, Cosmo stiffly crossed the small room. As he pulled open the door and Lucinda swept past him into the corridor, he said, "You are a vexing woman, Mrs. Partridge."

She pretended not to hear.

Turning sideways, Lucinda carefully dodged the theater people streaming through the narrow passageways behind the stage. It would be another hour before the opera house was empty of all the performers and behind-the-scenes workers. Checking the scenery, preparing the stage for the next performance, cleaning and putting away costumes would go on for some time yet.

She allowed Sir Cosmo to move around her and push open the back door that led to the alley behind the opera house. A gust of icy wind sliced through her cloak and gown like a knife. Stunned, she stumbled back a step and, realizing she was trampling someone's toes, looked over her shoulder at Mr. Ivan Pavlov.

The bearded man, clad in black breeches and a fine lawn shirt with flowing sleeves and an elaborately tied cravat, caught her arm and steadied her. "It is too cold for you out there, babushka!"

Sir Cosmo, drawing the door shut, grasped Lucinda's other elbow. "Are you all right, Mrs. Partridge?"

Supported on either side by Cosmo and Ivan, she felt a little foolish. "Of course! I didn't expect that blast of cold air, that is all. It is stifling hot on stage beneath those chandeliers, and my dressing room is nearly as stuffy. I'm afraid the sudden change in temperature put me off my mark a bit."

"I shall buy for you a mink coat," Ivan said, his English heavily accented.

"Oh, Ivan. You have bought enough for me." Indeed, the Russian lyricist had been extremely generous, courting her with gifts of fur caps, muffs and even the ermine-lined coat she wore that evening.

"Until then, a little vodka . . . it will warm your blood!" Ivan tightened his grasp on Lucinda's arm, as if to lead her toward his own offices where a ready stash of vodka and caviar always awaited.

"Ivan!" Lucinda wrested her arm from his grip. "You have not been introduced to my friend, Sir Cosmo Fairchild."

The Russian looked at Cosmo as if he hadn't noticed him before. Which, of course, was impossible, thought Lucinda. How could anyone miss noticing Cosmo Fairchild's dark gaze and silver hair? He was a most imposing figure, indeed.

Releasing Lucinda's elbow, Cosmo shook Ivan's hand. "If I recall correctly what Mrs. Partridge told me, you are the lyricist who translates the Italian librettos into English."

Ivan pulled a long face. "You call it English. It is garbage!"

"Ivan!" Lucinda touched the Russian's arm. "Your words are beautiful. Everyone thinks so."

"They are beautiful when they come from your mouth, my sweet one. But Italian opera is not opera when it is sung in English. It is tragedy, this English refusal to attend Italian opera. And so we translate for the . . . what is the word?"

"Papersculls?" Lucinda suggested.

"Yes! The papersculls who would have an opera butchered rather than learn a little Italian!"

"Then, why do you do it?" Cosmo asked.

"Because I love opera!" The Russian's pale-blue eyes sparkled, and his hands gestured wildly in the air as if he were conducting an orchestra himself. "I will do anything to work in the opera, even if it is to work in this cheap arena, which is a poor excuse for an opera."

"It's not the King's Theater," admitted Lucinda.

"No," agreed Cosmo. "But there is no place in London where opera is greeted with as much enthusiasm. That is why I chose this place when I decided to conduct an in-depth study of the London opera scene."

Ivan's brow shot up. "In-depth study? You are student of opera, perhaps? An aspiring tenor, or baritone?"

"Hardly. I am writing a book about Mrs. Partridge's life as a diva. She has kindly agreed to assist me."

"Is your book . . ." The Russian's hands made circles in the air as he searched for the correct words. "How do they say? Is it a scandal paper?"

"On the contrary. I plan to publish only the truth."

Ivan nodded. "Then, you must listen very closely to Mrs. Partridge. For she tells only the truth!"

Lucinda chuckled. When Ivan wanted to be, he was irresistibly charming. "As writers, you two seem to have found some common ground. Perhaps, Cosmo, you should be interviewing Ivan, and not me!"

Smiling, Cosmo took her arm again. "Forgive me for saying so, Mr. Pavlov, but I would far rather interrogate a pretty lady."

"I am not offended!" The Russian jabbed the air for emphasis. "You are a wise man, Sir Cosmo. I could not agree more. And may I remind you, Mrs. Partridge, that you have a performance tomorrow night, and you must protect your delicate little voice. So, do not permit this curious writer to keep you out very late!"

Lucinda patted Ivan's arm. "You must have noticed my voice was a trifle scratchy tonight. Oh, dear. I shall be certain to drink nothing but hot tea tonight, Ivan."

"A little vodka would be all right," he replied, leaning over to deliver Lucinda a peck on the cheek.

Cosmo pushed open the door again; but this time he clung tightly to Lucinda's arm, and they stepped into the night with Ivan calling out well wishes behind them.

Inside Cosmo's rented carriage, he turned to Lucinda. "A very charming man, that Mr. Pavlov. And is he on your short list of suitors? Um, babushka?"

She was grateful for the darkness, as she felt heat diffuse her cheeks. "Yes, he is. Along with Lord Wynne-Ascott, and Mr. Pugh."

Cosmo leaned back against the squabs. "What an interesting array of potential husbands you have assembled. An insufferable, stuffed-shirt aristocrat—"

"But Lord Wynne-Ascott is excessively generous. You wouldn't believe what he has offered me if I would—"

"If you would what? Become his mistress? But, you are holding out for the position of wife, are you not? A most prudent business move on your part, Mrs. Partridge. I applaud you."

She inhaled deeply. "I will not allow you to offend me, Sir Cosmo. You have no knowledge of my motivation and therefore are in no position to judge me."

After a moment, he replied softly. "I am in no position to judge, that is true."

"As to the other men on my list, as you call it, they include Mr. Lawrence Pugh, who has made a fortune in cattle and dairy farming."

"And appears to be no stranger to the dinner table, himself," noted Cosmo.

"But he is monstrous kind. Very good-hearted. La, if I were to marry him, I do believe he would let me do whatever I wanted."

"Sing in the opera?"

"Perhaps. Or simply be a housewife."

"I cannot envision you giving instructions on how to polish the silver, or fretting over whether nanny is giving Junior too much tapioca and causing him to be fat. He would be fat, you know. Any children you have with Mr. Pugh, that is. Egads, I don't think I've ever seen a bigger—"

"That is quite enough, Cosmo," interrupted Lucinda. But Cosmo was right. Pugh was fat, so fat that Lucinda didn't know whether she would be able to consummate her marriage to him, even if he did offer for her hand. Which he certainly would if she gave him any indication his suit would be welcome.

"Mr. Pugh is very sweet," she said in his defense.

"Yes, and Mr. Pavlov?" Cosmo inched forward on the bench seat of the carriage as it rumbled to a halt.

Grasping his hand, Lucinda stepped out carefully. On the street, she faced Sir Cosmo. "Ivan Pavlov is a fine gentleman, artistic, talented and the most intelligent man I've ever met."

"Well, that is a high recommendation for the man. And he has all that Russian family money. Doesn't hurt that he is rich, eh?"

"It doesn't hurt," said Lucinda.

"You mean his family didn't disown him when he announced his intentions to become an opera fanatic, rather than manage the family estates, wed the family virgin and perpetuate the family name, fortune and distinctive physical characteristics?"

The torchlights on the carriage illuminated Sir Cosmo's

expression. Once again, his mood had changed from lighthearted to bitter. In a flash.

"My, but you are an unhappy man," Lucinda said.

"That, Mrs. Partridge, may be the understatement of the century. Come, now. Shall we dine and talk of something more pleasant?"

"Like the opera?" she asked, taking his arm as he turned her toward the small hotel he had chosen.

After a pause, he replied, "No, not the opera. We can talk about the opera anytime. Tonight, Mrs. Partridge, I should like to talk about you."

Lucinda felt Cosmo's hand tighten on her arm. His nearness—the sensation of his leg brushing against hers as they walked—was disturbing. In the dim starlight, she could not make out his expression, but she saw the tight set of his lips. Tension surrounded this man. Did he never relax?

She placed her hand over his and gently slid her elbow from his grasp. Avoiding his touch was prudent. It didn't matter that his black gaze held her in its thrall, or that his mercurial moods seized her imagination. Walking beside him, shoulder to shoulder, she found she craved the warmth of his presence. But giving in to those feelings would lead her down a dangerous path, a path that would veer wildly from the one she had chosen.

His body stiffened in response to her withdrawal. Lucinda was saddened; she didn't want to wound Cosmo's feelings. She liked this mysterious writer who had chosen honor over wealth. And despite his sedentary life-style and the slightly strained gait of a man not accustomed to regular exercise, he possessed an almost overwhelming masculine air. She felt safe beside him. Even though he carried a cane, and leaned more heavily on it when he thought she didn't notice, Lucinda instinctively knew Sir Cosmo could take care of himself, as well as any woman he loved.

She halted just before they ascended the marble steps that led to the black lacquered door of the hotel. She wanted to say something to Cosmo, something to explain her contradictory actions. She wanted him to know that she found him attractive, but that she couldn't afford to encourage a more intimate friendship with him.

The words were slow in coming, however. Lucinda didn't know how to phrase such an emotion. Would she sound crass and materialistic? She knew she would, even if she confided in Cosmo her desire to build a women's shelter. No man would welcome hearing that he had been disregarded as a suitor because his pockets were not plump enough.

Still, there must be something she could say. . . .

She stepped back an inch, regarding him.

The bullet that grazed his forehead missed Lucinda's nose by an inch.

Five

A breeze lifted the fringe of silver on Cosmo's brow. Gunfire cracked the night air. A second later, Cosmo's forehead stung like mad, and he discovered blood on his fingertips when he raked his hand through his hair.

"Oh, Cosmo! You've been shot in the head!"

He had the good sense to realize that if someone fired a shot at him, they might fire another as soon as they realized they had missed. "Hurry, get inside!" He threw his arm about Lucinda's shoulder and jerked her body in front of his. Shielding her, he practically pushed her up the steps and inside the hotel.

A liveried servant had thrown open the door at the sound of the gunshot. As soon as Lucinda and Cosmo dashed across the threshold, he pulled shut the door and bolted it. "Dear me! Are ye injured, Sir Cosmo? Shall I call a surgeon or a barber?"

Cosmo stood in the elegant foyer while drops of his blood spattered the black-and-white checkered floor. "Damme! My gloves are ruined," he said, inspecting his fingertips.

Lucinda's mouth fell open.

"Mrs. Partridge, are you all right?" Cosmo asked. He knew by now that he hadn't taken a bullet in the head, but had merely been grazed by a poorly aimed shot.

Lucinda, however, was staring at him as if he had sprouted horns.

The hotel doorman summoned an array of personnel to assist him in dealing with their customer's misfortune. A uniformed house maid dabbed at Cosmo's forehead with a linen towel while a waiter from the restaurant went to fetch a fortifying drink. A hubbub of activity and nervous clucking surrounded Lucinda and Cosmo.

The hotel manager, a Mr. Beaversham, appeared on the scene. "Are you quite all right, Sir Cosmo? I shall send a messenger to Bow Street right away to report this incident. The doorman tells me that he opened the door to admit you just as an unseen assailant fired a pistol shot at you and your companion."

The doorman bobbed his head. "Yes sir, didna' see a thing. But then I slammed the door soon as Sir Cosmo and his lady got inside!"

"Perhaps my tiger or driver saw something," said Cosmo, studying Lucinda. "In the meantime, however, I am afraid my companion is in shock. Ah, here is a glass of sherry. Come now, Lucinda, try to drink a sip. It will do you good."

Blinking, she took the small glass in trembling hands. After a few sips, she regained a bit of her color. Her expression eased. Then, to Cosmo's surprise, she threw back her head and completely drained the sherry glass. When she returned it to the waiting servant, she hiccoughed and shuddered.

Cosmo couldn't resist a chuckle. "Feeling better?"

"A little. Good heavens, Cosmo, how can you be so calm? You were very nearly killed!"

"And so were you, pet. Had you not withdrawn your arm from mine, and put some distance between us, that bullet would have passed through your beautiful head."

She paled at the thought, and held out her hand for another glass of sherry. The waiter, decanter in hand, accommodated her. This glass she drank more slowly, but as her senses returned, her body began to shiver.

"A most ordinary reaction to such a tremendous shock," Cosmo said. "Would you like to be returned home? Or shall I rent quarters here for you to spend the evening?"

She shook her head. "I should like to eat, sir. I have drunk more than I should have, and I do believe my nerves would be calmed by a hearty repast."

"Good idea!" Cosmo put his arm around her and gently guided her through the foyer and into the dining room. A small corner table had been reserved, and it was to this shadowy alcove that Mr. Beaversham led the couple.

"Your table, sir," said the manager, smiling conspiratorially as Cosmo palmed him a ten-pound note. "I shall take care of informing the authorities about tonight's event. And I shall instruct the house detective to consult with your driver and any other potential witnesses. I do hope justice is done in this matter, and that whatever nasty villain who dared attempt to shoot you spends the rest of his miserable life in Newgate."

"Thank you, Beaversham." Another note was discreetly passed to the man. "A bottle of my good claret, would you, old man?"

When the hotel manager had disappeared, Cosmo slid his hand across the table. Lucinda placed her tiny fingers in his palm.

"I am better now, thanks to you. You are very kind," she said, smiling wanly. She squeezed his hand, then withdrew her own. "I was half-frightened out of my mind, I must admit. That bullet could have killed either one of us."

"Do you know of anyone who would like to see you dead?" Cosmo asked her.

"Other than the critics?" she replied. "Of course not.

That bullet was meant for you, Cosmo. Who do *you* think fired it?"

He sat back, considering the question. He could think of several people who might want him dead, Monique's husband for one. But that rascal was in Paris, and Cosmo had no reason to think he would come looking for the man who had cuckolded him. After all, it wasn't as if Cosmo had ever been a serious threat to his marriage.

"You didn't answer my question, Cosmo."

Cosmo leaned forward. His mission to expose the spy at the opera had just become more urgent. "I have no idea who would have tried to kill me. Indeed, I think this entire incident may be a case of mistaken identity. The would-be assassin mistook me for someone else, don't you think? Um? Lucinda, are you quite certain you are all right?"

Her gaze had drifted to the sommelier who, having appeared tableside, expertly uncorked, decanted and poured Cosmo's fine claret. At the sound of her name, Lucinda's stare shot back to Cosmo. "What? Oh, yes! I am fine, now."

"Then, I shall propose a toast." Cosmo lifted his wineglass and clinked the rim of Lucinda's. "To the most beautiful songbird in all of London. I am forever in your debt, dear lady, for the opportunity to learn from you."

Lucinda's cheeks colored. "That is very kind, sir."

"There must be something I can do to return your favor."

She shook her head, sipping more delicately now that her nerves were assuaged.

Lowering his glass, he leaned forward. "Your list of suitors, Wynne-Ascott, Pugh and Pavlov—"

"What about them?"

"You are determined to marry one of them, is that it?"

She lifted her chin a notch. "I am."

"Why the urgency, Mrs. Partridge, if you don't mind my asking."

She shrugged one shoulder. "Look at me, Sir Cosmo. I am nearly on the shelf as a woman and as an opera singer. Didn't you hear my voice crack last night when I missed that high C? You might as well learn this now, since you are so interested in the life of a diva. That life is frighteningly short, sir. There is always a younger woman, a more fulsome figure, a fresher voice, waiting in the wings to steal my parts."

"But you have a devoted audience," argued Cosmo.

"So does Madame Bartoli, who plays Cleopatra. She could easily sing the role of Caesar."

"Your fans love you."

"Have you seen the empty seats, Cosmo? The empty boxes? Well, perhaps you haven't. Lately, the theater has been full. But that is due to the popularity of the opera, *Julius Caesar,* and not to my performance. That is what Mr. Pavlov says, and he must be right because the last opera we performed wasn't nearly as successful. Don't you think the owners of the theater have asked themselves whether another star could bring in more patrons . . . all the time, no matter what opera is being staged?"

"Don't you have a contract? They can't just toss you out on the street! Can they?"

Lucinda smiled ruefully. "My contract is nearing its expiration date. And for all his efforts, poor Mr. Pavlov has been unsuccessful in obtaining a renewal for me. So, I have another month, Sir Cosmo. And after that, well . . . I may be tossed into the streets, indeed!"

"Have you not saved your money all these years?" Cosmo waved the sommelier to the table and instructed him to pour more wine.

With her finger, Lucinda pensively traced the rim of her filled glass. At length, her lashes flickered, and she met Sir Cosmo's gaze. "I fear I have not managed my money very well. You see, I have given most of it away—"

"Given it away?" Cosmo's mouth fell open in undisguised astonishment. "To whom, might I ask?"

"To friends," Lucinda replied lightly, as if it were the most perfectly natural thing to have done. "When it comes to money, you see, I am rather philosophical. Perhaps it was arrogant of me to believe that I would always have money, but I didn't realize, until it was too late, that my career on the stage would not last forever. So, whenever my friends were in need of money, I gave it to them."

Cosmo was nearly at a loss for words. He drank deeply, falling into ruminative thought as the waiter served dinner, two healthy portions of pan-seared turbot and wilted green vegetables. Mrs. Partridge's appetite, he noticed, seemed none the worse for his having engaged her in this unpleasant conversation, but Cosmo's need to understand her supplanted his need for nourishment.

"Mrs. Partridge, are you telling me that you are on the edge of being . . . unemployed?"

"And poor." She took a big bite of fish, then looked him straight in the eye, chewing unself-consciously.

He thought her epicurean gusto charming. Creeping over him was a warmth for this slightly eccentric young lady, coupled with an unquenchable curiosity as to how anyone could be so cavalier with their hard-earned money.

It wasn't as if she had inherited a fortune, like the one he had given up. Good heavens, she lacked even the family connections to live comfortably as a perennial houseguest, or to find accommodations as a glorified nanny in some cousin's remote country manor. Her only real connection to the *ton* was her friendship with Lord Wynne-Ascott, who, Cosmo firmly believed, would never marry the likes of her. She was certainly pinning her hopes on the wrong man if she expected that stiff-rumped dandy to leg-shackle himself to her.

But how could he tell her such a thing? How could he dash her hopes of securing a future for herself?

"I can certainly see the urgency of your situation," he murmured. "A female in destitute circumstances, without family to call upon . . . you don't have family in Town, I presume?"

"None." She calmly continued eating her fish.

"Are you not terrified of being poor, Mrs. Partridge?"

"I've been poor, Sir Cosmo. And I've been rich. I much prefer being rich, and to that end, I intend to marry a rich husband."

She said it so matter-of-factly that Cosmo was at first taken aback. He picked at his turbot, attempting to reconcile his warring feelings. On the one hand, his male instincts were fully aroused and outraged that this talented and beautiful songbird would be treated so cruelly by the theater's owners. Her own naivete in giving away her money—to friends in need, no less—intensified his sympathy for her.

On the other hand, he was offended by her bald remark that she intended to marry a rich husband. She was beginning to remind him of every woman he had ever encountered in his life. Those women included Monique, his horsey cousin Hilda, and his own mother, whose blind ambition had resulted in a parental ultimatum: marry your wealthy and very fat little cousin or you shall yourself be disinherited.

In retrospect, he thought he shouldn't cast Hilda into the same pot with his mother and Monique. After all, Hilda, in her own Machiavellian efforts to forge an alliance with him, had merely bent to the pressure of her own parents, who wanted her to marry a man with a small amount of respectability and a large amount of arable pastureland. Hilda wasn't of the same ilk as

Monique, that was certain. Monique, he realized, was in a category all to herself.

Cosmo shook his head, forcibly dispelling the disturbing images of Monique that popped into his head.

"It is my turn to ask you, sir," Lucinda said, interrupting his thoughts. "Are you all right? Perhaps the shock of being shot at has affected your appetite."

He stared down at his half-uneaten plate of food. Old feelings of resentment burned in his chest. His anger toward his overbearing mother, a woman who put her own aspirations above her son's happiness, roared to life. Bitterness toward the double-crossing Monique, the only woman who had ever seduced him body, soul and mind, flared up.

But, most of all, self-hatred burned within him. Perhaps he had never trusted women because he hadn't met one worthy of his trust. Or, perhaps it was because he was not trustworthy himself. Hadn't he set out to double-cross Monique, after all? Hadn't he seduced her in the first place because she was married to a powerful Frenchman who had Masséna's ear and who told his unfaithful vixen of a wife every military move Boney was going to make before he made it?

Hadn't he pursued Monique simply because she was a duplicitous wanton notorious for divulging her husband's secrets to her lovers? What was it about him that compelled him to fall in love with the wrong women? Why did he always learn to despise the very qualities that attracted him?

What was it that Sir Milburn Sinclair had once said? *Don't take out your anger on the next woman you meet, son.* Well, that was the rub, wasn't it? Staring into Lucinda's pretty blue eyes, Cosmo saw a woman who had all the characteristics of an opportunist. It was impossible not to transfer all his resentment toward his mother and Monique to this woman.

His mind churned. Suddenly, he could think of nothing that was good about Lucinda Partridge. He saw her as a mercenary little fortune hunter, a woman who would never be interested in the likes of him because she had written him off as an impoverished scribbler. Having squandered her own earnings, she was now determined to marry a rich man and spend all his money, too.

Was that what all women were about? he wondered. Wasn't there a woman anywhere whose affections and emotions were true, sincere and unadulterated by love of money?

A feeling of distaste roiled through his stomach. He touched the corner of his serviette to his mouth. "In answer to your question, Mrs. Partridge, I am indeed all right. But, I am suddenly very tired. If you are finished, I should like to take my leave of this place."

She looked startled, slightly wounded. "Yes, I am tired, too."

As they left the hotel, Cosmo was very careful not to touch her, not to rub shoulders with her or, God forbid, allow his leg to brush against her skirts as they walked. His tiger handed her into the carriage; then Cosmo hopped inside, seating himself opposite Lucinda. In the half darkness, lit only by the torches on the outside of the carriage, he caught glimpses of her expression. He had hurt her feelings. Her silence was eloquent and should have filled him with reproach.

But his bitterness was so strong that for a fleeting instant, he took a perverse pleasure in Mrs. Partridge's confused and wounded silence. Then, like the aftereffect a drunkard has after a night's debauchery, the implications of his actions hit home. A sickness overwhelmed him, and his gut twisted with shame. He had wounded Lucinda. He had allowed his private anger to so consume him that in his fury, he had lashed out at an innocent woman, a woman to whom he was greatly attracted. What sort of paperscull punished one woman for something another had done?

Mounting the steps slowly, Lucinda felt the weariness of her depression seep into her bones. Cosmo's sudden coldness had overset her. Why should she care whether the handsome writer liked her, she asked herself, thrusting her key into the lock. Why did his mood swings affect her at all?

Belatedly, she realized her apartment was awash in light. An oil lamp burned on the small table in her sitting room. A fire in the hearth crackled a warm greeting. Emerging from the tiny cooking area—a closet, really, barely large enough in which to store a few staples, such as flour, tea and chocolate—was Clarissa, her face split in a gap-toothed smile.

"Well, there ye are, missus. Here's a cup a tea fer ye! I heard ye coming up the stairs!"

The rusty-haired woman placed a delicate bone china cup and saucer on the round table, then settled down beside it to a cup of her own. Lucinda tossed off her cloak and hat, then pulled off her gloves and sat down. As the steam of the hot tea tickled her nose, she sighed. Clarissa had indeed become a fixture in her life. She often wondered if it wasn't she who needed Clarissa's charity . . . rather than the other way around.

"Have a bad night, did ye, lovie?"

"I missed the high C again, Clarissa. I don't know how many people noticed, but I certainly did. And my regular fans did, too, I'm sure."

"Not to mention the critics," added Clarissa.

"Thank you for reminding me."

"Don't mention it, missus. You've always got Clarissa

here to give you the unspoiled truth. Truth, with a capital T. I ain't nothin' if I ain't willin' to tell the truth."

Lucinda smiled, her mood quickly improving as the hot tea warmed her limbs and Clarissa's irrepressible cheerfulness buoyed her spirits. "Tell me something, Clarissa. What makes a man suddenly go cold, his mood totally alter in a matter of seconds?"

"Sometimes a man thinks he's ready for bed play; then all of a sudden, he realizes he cannot—"

"No, no! I'm not talking about that!" Lucinda might have liked to explore that topic further with Clarissa. The young woman was a fountain of information concerning the differences between the two sexes. She no doubt knew many things about men that Lucinda had never discovered, or dared speculate on, even after two failed marriages. But tonight was not the night to indulge herself in such a titillating conversation.

"I was having dinner with this gentleman," she said.

"What gentleman?"

"His name is Sir Cosmo Fairchild, and he's a writer. He's researching a book about divas, and he wants to spend a great deal of time with me, seeing how I live, what being an opera star is all about."

"Uh-um. Fergive me fer soundin' skeptical—ye didna' know I knew them big words, did ye?—but somethin' about this gent sounds fishy awready."

"You're always skeptical about men, Clarissa."

"And I'm usually right, ain't I?"

Lucinda paused, reluctant to admit the truth of that remark. "Oh, well. We had dinner tonight. And everything was going well. After we got shot at, that is."

"Shot at! Well, that's a little fly in the ointment, ain't it? Is it every night, then, that ye get shot at, Mrs. Partridge? Were ye really that frightful on stage? Dear God, I knew the groundlings sometimes tossed peanuts, or threw rotten oranges, but have they started shootin' at ye, now? Just for missing yer bloomin' high C? *Everything went well, she says, after we got ourselves shot at, that is.*"

"It wasn't like that, Clarissa. Someone mistook us for someone else, that's all. A pistol shot was fired in our direction as we entered the hotel. Luckily, the shot missed my nose by an inch, although it grazed Sir Cosmo's head and left him with a scratch, no worse than a nick from a shaving razor."

Clarissa leaned back in her chair and crossed her arms over her chest. "Someone mistook ye fer someone else, uh? Ye'd think murderers would be more careful, wouldn't ye?"

"Anyway, dinner was going fine."

"Until the hotel caught on fire, I s'pose. Not that a minor incident such as that would cool *yer* ardor!"

"What sort of remark is that, Clarissa? I don't like this man in the least!"

"Bullets was flyin' past yer head, lovie, and yer frettin' 'cause this handsome writer named Sir Cosmo fell into a pout over dinner."

"I was talking, and he was listening, and—"

"Men can only listen to a pretty face for so long; then they lose interest. In the talkin', anyway. Don't matter what yer talkin' about, could be as fascinatin' as Prinny's sex life, or as dull as the price of horseflesh at Tattersall's. But, all I'm sayin', dearie, is dumb men are easily bored by a woman's talk, and the really smart ones are offended by it."

"I don't understand."

"Of course ye don't." Clarissa sighed. "Never mind. Ye just talked too much, probably. The poor man was settin' there starin' at ye, wishin' he could tear off yer clothes, and—"

"Clarissa!" Lucinda's teacup clattered to the saucer.

"And there ye were, flappin' yer jaw, lookin' fer all

the world like ye wasn't gonna stop till daybreak. What was ye talkin' about anyways?"

"About my three suitors."

"Excuse me?" Clarissa cupped her hand to her ear.

"Lord Wynne-Ascott, Mr. Pugh and Mr. Pavlov. I was discussing which one of them would be the most fitting husband. And I was just about to tell Sir Cosmo about my plans for a women's shelter, and that I needed to marry a rich man so that I could finance my dream to build a place where underprivileged women could go—"

Clarissa's palm slapped the table, cutting off Lucinda's speech. Picking up her cup and saucer, the prostitute stood, staring down at the pretty opera diva with a mixture of amusement and sympathy in her tired gaze. "Oh, my, ye really are a green girl, even after two marriages."

"What do you mean, Clarissa? What have I done wrong now?"

"Have ye taken leave of yer senses, gel? Talking about those three men to the one yer in love with?"

"But, Clarissa, I am not in love with Sir Cosmo Fairchild. I'm not certain I even like him. Our arrangement is a business deal, only. He is going to split his profits with me when his book is published. And until I am married, I cannot afford to turn down any offers of financial remuneration. I am determined to build that women's shelter! I am!"

"But, he's very handsome, ain't he?" Clarissa tilted her head, staring at Lucinda as one would gaze at a slow, but loveable, child.

"Yes." Heat suffused Lucinda's cheeks. "Very handsome."

"Does yer stomach feel as if it is tied in knots each time yer around him?"

"Yes."

"And when he touches ye—he has touched ye, hasn't

he?—did ye feel as if ye'd explode if he didn't keep on . . . touchin' ye, that is?"

Lucinda dipped her head, embarrassed to admit that what Clarissa described was precisely what she had felt when Cosmo had touched the back of her neck in her dressing room.

"And when those bullets came flyin' by yer head, Mrs. Partridge, tell me something. What was the first thing that flashed in yer mind the instant ye realized someone had fired a pistol at ye and yer handsome writer?"

Lucinda lifted her head, and as she stared into Clarissa's weary eyes, hot tears streamed down her cheeks. "Oh, Clarissa. I just couldn't bear to think that my dear Sir Cosmo had been hurt. To think that someone would want to do him harm . . ."

She buried her face in her hands and sobbed as Clarissa cleared the table. After a few moments, the red-haired prostitute handed her a square of linen, patted her on the shoulder and sat opposite her at the table.

Lucinda looked up and met her friend's sympathetic gaze. Sniffling, the diva managed a wan smile. "The truth is, Clarissa, I cannot afford to love that man."

"The question is, dearie, can you afford not to?"

Ivan Pavlov's pulse raced. Alone in Lucinda's dressing room, he felt a twinge of guilt, and a stab of erotic pleasure. Silk stockings, lacy bustiers and gauzy undergarments littered the small room. Makeup, wigs and all the accouterments associated with a diva's stage appearance were strewn across Lucinda's dressing table. The perfume of flowers, sent on a daily basis from Lucinda's admirers, filled the air.

Fingering the vellum note card attached to one particularly spectacular bunch of red hothouse roses, Ivan experienced a surge of jealousy. His gut twisted as he read the elaborately scripted words:

Not to worry, songbird. Your voice is as sweet as rose water, and your cheeks as fine as Meissen porcelain . . . take care of yourself, love.

> Yours forever,
> Nathaniel

A cruel smirk tugged at his lips. That haughty aristocrat was consoling Lucinda, telling her that she shouldn't worry about missing that high C the previous evening. Obviously, he didn't understand the mental processes of a diva. Reminding the famous Mrs. Partridge that her stage performance had been anything less than perfect would no doubt rattle her nerves and make her as angry as a viper.

Which suited Ivan's purposes just fine. All these nosey men, these hangers-on who had attached themselves to Lucinda in the past year, were beginning to annoy him. Why, even that porcine Mr. Pugh was becoming a pest, showing up backstage after performances, watching every move Lucinda made, taking up as much of her time as the diva would allot to him. Ivan had begun to think that these suitors were a nuisance, indeed. They impinged on his time with Lucinda. They made him nervous. And, with the addition of Sir Cosmo Fairchild, they were very definitely posing a threat to Ivan's future plans for the great opera star.

He picked up a few letters lying about on Lucinda's dressing table. All plaintive missives from lovesick boys, infatuated opera lovers, and hopeless romantics. Scattered among them were unpaid bills from Lucinda's grocer, butcher, coal vendor, modiste and shoemaker. Already, the poor woman was having difficulty paying her bills. He was saddened by the thought that her imminent impoverishment would cause her heartache. But, if everything went according to his plans, there would come a day when Lucinda would not have to worry about a thing, ever again.

The dressing room door opened with a harsh grate along the wooden floor and a crash against the wall. Ivan's gaze shot to the mirror above the dressing table. Lucinda stood in the threshold, staring back at him.

Ivan did not attempt to hide the cobbler's bill he held. Rather, he turned and looked at the diva approvingly from head to toe. She really was a beauty, with her blond hair, tiny waist and ample bust line. He wasn't surprised that suitors swarmed around her like honeybees.

"What are you doing in my dressing room, Ivan?" Her voice was but a whisper, but her expression was piqued.

"I am waiting for you, babushka. Please forgive me for intruding on your private quarters. However, I have a matter of grave importance which I must discuss with you."

She closed the door, crossed the room and stood before her dressing table. Chagrined to find the Russian in her room, she slanted him an icy stare while yanking off her gloves. Shrugging off his offer of assistance, she threw her coat onto a nearby divan. Quickly, she slipped behind her tole screen, removed her gown and donned a silk dressing robe. Then she sat before her table and, with a sigh, studied her reflection in the mirror.

Her eyes were puffy and her jowls were swollen. Sleepless nights wreaked havoc on Lucinda's complexion and skin tone. She shouldn't have stayed awake crying over Sir Cosmo Fairchild. He wasn't worth it. As Clarissa had succinctly pointed out, *"Isn't no man worth that sorta carryin' on!"*

Her all-night crying spell had one positive effect, however. Lucinda was quite certain she had got Sir Cosmo out of her system. He had only been an infatuation, anyway, a passing interest that had tweaked her imagination and caused her to wonder what it would be like if she were free to fall in love with anyone she fancied. But, as dawn approached, she had convinced herself that finding a rich husband was not only necessary, but, in her case, a downright noble endeavor, given that she intended to spend her future mate's money on a worthy cause. She was resigned to marrying—not for love, but for money.

Another sigh, another shrug. *Well, life is full of compromises, isn't it? A wise woman knows she can't have everything she wants.*

"Babushka," Ivan said tenderly, "we must talk."

She shook her head no. She had missed her high C the night before, and she had no intention of straining her voice before tonight's performance.

"I understand. Then I will talk and you will listen, eh?"

Nodding, Lucinda watched Ivan in the mirror. Of all her suitors, he was the most talented. The eldest son of a Russian nobleman, he, like Sir Cosmo, had opted to pursue a career in the arts rather than manage his family's estate. Unlike Cosmo, Ivan's family had not punished his defection; the Russian lyricist worked at the Orange Street Opera because he loved opera, not because he needed the money.

He stroked his russet beard, searching for the correct words. Glancing at him, Lucinda couldn't resist a small smile. Ivan translated Italian lyrics into English, a language he spoke with some difficulty. That, of course, accounted for some of the awkward phraseology of the operas Lucinda performed.

Not that the owners cared, thought Lucinda as she patted makeup onto her face. Ivan wrote passable lyrics that satisfied his audience; most of the London opera-goers were illiterate in Italian and asleep by the third act, anyway. As for Lucinda, she was hardly such a purist that she would demand more literal translations of the Italian librettos. All she cared was that her voice had an outlet; as long as she could sing, she could express the emotion of the story through her voice, even if the words were not quite right.

Ivan pulled a sheaf of papers from his inner coat pocket. "I have changed a few of the lyrics for tonight's performance. It is in the scene where Cleopatra has been told that Julius Caesar has drowned. Instead of crying, *'Oh, the death of my beloved has robbed me of the chance for eternal love,'* Cleopatra will sing, *'Oh, the death of my conqueror has left me a widow in the Russian winter of my life.'* "

Lucinda laid down a small eyeliner brush and took the revisions Ivan proffered. "Russian winter, Ivan? Handel would roll over in his grave."

"Russian winters are the harshest of all, Mrs. Partridge. Our audience will appreciate the reference, trust me."

She frowned. For one thing, the new words would be difficult for Madame Bartoli to sing. For another, the altered phraseology changed the original librettist's meaning.

With a ready protest on her lips, she looked at Ivan. But she was silenced by his cold expression, an expression that was, indeed, as cold as a Russian winter, she silently concluded. Unpinning her tousled coiffure, Lucinda brushed her long golden hair until it crackled with friction.

Color rose to Ivan's cheeks. His brow knit in a straight line, and his high forehead deeply furrowed. His tension was so palpable that Lucinda ached for him. Whatever was troubling her Russian friend, she decided not to compound it by quibbling over these trivial line changes.

Instead, she piled her hair atop her head, then reached for a pin to secure it.

"The other thing I wanted to say," he continued haltingly, his eyes averted, "is . . . I don't know how to say—"

"What is it, Ivan?"

"Shhh! You must conserve your voice, my love. Perhaps I chose this moment to tell you of my feelings because I knew you would not be able to silence my silly ramblings. It is that I love you, you see. I love you, and I want you to be my wife."

Lucinda stared at him in stunned silence.

"Will you marry me, babushka?"

Six

A hairpin slipped from the blond pile of curls atop Lucinda's head. Her hands froze in midair, and a long golden braid tumbled down her shoulder. Turning from Ivan's reflection, she looked him full in the face.

Will you marry me? Was it possible that after all this time Ivan Pavlov wanted to make her his wife?

Her pulse pounded out a staccato tempo. Lucinda opened her mouth to speak, but couldn't find the words to express her shock.

More shocking than Ivan's proposal, however, was Lucinda's reaction. She didn't know whether to say yes or no.

Her lips moved, but no sound emerged.

"Well? Will you be my wife?" he asked, his expression full of nervous anticipation.

A marriage proposal was precisely what she had been angling for, wasn't it? And Ivan Pavlov was one of her three most likely prospects for a husband, wasn't he? So, she could hardly afford to rebuff him, or waste her time waiting for a better offer . . . could she?

Her head told her to shout yes!

But her heart wouldn't let her accept Ivan's proposal so quickly. Blinking back hot tears, Lucinda turned toward the mirror. She clutched her throat and stared at her suitor's reflected gaze.

"I see that my offer has surprised you," he said gently. She nodded.

He laid his hand on her shoulder, caressing her bare neck, toying with the strands of hair that had tumbled from her coiffure.

"Ivan, you mustn't," she gasped.

The sharp breath she took emboldened him, and he bent over her, slipping his fingers beneath the neck of her robe. He kissed her shoulder, pressing his warm lips against her delicate skin. His beard chafed and tickled, drawing chill bumps and causing her to shudder, a response the Russian mistook as desire.

She felt his hot breath and the scrape of his teeth along her shoulder.

A horrible realization assailed her. Ivan Pavlov's touch left her cold and empty. The contrast between the way this man made her feel, and the way Cosmo had made her feel when he touched her, was as dramatic as a Greek tragedy. Something inside her seemed to shrivel and die; that she felt no warmth at all beneath this man's touch terrified her.

What was wrong with her? After all, she liked Ivan, and he had been a good friend to her. He had done everything he could to extend her contract at the Orange Street Opera House, and when it was clear the owners refused to keep her on, he had promised he would help her secure another singing engagement.

And she had every reason to believe that his promise had been genuine, despite the fact that she was one month away from termination and there was no job offer in sight. Of course, if he married her, he would also support her financially. That was the traditional arrangement, was it not? In which case, Lucinda wouldn't have to worry about finding another position with another opera house. As Mrs. Ivan Pavlov, she could devote her energies to building her dream. As Mrs. Ivan Pavlov, she would never have to worry about money again.

Yet, she recoiled from his touch, clasping her robe more tightly around her waist. "No, Ivan, not now," she whispered hoarsely.

He straightened, standing behind her with his hands resting gently on her shoulders. "You are well within your rights to make me wait, Lucinda. A woman of your caliber cannot be trifled with, I understand."

The irony of Ivan's remark drew a wan smile to her lips. Touching her throat again, she shrugged. "I must sing tonight," she murmured.

"I understand. And I understand that the suddenness of my proposal has caught you off guard. So, I will not press you for an answer. I will wait." His hands slipped off her shoulders, and he took a step backward, so that Lucinda could not see his face in the mirror. "Till the end of your contract, babushka. One month. And then I shall demand an answer of you. That is fair, no?"

She nodded. Yes, that was fair. She knew it was, and yet she was relieved to have been granted a reprieve by the Russian. One month. That was a very long time, she told herself as she watched Ivan depart her dressing room. Many things could happen in one month's time. Sighing, she went to work pinning up her hair. A great burden had just been removed from her shoulders. She had at least one offer of marriage, and so she needn't fear impoverishment when her contract expired.

She should be happy. But, as Lucinda Partridge slipped into Caesar's tunic that evening, she experienced a sense of panic. Beneath the tight girdle that compressed her bosom, a cold sweat licked her skin. And it was a dread that had nothing to do with whether she would hit her high notes.

* * *

"Lucinda?" Mr. Lawrence Pugh's muffled voice sounded from the opposite side of her dressing room door. "Mrs. Partridge? May I come in?"

A well of hope sprang in Lucinda's heart. If nothing else, Mr. Pugh represented an alternative to Ivan Pavlov. Barefooted, she rushed to her dressing room door and admitted the heavy-set gentleman.

His gaze took in her gauzy costume and her unshod feet. "Hello, dumpling. My God, but you are beautiful!"

As Lucinda retreated, he entered, shutting the door behind him. For a moment, he simply stood and stared, mostly, Lucinda noticed, at her naked toes.

"Lawrence, it is so unlike you to visit me before a performance. Is everything all right?" Self-consciously, she moved to her dressing table and sat down to lace up the golden sandals she wore on stage.

His gaze was riveted to her feet. Suddenly, as if he were suffocating, he jerked off his hat. Then he shrugged out of his elegant black woolen cloak and draped it over his arm. Between gulps, he managed, "Please forgive me, but I have a matter that I would like to discuss with you."

"Go right ahead, Lawrence." She crossed one leg over the other and drew her knee to her bosom. The long, golden straps which laced from her ankles to her knees required not a little expertise in crossing and tying just right.

"How long has it been that I have courted you, Lucinda? A couple of years, at least, has it not?" In his nervousness, he worked the rim of his hat.

Lucinda's fingers froze. Looking up, she said, "Go on."

"Lord knows, I am not a handsome man. But I am, to put it bluntly, plump in the pockets."

Lucinda didn't mention that he was plump everywhere else, too.

"And I am a patient man, Lucinda. Generous. And kind."

"To be sure, Lawrence." Lucinda straightened, staring at Mr. Pugh with a mixture of alarm, sympathy and amusement. "Darling, you are ruining your hat."

"Lucinda, I love you, and I want to marry you. There, I've said it! Can you ever love me, dumpling? Oh, I know you don't love me now. I can see it in your face. I know that I am not every woman's dream. I know, too, that you could choose from a hundred suitors. But, if you marry me, Lucinda, you'll never want for a thing! You'll be rich beyond your wildest dreams—"

"Lawrence, I don't know what to say!" Lucinda stood, one sandal on and one off.

"Don't say anything now. Take your time, Lucinda. I am a patient man."

For a moment, the two stared at one another across the small room. Then Mr. Pugh, his bald head crimson, nodded. Lucinda thought if he had a forelock, he would have yanked it to show his deference and respect. He bid her good night and wished her the best of luck on stage. "And don't worry about your high C, dumpling. Tonight, you'll do it! I swear!"

As he passed over the threshold, her fist tightened around a golden sandal. It took every ounce of restraint she had to keep from throwing it at the closing door.

The opera house was unusually crowded for a weeknight. Lucinda was surprised that so many people would come out on an evening as blustery as this one. But operagoers were an enthusiastic lot, and the Orange Street Opera House's patrons were more faithful than most. Over the years, Lucinda had built up a loyal following among those Londoners who loved opera. She supposed that word had got out that she would only be performing Caesar for one more month; perhaps that accounted for her sudden swell in popularity.

The groundlings cheered raucously as the curtain went up. Through the first two acts, Lucinda sang well. But she avoided her high notes, and opted instead to take her voice down a note rather than reach for an unobtainable C. The conductor shot her curious looks, and members of the symphony frowned their disapproval. Beneath the sweltering candlelight, Lucinda noticed a few of her admirers shrug, or whisper to one another behind cupped hands or spread fans. Inwardly, she shuddered to think she was disappointing her faithful crowd. Another missed note, however, would shatter her self-confidence.

The huge chandelier that hung from the ceiling directly over the orchestra pit gave audience and performers equal opportunity to view one another. Mr. Pugh sat in the front row, clapping loudly at the close of the first and second acts. Meeting his gaze whenever she wandered close to the edge of the stage, Lucinda offered him a tepid smile.

Above her, on her right, ensconced in his private box with a middle-aged female companion, was Nathaniel Upham, Lord Wynne-Ascott. His searing gaze never tore itself from her. Lucinda acknowledged the aristocrat several times with a bat of her eyelashes and a coy nod. But, fearing to provoke the jealousies of the elegantly dressed lady beside him, she smiled sparingly in his direction.

His mother, Lucinda surmised. She wouldn't want to appear too brazen by flirting with Lord Wynne-Ascott right beneath his mother's nose.

On her left, seated in another private box, was Sir Cosmo Fairchild. During the final act, Lucinda gravitated toward his side of the stage, pulled by forces she did not understand. She sang to him, staring at him over Madonna Bartoli's raven-haired head.

Cosmo leaned forward, resting his arms on the edge of the box. His dark gaze was fixed on Lucinda, thrilling her with its feral intensity. Her focus became Cosmo; there was an intimate connection that formed between them. And, though the opera house was packed with people, Lucinda sang her final aria—Caesar's love song to Cleopatra—for Cosmo and no one else.

She sang with passion, with emotion she hadn't felt in years. It was as if she had never sung the words before, yet she felt them as if they resonated from her very soul. Looking at Cosmo, she forgot her fear, forgot last night's performance. Suddenly, she felt she could do anything. Her voice strengthened and filled the opera house; she knew she was giving the performance of her life, and it was all because she was singing to Cosmo.

Her voice shook the rafters. Lucinda reached toward Cosmo, yearning to embrace him. The groundlings fell quiet, and even the orange vendors came to a halt in the aisles. This was the best soprano voice London had ever heard. Lucinda's singing had never been so strong, or so pure.

Then came the verse in the aria when Lucinda had to decide whether to reach for her high C. The chorus behind her swelled; the orchestra worked toward its crescendo. Lucinda paused, drawing in a deep breath. She met Cosmo's gaze, and some sweet, unspeakable intimacy passed between them. Liquid heat spilled through her body. Her heart ached, and there was nothing for it but to loosen all the emotions she had buried deep within her, to let them go.

He sat still as a statue, his jaw hewn in granite. Yet, heat radiated from him. Though she couldn't touch him, Lucinda felt his silent urgings. She drew her strength from him. Finding her voice, she sang with her heart. Her high C rattled the windowpanes in the opera house.

The applause was deafening. Roses were tossed at Lucinda's feet, and shouts of, "Brava! Brava!" filled the opera house. She had done it! After missing her high note the night before, Lucinda Partridge had hit that C with the strength and vitality she'd possessed ten years ago. Exhilaration flowed through her veins, and tears of gratitude streamed down her face. Her accomplishment was a physical release that left her knees weak and her heart pounding.

For the first time ever, she saw Sir Cosmo Fairchild's handsome face transformed by a genuine smile.

Slowly standing, he offered her a little bow from within his box seat. And though she couldn't hear his voice above the din of her thunderous applause, she knew exactly what he said.

"Bellisimo, Mrs. Partridge. Brava!"

As the curtain fell on the final scene, Cosmo scanned the opera house. Lord Wynne-Ascott's box was empty; he and his companion had apparently left during Lucinda's final aria. Looking down, Cosmo spotted Mr. Pugh's bald crown, shiny beneath the heat of the chandelier. The rotund man clapped furiously, long after Lucinda had left the stage. Cosmo hardly faulted the man his adulation of Mrs. Partridge, but he wondered whether Pugh's ostentatious presence at the opera had anything to do with the spy ring operating out of the Orange Street theater.

Reaching for his cane, Cosmo moved without the faintest twinge of discomfort. Lucinda's voice soothed not only his nerves, but alleviated his physical pain as well.

Below him, the groundlings moved restlessly toward the doors leading to the streets. Mr. Pugh abandoned his solitary cries of, "Encore!" The post performance cacophony was a mingling of laughter, shuffling feet, and the clatter of an orchestra packing its instruments and sheet music.

The rear of Cosmo's private box was draped in burgundy-colored velvet curtains. The thick blanketing served to enhance the acoustics of the opera house, but if one didn't know precisely where the door was, exiting could be a confusing affair. Cosmo reached for the handle, noting belatedly that his curtains had been rearranged. His hand fumbled in the velvet panel. Just as his fingers grasped the brass knob, the curtains on his right rustled and parted.

In an instant, Cosmo knew he had made a dreadful mistake. He had allowed himself to become so caught up in Lucinda's singing that he had failed to pay attention to his surroundings. Failings such as these cost clandestine operatives their lives, he reminded himself. In the next split second, a man clad entirely in black emerged from between the wall and the curtains and rushed Cosmo from his right side.

A knife blade flashed. Instinctively, Cosmo raised his right arm—and his gold-headed cane. The knife ripped through curtains with a horrifying slash before it arced downward, aimed straight for Cosmo's heart. Wielding his cane like a sword, however, Cosmo made a quick defensive move that left the knife embedded in the shaft of his walking stick.

With his weapon wedged in Cosmo's cane, the attacker, his face disguised behind a black mask, sucked in a jagged breath, then strengthened his grip on his knife hilt. For a moment, the men froze in their struggle, their arms lifted, their breathing deep and labored. Cosmo gripped both ends of his cane while the assailant tried vainly to extract his knife.

Recognizing the chink in his enemy's armor, Cosmo let go of the cane and punched his foe in the belly.

Tremendous upper body strength gave Cosmo's blow devastating force. The knife and cane fell with a thud to the carpet while the black-clad attacker doubled over.

So, this was the spy he had been looking for! Cosmo gripped the man's cloak, preventing him from crumpling to his knees. With one hand, he pulled at the black woolen cloak; with his other, he grappled for the assailant's mask. The villain who had been passing England's military secrets to the French was about to be revealed.

The man's head lolled. Cosmo's fingers grasped the hem of the black silken mask. He gave it a tug.

The door to his private box flew open. A feminine scream erupted, and Cosmo froze, his fingers clutching the attacker's mask. His hesitation was just long enough to allow the black-clad villain to wrench himself free and bolt for the door, knocking over the woman who stood in the threshold.

As Cosmo went to follow his attacker, the woman in the doorway collapsed in a faint. He caught her in his arms just before she hit the floor.

Her weight surprised him. Gently lowering the unconscious woman to the carpet, Cosmo pressed his fingers to the pulse point in her throat. Pursuing his attacker was out of the question now. The man had a good head start on him, and Cosmo was hardly fleet of foot with his bad leg and awkward gait. Not to mention the fact that stepping over a woman in a dead faint, even to chase a villainous spy, seemed somewhat callous. His chivalrous instincts would not allow him to abandon her until he was satisfied she was not seriously injured, and her escort or chaperone was located.

Cosmo's right leg ached as he squatted beside the woman. He wished he had a vial of hartshorn in his jacket pocket.

Footsteps in the corridor relieved his growing anxiety. The woman had been unconscious a good five minutes, and though he was loath to leave her, Cosmo was becoming increasingly uncomfortable. Being alone with an unchaperoned woman was scandalous enough; add to that her unconscious state, and the scene had all the makings of a terrible misunderstanding. He was glad that someone else had finally arrived.

Until he heard the familiar voice of Lord Wynne-Ascott.

"What in the devil's name is going on here?"

"What does it look like?" Cosmo retorted. "The woman fainted."

"I can see that." Wynne-Ascott remained standing, his shiny Hessians just inches from the woman's head.

"Do you know her?" Cosmo asked.

"Of course I know her. I brought her to the opera tonight, for heaven's sake. That is Lady Sapho Drummond, wife of Sir Nigel Drummond."

Cosmo frowned. "Nigel Drummond? Wasn't he recently knighted for his service to the crown?"

Wynne-Ascott shrugged. "A parvenu to be sure. His title's as fresh as Brummel's latest cravat. But, I suppose it is petty and unpatriotic to begrudge the man his honor. After all, he served Wellesley quite admirably, from what I heard."

"Good lord, wasn't he a barber?"

"He was an excellent haircutter," Wynne-Ascott replied with a sniff.

"Well, it's a fine thing when a man can get knighted for trimming the hairs of an English warrior."

"No, no, he wasn't knighted for that." Wynne-Ascott snorted derisively. "If you've seen Wellesley's hair, for God's sake, you'd know better. On the contrary, Drummond happened to be at Ciudad Rodrigo when Wellesley came down with a dreadful case of the flux. Almost perished from dehydration and weakness, from eating that revolting Spanish food, no doubt. Drummond cured him with some sort of vile concoction of candied ginger, almond oil and absinthe. He later denied it was a hair tonic . . . in fact, he denies he ever was a barber, now that he's been knighted. But, there you have it. It's a sad day when common scissor men can wheedle their way into the fringes of the aristocracy."

"War is a hellish thing," Cosmo murmured. His haunches were growing stiff, and he was tiring of Wynne-Ascott's impeccably well-ordered view of the world. "What about you, my lord? Ever consider serving your country by joining one of Wellesley's regiments? Some of your ilk have done it, if only to experience the excitement of a battlefield. Although, I dare say those fellows learned quickly enough there is nothing glamorous about war."

"I've suffered enough for my country," Wynne-Ascott said. "My cook was conscripted to serve, and there was nothing I could do to buy him out of it. Damndest thing, but the foolhardy man actually wanted to go to war. Got himself killed at Oporto, silly bastard. I haven't had a decent roasted grouse since 1808!"

"You've sacrificed more than a man should be asked to give up for his country," Cosmo answered, without the slightest trace of a smile.

A slight mewling sound drew his attention to the poor Lady Drummond, whose dead faint, however spectacular, had somehow been eclipsed by Wynne-Ascott's unique perspective on the hardships of war. He watched her eyes flicker open, and smiled as her pale blue gaze slowly took focus.

She was a woman of late middle-age, sturdy of frame and feature. Unremarkable in her appearance, she overcompensated by piling on the jewelry; strands of pearls choked her thick neck while big, sparkly diamonds dripped from her fleshy earlobes. Her pudgy fingers were studded with emeralds, rubies and sapphires. A gaudy tiara nestled in her expertly crafted, silver-haired coiffure. Cosmo was hardly surprised the woman had fainted. Indeed, with all that hardware weighting her body, he wondered that she could hold up her head without suffering severe injury.

She stared at him with an expression of confusion and apprehension. "Dear me, what happened?"

"You fainted, Sapho," answered Wynne-Ascott. He made no move to comfort her, or bend down to offer his assistance.

"Permit me to introduce myself. Sir Cosmo Fairchild at your service, ma'am. You did interrupt a rather frightening scene, and for the part I played in causing you upset, I am terribly sorry."

Her eyes rounded. "I remember now! Oh, it was terrible, Nathaniel! A phantom dressed in black was attacking this nice gentleman. It gave me such a fright I thought my heart was going to explode!"

"Sapho, you have quite an imagination," Wynne-Ascott said.

"It wasn't her imagination," Cosmo said.

Wynne-Ascott looked astounded. "Someone attacked you? In your opera box? Egads! Robbed you, no doubt. Crying shame when the riffraff get bold enough to haunt the opera, preying on respectable men like you and me . . . well, like you, anyway. Even a desperate jackanapes wouldn't have little enough sense to try and shake me down."

"Oh, and why is that, my lord?" Lady Drummond asked.

He produced a tiny black revolver from inside his coat pocket. "Because I would shoot him first."

Lady Drummond's lashes fluttered. "Just to save your money?"

"No, dear lady, to preserve my honor," Wynne-Ascott

replied. "Cosmo, I hope you didn't lose your bankroll in this madcap skirmish."

Cosmo wondered if the lord might know more about the attack than he was letting on. Clearly, the villain's motivation hadn't been robbery. "Luckily, my lord, I managed to hold on to my blunt as well as my honor."

"Good for you!" said Lady Drummond, with more heartiness than Cosmo would have expected from a woman who had passed out cold on the floor.

"Can you stand now?" Cosmo straightened and, with Wynne-Ascott's assistance, got Lady Drummond to her feet.

She tottered a bit, then leaned heavily on her escort's arm. Cosmo retrieved his fallen cane from within the private box, and discreetly removed the knife and slipped it into his pocket. Then the three strolled slowly down the corridor. By the time they reached the landing of the stairs that led to the opera house lobby, Lady Drummond appeared to have completely regained her equilibrium.

"I am happy to see you are recovered," Cosmo remarked as they descended the staircase.

Lord Wynne-Ascott produced a numbered chit and collected their cloaks and hats from the uniformed valet in the vestibule. While he was absent, Lady Drummond waited with Cosmo.

"Thank you, sir, for your kindness. I do hope you weren't injured in the fray."

"I fought in Spain, dear lady. I have encountered far more treacherous adversaries than the man I met to-night."

"Undoubtedly," she said softly, touching Cosmo's arm.

Her intense stare piqued Cosmo's amusement. Older women often found him interesting; his war wound seemed to arouse their maternal instincts. Lady Drummond, however, was definitely not his type. Despite her familiarity, there was not a hint of warmth in her pale-blue gaze.

"Nonetheless, I apologize that you witnessed such a crude display of behavior." Cosmo donned his beaver hat while Wynne-Ascott assisted Lady Drummond with her cloak. "I pray you do not suffer any lasting consequences as a result of your fainting spell."

She laughed heartily as a valet held open the door. Outside, pedestrians rushed past, hunched against the wind, hats pulled low over their eyes, and coats clutched tightly about them. Wynne-Ascott lifted a hand to summon his carriage, parked half a block down the street. Instantly, his liveried driver slapped the reins on the rumps of four matching greys.

"I dare say that when you get to know me better, Sir Cosmo, you will realize that I am not a missish woman. 'Twas most uncharacteristic of me to fall out like that simply at the sight of two men fighting."

"I found it rather odd, I must admit." Wynne-Ascott muttered this aside through clattering teeth. Eyeing his approaching rig, he appeared impatient—and chilled to the bone. "Never seen you act so girlish, Sapho."

An elegant carriage rumbled to a stop in front of the theater. Wynne-Ascott's tiger, a young boy dressed in a striped waistcoat, leapt from the driver's perch and produced a small step.

Lady Drummond offered her hand to Cosmo. Shaking it, he noticed that her gloves were specially made to accommodate the dimensions of a chubby forearm made even bigger by the ropes of diamonds wound around it. Though he sensed the woman would have been pleased if he brushed his lips across her knuckles, he couldn't bring himself to do it. The idea of kissing the precious gemstones that bulged beneath Lady Drummond's black lambskin glove offended him.

"Do come around to see me, Sir Cosmo. You intrigue

me," she said, before a blast of icy wind cut short any further conversation, and Wynne-Ascott practically pushed her into the carriage.

Cosmo touched the brim of his hat and bid the couple good night. He watched the coach roll smoothly down the street and merge with the late night theater traffic. When he was certain he could not be seen out the rear window by either of the rig's occupants, he turned and reentered the Orange Street Opera House. He couldn't explain his actions. But he knew that he would be miserable, that his heart would feel as heavy as a stone, until he saw Mrs. Lucinda Partridge and spoke to her once again.

Seven

In the corridor leading to Lucinda's dressing room, Cosmo passed Mr. Pugh. The men acknowledged one another with a brusque nod, but it was apparent to Cosmo that Pugh wasn't happy; the fat man wore a very unjolly-looking scowl. Well, perhaps Mrs. Partridge had turned down another dinner invitation, or even denied him entrance to her private quarters. Whatever the case, Cosmo was glad to see the man heading toward the exit doors.

As he lifted his hand to knock on the diva's door, it swung open. Mr. Pavlov, standing on the opposite side of the threshold, appeared slightly startled.

"Hello, Sir Cosmo, I was just leaving. Mrs. Partridge is quite weary tonight, so I suggest that she not be disturbed." The bearded Russian stepped into the corridor and pulled the dressing room door shut behind him.

Brushing shoulders with Pavlov, Cosmo reached for the doorknob. "I appreciate your concern for Lucinda, and I assure you I will do nothing to endanger her health. Good night." Then he stepped inside Lucinda's dressing room and closed the door.

Clad in her silken robe, hair pushed from her face by a cotton bandeau, the diva sat at her vanity table. She lowered the wet towel she had used to cleanse her face of makeup. Her skin glowed pink and fresh in the candlelight. Tears sparkled on her eyelashes.

She stared at Cosmo's reflection in her mirror. Then, as he slowly crossed the floor, she turned and lifted her face to him. He drew up a chair and sat beside her, his knees touching hers, his hands grasping hers.

"Lucinda, you've been crying. And on such a marvelous night, when your voice was as sweet as a dove's."

His hands, covering hers, felt so strong and warm. Emotions, so many of them that Lucinda couldn't possibly articulate her feelings, roiled inside her. Yet, she wanted more than anything to communicate those feelings to Cosmo.

"I am so happy," she whispered. "I know now that my voice hasn't deserted me."

"You are the finest soprano in all of London." His voice was husky, and his eyes, black beneath that fringe of silver hair, were as hungry as a panther's.

Lucinda felt the heat of his gaze. Her torturous undergarments had been removed, and her bosom swelled beneath the thin silk of her robe. No green girl, she recognized Cosmo's heavy-lidded stare and raspy voice for what it was. A physical awareness opened up between them and held them in an invisible, erotic thrall. Lucinda's fingers tightened around his. She leaned toward him and touched his jaw. The quick, jagged breath he drew at her touch filled her with longing.

"But, Cosmo," she said softly, watching him. She could have watched him forever. Her heart leapt when his breathing altered. His response to her—so primeval, so poignant and so thoroughly masculine—thrilled her. She savored the warmth of his skin, the bristle of his whiskers. And when he pressed his lips to her palm, a ribbon of desire unfurled in the pit of her stomach.

"What, Lucinda?"

"I was so sad, too."

"Tell me why. You can tell me anything. I want to know everything about you."

"Last night, when we parted, I felt so alone. I thought you were angry with me, and I couldn't understand my feelings."

His forehead creased, and he averted his gaze. "I don't understand what is happening either. Tonight, when you sang, I almost forgot I was in a packed opera house."

"You were the only person in the theater tonight, Cosmo. It was as if you were right beside me, holding my hand, urging me on every step of the way. When I felt you there—beside me, *within me*—I knew I could do anything."

He stared at her for a heartbeat. His jaw worked, but he said nothing more. Then, releasing her hand, he turned his head from her.

Lucinda's chest ached with the need to touch him, to know him, to understand him. But, in an instant, he seemed to have removed himself from her reach. He had begun to respond, but then he had clamped shut his lips, retreating into some private cave. He hung his head between slumped shoulders. Lucinda listened to his labored breathing, but she knew she could not bring Cosmo back to the private place they had shared just a moment before.

Confused, she wavered. Should she touch him, throw her arms around him, and draw him to her? She hesitated. What if he rebuffed her? Perhaps he needed to be left alone. Some men were that way.

At last, she placed her hand on his arm. "I would like to be your friend, Cosmo."

He caught her hand, and squeezed her fingers. Gazing at the floor, he spoke in a strangled voice. "I should be honored to count you among my friends, Lucinda. You are a good woman."

"Do you really think so? I got the distinct impression last night that you didn't think so highly of me. You were put off by my talk of finding a husband, isn't that so?"

He shrugged.

"Do you think it brazen of me to admit that I am looking for a wealthy man, Cosmo?"

He lifted his head and looked at her. "I confess that I do not understand it. Why would a woman such as yourself settle for so little? Why wouldn't you demand integrity and honor from the man you intend to spend your life with? Doesn't love count for anything?"

Lucinda chuckled, then leaned forward and gave Cosmo a kiss on his cheek. Withdrawing her hand from his, she sat back in her chair and studied him. "You are a man of many contradictions, sir. You are a romantic in theory, yet you have difficulty expressing your innermost feelings."

"I can say whatever I want. Some feelings should be kept to oneself, however, for to bring them out in the open only causes misunderstanding."

Lucinda nodded, fairly certain what Cosmo really meant: *To bring certain feelings out in the open might make a man appear weak.*

He continued: "I do believe, however, that a man and a woman ought not to be together unless they are in love. Truly, madly, passionately in love. Forever, all the time."

"Do you think that is possible, Cosmo? Were your parents in love, passionately, all the time?"

"No, of course not." He frowned. "But I will never marry a woman like my mother. She was demanding, overbearing. She placed so many conditions on her approval of me. No, I shall marry a woman who loves me simply for myself. Not for fame, not for social standing, and certainly not for wealth."

"Are you saying that the woman you will marry must love you solely for yourself, the way you are exactly, with no conditions or restrictions whatsoever?"

"Yes, that is precisely what I am saying."

Lucinda smiled. Suddenly, Sir Cosmo Fairchild for all his grey hair and brooding scowls and deep worry lines appeared so young and boyish. "Dear Cosmo. Don't you know that love and marriage are living things that require nourishment and understanding and careful cultivation? A woman must work diligently to keep a man in love with her; a man should work equally hard to keep his lady entranced."

"Love should come naturally," argued Cosmo.

She sighed. "I have been married twice. I know that it takes more than love to make a marriage successful."

" 'Tis you who are the cynic, Lucinda."

"Perhaps. And you, the dashing romantic. With a mysterious past. La, your eyes look as if they have seen true suffering, and your creased brow bespeaks a troubled conscience. If I were one of those silly addlepates who reads tea leaves or palms, I suspect I would tell you that you have seen much tragedy in your life."

"Any charlatan worth her crystal ball could safely make such a statement to a man of my age."

"But, then, I have no idea how old you are, sir."

"No doubt we are very nearly the same age, Lucinda."

She smiled. "Then, I should be thankful my hair hasn't turned to grey. Not that yours isn't attractive. On the contrary, it lends you a world-weary look that is quite appealing."

"To some women, I suppose."

To any red-blooded woman who is alive, Lucinda thought. She stopped short of telling him how compellingly handsome his rough-hewn features were, or how comforting was the physical presence of his broad shoulders and long, lean legs. No use in swelling his head too much.

After all, they had just made a compact to be friends, not eternal soul mates.

He sighed deeply, straightened, and threw one booted leg over the other. Smiling roguishly, he said, "And how dare you label me a romantic? Has love now become nothing more than a literary device?"

"Oh, now, you have been reading too much of Lord Byron! How is it that a cynic like you could fail to realize that when a woman chooses a mate, she must think of matters other than her heart? The realities of life, dear boy, are sometimes harsh."

"You consider *me* a cynic? The man who gave up his family fortune to become a penniless writer?"

The word *penniless* struck fear in Lucinda's heart. "Well, I dare say, I do not quite understand why you would do such a thing. Could you not have written *and* managed your family's estates?"

"Wasn't it Shakespeare who said, *'To thine own self be true?'* "

"Shakespeare was no pauper."

"I am happy with a roof over my head, enough food to eat and enough paper and ink to write with."

" 'Twas money that bought your fine cache of French Bordeaux, Cosmo."

"Relics of my past, Mrs. Partridge. As I told you, I haven't always been this impecunious. My coats are the most expensive money can buy, too, but I haven't bought a new one in four years. I have learned the hard way, dear lady, that money can not buy happiness."

"But it is useful when the bill collectors are knocking down the door." Lucinda laughed along with the handsome writer. She found herself wanting to know more about him. Yet his diffident attitude toward wealth daunted her. His philosophy was completely at odds with her own objectives.

She faced her mirror with a sober expression. When

she pulled her bandeau from her head, scads of golden hair tumbled to her shoulders. "Do you really want to know why I need to marry a rich man?"

Cosmo's gaze was riveted to Lucinda's hands and the brushing she was giving her thick, lustrous hair. "Yes," he murmured.

"I intend to open a women's shelter. A place where women who have been cast out of their homes can go for refuge. A place where homeless women can live until they find employment. A sanctuary for prostitutes who are trying to change their circumstances."

Cosmo's expression was one of astonishment. After a beat, he let out a bark of laughter. "Good God! I should say that you are full of contradictions, too. But, on second thought, perhaps your reformist politics are quite consistent with your cynical attitudes toward men. Convinced that men cannot change their ways, you have decided to provide women with a safe refuge from their tyrannies."

"And what is wrong with that?"

"Why not leave social reform to the members of Parliament?"

"Because I don't see them doing much about it."

"And you believe that you can make a difference? You? One person? One woman?"

Lucinda laid her brush on the top of her vanity table and faced Cosmo. "It is a beginning, Cosmo. And it is what I want to do. Just as you have given up wealth in favor of your writing career, I am willing to give up everything to pursue my dream of helping these women."

"Are you prepared to give up your chance at love, Lucinda?"

His question and, as always, that dark, challenging stare of his slammed into her like a runaway curricle. "How dare you challenge my integrity, sir."

He laced his fingers around his knee. A tense silence

hung in the air. Finally, Lucinda resumed brushing her hair, and Cosmo watched her reflection in the mirror. A considerable amount of time passed before anyone spoke.

"Let us have a more serious discussion," Cosmo said, at last.

She slanted her gaze at him. She thought that was what they *had* been having. Cosmo clearly wasn't interested in her so-called reformist ideas.

"You are determined to marry one of your three gentleman callers, is that not so?" he asked.

"That is correct. I haven't much time to make a decision, either. My contract expires in a very short time, you know, and then I shall be totally without funds. With no savings and no income, I won't be able to support myself, much less help anyone else."

"And with two failed marriages behind you, you had best be certain you make the right choice this time."

"I resent your reminding me of my past, Cosmo."

"It seems we have turned the tables, dear. You have gone out of your way to question the judgment I have used in my past."

Lucinda held her tongue. Cosmo's playful tone contained a note of maliciousness; she wasn't certain whether he was mocking her, or whether he was mocking himself. Perhaps both. He hadn't said or done anything that she could declare was "ungentlemanly," or outside the bounds of decorum. But there was something about his incisive questions, something about his willingness to challenge her motivations and her character, that made her uncomfortable.

In the past, the men she had known cared not a whit whether she was honest, straightforward, trustworthy or kind. All the men Lucinda knew had valued her pretty looks, her voice, her income, her fame and her ample body. Cosmo was the first man she had ever met who seemed to be forming an opinion of her based on what was inside her heart and head. And, for that reason, she realized, his opinion of her *mattered*.

"I should tell you that just today I have been proposed to by both Mr. Pugh and Mr. Pavlov."

"Two proposals in one day?" Cosmo scratched his chin. "Well, that does complicate the matter, doesn't it? Which one shall you choose? Or should you hold out for Lord Wynne-Ascott?"

"I am having a late dinner with him this evening."

Cosmo arched one shaggy, black brow. "That man does make the rounds, doesn't he?"

"If you are referring to his friendship with Lady Drummond, I know all about it, Cosmo. He came around right after the performance—"

"My, the traffic has been thick in here tonight!"

"And he explained everything to me. He and Lady Drummond are merely friends. He has no romantic interest in her. Good heavens, she is too old by far, and not at all his type."

"I should think that she is far below his social station, as well. But, perhaps her obvious wealth compensates for her parvenue status."

"Don't be rude, Cosmo. Just because you care nothing for money doesn't give you license to brand all rich people as shallow or hypocritical."

"Your words, Lucinda, not mine. At any rate, I have a proposition for you. It is a mad scheme, but one that I think will serve us both well. It has to do with your decision, Mrs. Partridge. You see, I feel I also have a stake in seeing that you make the right one."

"Why, Cosmo? You are writing a book about a diva's life. That does not make you responsible for my future happiness."

"No, but I have decided that I like you. I shouldn't care to see you marry the wrong man. If you will permit me to act in the role of, say, an older brother or guardian, I should be honored to help you make the right decision about whom to marry. Besides, your plan to build a women's shelter is a laudable one, and I should be proud to know that I had the slightest role in making that possible."

Astonishment stole Lucinda's breath. She gaped at Cosmo, half-certain she had misunderstood what he had said. "Are you quite serious, sir?"

He nodded.

She was flattered and confused. Despite the short time she had known Cosmo, she, too, felt that they could form a lasting friendship. Sometimes, the bonds of friendship were forged quickly, but that made them no less strong. Still, she didn't recall ever having a friend who was willing to do something so unselfish for her. She was so overwhelmed by gratitude that she could hardly speak.

Her eyes blurred with hot tears. Reaching out to grasp Cosmo's hand, she murmured, "That is very kind, sir."

"Now, don't be maudlin, Mrs. Partridge," he teased her softly. "You must save those tears for the stage."

She let go his hand, and found a damp towel on her dressing table. Quickly, she dried her eyes, then smiled brightly at Cosmo. "What precisely do you propose to do, sir? To help me make my decision, that is."

His crooked smile held a promise of mischief. "I propose to conduct a surveillance of all three of your suitors. I will investigate them as if they were suspects in a heinous crime and I were a Bow Street runner. Believe me, before my investigation is concluded, you will know everything there is to know about each gentleman. All the facts you need to have in order to make an informed decision will be yours. There will be no guesswork involved, Lucinda. You will marry the right man, that I assure you."

She burst out laughing. "Oh, how dreadful. And how utterly delicious!"

His throaty laughter thrilled Lucinda's senses. "Are you in agreement, then?"

She didn't hesitate. "I should feel like the lowest tabby for allowing such a thing. But your proposition has its merits. How else is a woman to know what sort of man a man really is? Other than what he chooses to tell, there is no way to gauge a man's sincerity or his credibility."

"I believe you have learned that lesson the hard way," Cosmo said.

"Don't remind me." Lucinda shuddered at the memory of her second husband, the handsome man in shining armor who turned out to be a bigamist. "It is settled, then. I accept your offer, Sir Cosmo."

He stood, bent low over her hand, and grazed her knuckles with his lips. "Good. Then I shall bid you good night. Your late-dinner companion will be arriving soon, and I have no wish to see Lord Wynne-Ascott again this evening. I will begin my investigation tomorrow, Mrs. Partridge."

"Good night." She drew a deep breath, confounded by the sensation of his warm lips on her skin. Watching him cross the floor with his elegant cane, she thought him the most handsome, enigmatic man she had ever met. His departure incited a momentary panic. She didn't want him to go away, and that realization rattled her nerves.

Standing in the threshold of her dressing room, he turned and met her gaze. In her heart, Lucinda experienced a quickening. Knowing that Cosmo cared enough about her to assist her in finding the proper husband gave her an incredible feeling of safety and warmth. But she couldn't help wondering how different her future might be if Cosmo had enough money to qualify as marriage material.

* * *

In a maroon dressing gown, hastily thrown on pantaloons and velvet slippers, Milburn Sinclair appeared the epitome of effortless elegance. The silver-haired gentleman sat in a plush leather wing chair positioned cattycornered to an ornately carved mantelpiece. The fire which his servants had quickly stoked now crackled with vibrance.

Sir Cosmo's unexpected visit had put the night staff of Sinclair's Curzon Street town house into a minor frenzy. Hot tea was being brewed, port had already been served, and a plate of cold meats and sliced bread was on its way. But the elder government servant appeared not the least harried by the arrival of one of his most trusted agents. He patiently waited while Cosmo drank his port. Whatever the younger man needed to get off his chest, Sinclair had no intention of rushing him.

Mahogany-paneled walls, heavy claw-footed furniture and an imposing partner's desk created a somber, masculine ambience. Flickering candles washed the room in muted, golden tones. In a matching chair opposite Sinclair's, Sir Cosmo Fairchild stared at the marble hearth and gathered his thoughts. He wasn't even sure why he had roused Sir Milburn at one o'clock in the morning. He knew only that his feelings toward Lucinda Partridge were incredibly muddled, and he feared that he was falling in love, once again, with the wrong woman.

Outside, the wind howled. Fist-sized nuggets of hail barraged the windows facing Curzon Street. And Cosmo couldn't help but worry that Lucinda, wherever she and Wynne-Ascott were by now, was safe and warm.

Squeezing shut his eyes, he silently lambasted himself. Fool! He should be thinking about his duties! His job was to unveil and apprehend a spy ring, not to protect

Lucinda Partridge. Indeed, her welfare should be of no concern to him.

He drained his glass, reached for the decanter and poured himself another drink.

"Care for a pinch of snuff?" Sir Milburn asked.

"Thank you, but I prefer to numb my senses rather than heighten my awareness."

Milburn gave the younger man a sympathetic smile. "Is your situation that grave, Cosmo? Well, then, perhaps it is time you speak about it. I know you didn't get me out of bed at this hour of the morning to share a glass of port with me—or half a bottle, for that matter. Ease up, boy. Otherwise, you'll have the megrims come morning."

"An aching head is nothing compared to the way I feel now."

"Leg bothering you?"

"No more than usual." Cosmo stared at the fire but saw nothing of it; Lucinda's face was imprinted on his mind. Squeezing the bridge of his nose, he shut his eyes. When he opened them, Milburn's incisive stare demanded that he get on with the reason for his visit. "I just don't think I can do it, sir. Continue this mission, that is. I am in over my head as it is. I have no objectivity—"

"Dear God, you've gone and done it again. You've fallen in love with her, haven't you?"

"This isn't like last time. Lucinda is different."

"Let us hope so. The last time you fell in love with a woman you were supposed to be spying on, she turned out to be spying on you!"

Cosmo's stomach turned as sour as his mood. Swallowing the bitter taste that had surged up his throat, he said, "Monique learned nothing from me. And to set the record straight, it has never been proved she knowingly intended to infiltrate the British Home Office. I seduced her, and she came to my bed as a woman in love, not as an agent provocateur."

Milburn sighed. "I admit, she gave you quite a bit of good intelligence. *In the beginning.*"

"She was estranged from her husband, and eager to spill his secrets."

A long moment of silence passed before Milburn said, "What happened, Cosmo? What left you so bitter when that affair ended? You always knew it would; it had to. How could it have been any other way?"

A wave of hot regret swept over Cosmo as his mind flashed on Monique's lovely face. Their lovemaking had been so passionate, so intense and intimate, that he had come to believe she truly loved him. When she dropped him, his heart had nearly broken in two. And when the Home Office learned that she was a French intelligence agent, Cosmo's credibility had come into question. What sort of pillow talk had they really shared? Had she outwitted the English spy? Had she obtained more information from him than Cosmo got from her?

For a while, Cosmo's career had hung in the balance.

He drew in a deep breath, quelling his anger, willing himself to stay calm. "It could not have been different, Milburn. It was just that . . . I thought . . ."

"You thought she truly loved you. And you discovered that she had an affair with you merely to make her husband jealous. But, in the end, Cosmo, her information was reliable. She really was just a bored wife seeking an outlet for her passions. I'm quite certain she never knew the significance of what she told you. You were very skillful at getting that intelligence out of her without revealing your identity. We know now that she never suspected you were a spy. Everyone here in London believes that you did a magnificent job in Paris."

"Then, why did I feel like such a blasted fool?"

"Spying isn't easy, boy. By its very nature, it requires

you to do things that you've been taught are reprehensible. You betrayed Monique, and for that you feel guilty. The fact that she used you just as badly makes you feel like a fool. I wouldn't be too hard on myself if I were you, though. You seem to have a knack for making the ladies talk. Bloody hell, I've never seen anything like it—women practically swoon over you. Care to share that little secret with me?"

Cosmo gave a self-deprecating chuckle. He wasn't at all proud of his accomplishments. And though he wasn't immune to the fact that women seemed to be attracted to him, he believed not one of them had ever loved him for himself.

Horsey Hilda had loved him for his inheritance. Monique had loved him for his indomitable sexual appetite, not to mention a particular physical attribute that in Spain had earned him the moniker *El Grande*. Lucinda, if she cared for him at all, did so because she thought he was a true friend. But if she knew who he truly was, and why he had insinuated himself into her life, she would despise him.

"Bloody Hell!" Cosmo threw back his head and swallowed the remaining port in his glass.

At that moment, two servants appeared, one with a platter of food, the other with a tray of tea. When the late-night repast had been laid out on a small table between the two men, the servants retired from the room. Sir Milburn poured a cup of tea and handed it to Cosmo.

"I think you'd better drink this, boy. You've had enough port."

Accepting the cup and saucer, Cosmo said, "I would appreciate it if you'd cease calling me *boy*. I've as much grey hair as you, for God's sake."

"But you're years younger. Your dashing figure attests to that."

The hot tea soothed Cosmo's nerves. After a moment, he said, "I've agreed to surreptitiously follow Lucinda's suitors. She is determined to marry one of them, and since we have become friends, I have proposed to investigate the private habits of each."

Milburn laughed so hard his tea went down the wrong way. After his coughing spell abated, he said, "What a clever ruse, Cosmo. Upon my great-aunt's ghost, I think you are the slyest Romeo I've ever met."

Cosmo ignored the back-handed compliment. "There are three of them, all prime candidates for the spy we are looking for. If you ask me, Nathaniel Upham, Lord Wynne-Ascott, is the most suspicious of the group. Someone tried to kill me at the opera house last night, and he appeared on the scene just moments later. But, I've nothing solid to go on yet."

"Well, keep me informed, boy—I mean, Sir Cosmo."

Cosmo hungrily disposed of a couple of sandwiches, then washed them down with another cup of tea. When his belly was satisfied, and his mood much improved, he rose. Balancing his cane against his leg, he stood before the fire and chafed his hands. Sir Milburn pulled a bell cord and, when a servant appeared, ordered that Cosmo's cloak and hat be produced.

Before Cosmo left the warmth of Sir Milburn's study, the older man came and stood next to him. He spoke in low tones, as if he were afraid someone might overhear.

"I am glad you came here tonight, Cosmo. I should tell you that this case has taken on a new urgency."

"What? Not another of our agents? Has someone else's identity been compromised?"

"No, nothing like that. Our man in Paris, the one who replaced you, tells us that Napoleon is pulling out of Spain."

"Why? He's giving Wellington a run for his money.

The conflict there is not yet decided. If he pulls out now, Wellington will have a clear victory—"

"I know, I know. That is what makes it so damned confusing. What is Puss'n Boots up to now? What in the hell has he got up his sleeve?"

Cosmo thought for a moment. There was only one answer. "Russia?" he asked.

Milburn nodded, but fell silent when his valet entered the room with Cosmo's cloak. When the servant had departed, he continued. "With Boney headed for Moscow, it is all the more important we shut down this operatic spy ring. It seems the French know every move we make before we make it. And we can't afford to have Russia in the emperor's hands, Cosmo. We simply can not!"

Then, it was settled. Cosmo left Milburn Sinclair's house with a renewed sense of purpose. Betraying Lucinda was no more palatable than it had been before. It was simply more urgent. And suddenly Cosmo's aching heart—and the beautiful diva's future—were inconsequential. England's security was at stake.

And Cosmo couldn't afford to let his chivalric principles interfere with his duty—which was to root out the spy at the opera house. Notwithstanding the emotional carnage that was sure to follow when Lucinda discovered who, and what, he really was.

Eight

Lucinda knew she should not have allowed Nathaniel Upham, Lord Wynne-Ascott, to persuade her to accompany him to his town house. Despite his reassurances—indeed, quite to the contrary—there were no chaperones present to monitor their visit, no servants milling about to lend propriety to their late-night private party.

Wynne-Ascott had even closed the door behind him when they had entered the drawing room. And now he was seated beside Lucinda on a chintz-covered sofa, his body slanted toward hers, one arm draped along the sofa's camel back, and an unequivocally predatory gleam in his eyes.

"Care for some more sherry, songbird?"

She inched farther down the length of the sofa. "No thank you, my lord. It is frightfully indecorous that I should be alone with you."

"I'm afraid my butler has come down with the flux. I had no way of knowing we would be abandoned to our own devices. But, I will not say that I am sorry."

"You should be."

"No one knows you are here, Mrs. Partridge. No one at all."

A finger of apprehension ran up her spine. "It is getting late, you know. I must go soon."

The lord leaned forward, and his fingertips found the

back of Lucinda's neck. Gently playing with the tendrils at her nape, he said, "Please don't go, Lucinda. I want you here with me. I have been thinking about this moment for months."

Lucinda sipped her sherry nervously, her fear at being alone with Wynne-Ascott warring with her desire to hear him out. "Whatever are you talking about?"

"You must know that I love you, Lucinda."

" 'Struth, you catch me quite unawares."

" 'Tis true. I think of you ceaselessly. My friends at Brooks's say I am woolgathering when I should be paying attention to the cards. My dear mother believes I am besotted because I spend more time at the opera house than I do at Tattersall's. And Lady Drummond said I had cow eyes at the theater last week; in her estimation, I was positively boring!"

"You? Boring?" Lucinda stifled a giggle. "Why, my lord, that is impossible."

"I would certainly hope so. Nevertheless, I am stricken with desire for you, Lucinda. And I have arrived at a very important decision, possibly the most important one I have made in my life."

The warmth of her sherry spread through Lucinda's veins, bolstering her courage. Otherwise, she might not have been able to hide her nervousness. Clearly, Lord Wynne-Ascott was head over heels in love. That he was on the verge of proposing to her filled her with fright. Was she certain, after all, that she wanted the man to marry her?

Good lord, three proposals in one day. Lucinda supposed there was some truth in the adage that good things come in threes. Except she wasn't entirely certain three proposals were a good thing.

Especially when she didn't know which one to accept.

Well, she had to accept one of them if she ever wanted to open her shelter. There was no way she could raise the money on her own—in one month, she wouldn't have an income. Moreover, her only talent was singing. Having been schooled and trained as an opera singer, Lucinda knew she couldn't do anything else. Which was in itself a terrifying thought. Already, she was having trouble hitting her high notes. A soprano's career could be monstrously short.

Thank goodness she had Sir Cosmo to depend upon, to assist her in determining which suitor was the most eligible. Soon enough, once his investigation was complete, she would know the true mettle of Lord Wynne-Ascott, as well as Messrs. Pugh and Pavlov. Then she would know which proposal to accept. Until then, she would simply hold off on making a decision. She would stall her suitors—if she could.

Lord Wynne-Ascott moved closer to her and took her sherry glass from her fingers. "Truly, I don't believe I can live without you."

"I am quite overtaken by surprise," Lucinda replied, pushing herself deeper into the corner of the sofa. "And emotion."

"Kiss me, then." The lord slid down the shiny chintz and wrapped his arms around Lucinda's shoulders. With lips puckered and eyelids at half-mast, he angled his head for a kiss.

Squirming, she deflected the advance. "Oh, no, my lord. It wouldn't be proper. I haven't given you my answer, after all. I have to think about your proposal, and that may take some time. This is a very important decision for me, also."

His eyes widened. "What is there to think about? I have pledged my undying devotion to you. What more could a woman of your stature ask for?"

"A woman of my stature? Whatever does that mean?" Lucinda grabbed a small pillow and held it in front of her like a shield.

Lord Wynne-Ascott shrugged and reared backward. "Well, songbird, you are a woman of the theater! One in your position must be realistic about her prospects. You can hardly afford to spurn a suitor who is willing to give you *carte blanche.* The fact that I love you—truly love you!—should make your heart sing. I wouldn't be cruel, dear, like so many other protectors would."

Lucinda's horror and hurt were too great to express. Yet her pride saved her from exhibiting too demonstrative a show of disappointment. Lord Wynne-Ascott would never know how badly he had hurt her feelings. He would know, however, how very wrong about her character he was. Lucinda wasn't certain how she would do it, but she knew instantly that before she cast him off permanently, she would see to it that Lord Wynne-Ascott would regret trifling with her.

Inhaling, she gathered her composure and forced a slight smile to her lips. "Yes, I see your point. I understand now. How very generous you are being, my lord. I hadn't thought it through in precisely those terms."

"You hadn't thought that I was proposing mar—" He let out a bark of laughter and moved away from her. "Dear God, you didn't think that I meant to make you my wife! Oh, dear woman, forgive me, but that is out of the question."

"Oh, yes, I know that it is. After all, you have your social position to worry about."

"Some have done it. Married undesirables, that is." Wynne-Ascott pushed off from the sofa and crossed the room. With a full glass of sherry in his hand, he returned, this time giving Lucinda a much wider berth on the chintz cushion. He seemed somewhat sobered by the word *marriage.* "I can not bring myself to such a folly as that. Mother would have my head!"

"Would displeasing Mother be so dangerous?"

He looked at her as if she had said something ludicrous. "Dear woman, my mother makes Robespierre look like Joan of Arc."

"Then, you are quite wise not to provoke her anger. I see why you must be careful whom you choose to marry. And marrying an opera singer, even a famous one, would surely ignite your mother's ire. Well, then, that is all there is to it. I will give you my decision as expeditiously as I am able."

"As expeditiously as you are able?" Lord Wynne-Ascott stuttered. "What sort of gammon is that? Why, you simply can't turn me down. I won't hear of it!"

Lucinda smiled serenely and stood. "Have you ever wanted something that you couldn't have, my lord?"

He stood also, his brow furrowed. "Of course. Why, yes. I mean, I suppose so. There must have been something. Why the devil would you ask me such a thing?"

"It occurs to me that you have grown accustomed to having everything you want, whenever you want. Well, my lord, you can not have me."

"I can, and I will."

Were all men little boys at heart? Lucinda felt a twinge of pity for this one, this petulant little rich boy who had every material possession he wanted, yet lived in fear of his mother's wrath. "How miserable you must be," she murmured, reaching out to touch his cheek.

Clasping her wrist, he drew her palm to his lips and pressed his lips to her skin. With his eyes tightly shut, he held her hand and kissed her fingers. His sigh was laden with emotion, and as he released her fingers, the handsome lord wore the most forlorn expression Lucinda had ever seen.

A long, tense silence stretched out between them. Lord Wynne-Ascott clenched his fists at his sides and seemed on the verge of saying something. The words were smothered by a cloud of repressed emotion, however, and never emerged.

"I have to go," Lucinda whispered at last.

"I shall have my driver take you home." He walked her to the entry hall, and as they stood waiting for his carriage to be brought around, he said, "I am sorry, Lucinda. 'Twas highly improper to bring you here to-night when there was no one to chaperone us."

"You cannot be blamed for your butler's illness."

He gave her a rueful grin, and shook his head. "You are a kind woman, songbird. You refuse to wound the feelings even of the veriest cad in London."

Offering him a soothing smile, she touched him on the shoulder. "Good night, my lord."

Outside, he saw her into the carriage. Before his tiger whisked away the portable steps, he leaned inside the compartment and stared wistfully at her. "I won't surrender," he said simply.

"I hope not," Lucinda replied.

At that moment, she thought she had never felt such sadness in her life. The wonder of it was, she was sadder for the rogue who had just offered her *carte blanche* than she was for herself.

Sir Cosmo's rented carriage bounced roughly along the country road. The recent freeze had left the highway in ruinous condition, and the horses were having a tough go of it. Every so often, the driver erupted in exclamations of warning and aggravation; then Lucinda and Cosmo would brace themselves, and the carriage would fall heavily into a deep rut before jolting out again.

If he were not so content to be in the company of Mrs. Partridge, Cosmo would have ordered the driver to turn back miles ago.

"Are you warm enough?" he asked.

She pulled her lap blanket tighter around her shoulders. "I believe my teeth have rattled loose, but I am sufficiently warm."

"You should be. I don't think I have ever seen a woman dressed in so many clothes."

Lucinda's chuckle reminded him of silver sleigh bells, tinkly and festive. "The wardrobe department was very curious about my wanting to borrow such a costume. Thick woolen stockings, heavy boots, a shapeless maid servant's gown and pinafore . . . I don't know how I managed to sing the part of a servant with so much wool and linen layered on my body."

"You certainly look the part. A smudge or two of ashes on your face and no one would ever guess you were a famous opera singer."

"Let us hope that I can convince the milk maidens who work for Mr. Pugh that I am one of them."

Sir Cosmo frowned, wondering whether he had made a mistake by allowing Lucinda to accompany him. He hadn't planned on bringing her along while he spied on her suitors. But when she learned that he was heading to Twickenham to pay a surprise visit to Lawrence Pugh's dairy farm, she refused to be left behind.

"Remember, Lucinda, we are to stay on the grounds only an hour or so. The longer we masquerade as hired hands, the greater our chances of being discovered. And I simply will not allow you to be found out. This Pugh fellow is likely to be very angry when he discovers what I've done."

"He shall never discover it," Lucinda replied, a mischievous gleam in her eyes. "You are quite convincing in your part, also. La, I think you could have had a wonderful career on the stage."

Cosmo looked down at his rough woven coat, patched mittens and thin-soled boots. His feet had been cold since he had donned this ridiculous outfit in London, and the chill was seeping through his bones, making his

right leg particularly stiff. He hadn't suffered this much
discomfort since he had taken the bullet in his thigh
and been rendered unfit for active military duty. Since
then, his life of espionage had actually provided the
most sumptuous of luxuries. Some men, like Sir Milburn,
actually envied him—after all, he had made a career, it
seemed, out of seducing women.

The carriage, encountering another deep pit in the
muddy road, slammed violently against the rocky
ground. Cosmo, his neck lashed like a leather whip, was
pitched forward. Lucinda slid off her own cushion and
screamed with fright. The horses whinnied their protests,
and the driver let out a stream of profanity that burned
even Cosmo's ears.

Lucinda and Cosmo tossed about the tiny cabin like
leaves in the wind. By the time the horses pulled the
carriage out of the trough, the passengers were on the
floor in a heap of old, tattered clothes. Lucinda landed
hard on her bottom with her arms wrapped around
Cosmo's neck. He crouched on his knees, pain shooting
through his right thigh, hands clasping Lucinda's waist.

The ache in his leg faded to the back of his mind.
Lucinda's weight in his arms awakened his awareness of
her. Even through the thick layers of woolen gowns,
aprons and cloaks, her round female figure was disturb-
ingly evident. Soft in all the right places, she nestled
against his body, as comfortable and warm as a familiar
lover.

Outside, the din of the driver and his horses dimin-
ished. The carriage tumbled down the road at a good
pace, apparently undamaged by the incident. Inside, Lucinda and Cosmo sat motionless, holding one another.
A long moment passed during which Cosmo closed his
eyes and allowed himself to savor the sensation of feeling
Lucinda in his arms. It was as delicious as old port, as

heady as young whiskey. He would have liked to stay that way forever.

She cleared her throat, forcing him back to his senses. "Excuse me, sir. I must be crushing your legs. If you will just, er, release me, I will return to my seat."

"Ah, yes." Stiffly, Cosmo rose, careful to avoid banging his head on the carriage roof.

Taking his proffered hand, Lucinda returned to her seat on the squabs. "I hope I didn't hurt you. I am hardly the waif that Madame Bartoli is."

"Thank God," he replied, sitting across from her. "I can only speak for myself, but I happen to prefer a woman with a little meat on her bones."

Lucinda smiled shyly, but did not meet his gaze. He wanted to sit beside her, to hold her hand and feel her leg pressed flush against his. Her demeanor, however, was no invitation; she appeared shaken by their close encounter, and Cosmo perceived that she wished to put distance between them.

She was right to do so, of course. Despite her living a far less sheltered life than the average woman of the *ton,* she was correct in maintaining a sense of decorum. She might be free to cavort around the countryside with a man not her husband—something most ladies would never do for fear of damaging their precious reputations—but she wasn't about to let herself be manhandled by a penniless scribbler.

Or anyone else for that matter.

A thought suddenly occurred to Cosmo that caused his jaw to clench. How did Lucinda manage to conduct her ongoing romances without chaperones, without a mother or father to protect her? The fact that she had been married before bespoke a certain worldliness on her part, but she was, after all, a woman alone in the world. How on earth did she fend off her suitors' unwanted advances?

"It will be another hour yet before we reach Twickenham," Cosmo said, removing his writing instruments and paper from his leather valise. "Let us not waste this time, Lucinda. Would you be opposed to my asking you some questions about your life, about the life of a diva?"

She appeared relieved. "Not at all."

"Tell me what a typical day is like for you. Start at the beginning, when you awaken." He watched her as she spoke, picturing her face in the morning light, imagining her hair loose and flowing across the pillows.

"I am not an early riser, sir. By the time I am out of bed, my maid servant has come and prepared hot tea and biscuits. I like to take a long, leisurely bath before I dress; then I spend the afternoon reading or, if I am performing a new opera, memorizing my lines."

"Do you sing during the day?"

"I try not to overexert my voice when I am performing. Of course, it is impossible to be totally quiet. I am a creature who likes to talk, after all. La, I chatter away sometimes; I hardly know how you tolerate it, sir."

Cosmo smiled as he wrote in his journal. Much of what Lucinda said, he transcribed verbatim. Often though, he wrote his own impression of what she said, impressions that might have surprised her. Sometimes he got so caught up in listening to her speak, his pen simply made illegible marks on his page. Frequently, he found himself mesmerized when Lucinda talked; he might consider it prattling in other women, but when she spoke, his gaze was riveted to her lips, his attention fixed on the melodious sound of her voice.

"Go on," he urged her. "Then, after the performance, you receive visitors in your dressing room. Your suitors often come to visit you there, do they not?"

She met his steady gaze. "I cannot refuse to see patrons of the opera house. The managers would be furious with me if I did. Patrons who deliver flowers, or bring gifts of chocolates and sweet-smelling things, are always thanked politely. I make it a point not to be overly friendly or familiar with these types of men, however."

"But, you are a woman alone in the world."

She arched her perfectly shaped brows. "I can take care of myself, sir. Madonna Bartoli is only a few feet away in her dressing room next to mine. In addition, Mr. Pavlov is always aware of everything that happens backstage."

Cosmo doubted that the manager of a busy opera production could be counted upon to mark the comings and goings of every person who ventured backstage.

"Forgive me for pressing the point, Lucinda, but what would you do if one of your suitors attempted to compromise your virtue?"

Lucinda's expression hardened. "I can take care of myself."

"You are quite the independent woman."

A look of surprise flashed in her eyes. "Independent? In some ways, I suppose." Then she turned her head and stared out the window at the passing countryside, bleak and wintry.

Realizing he had touched upon a sore subject, Cosmo perhaps should have backed away. But it wasn't in his nature, and besides, he was eager to know as much about Lucinda Partridge as he could. "Why would a woman as independent as yourself be so desperate to obtain a husband? Will you not feel constricted by married life? Will it not be a huge adjustment for you?"

At length, Lucinda replied, "Perhaps you are making assumptions without all the true facts, sir. In one month, I shall be without an income. And I have no savings whatsoever to subsist on. A fine job I have done taking care of myself."

"You could get on with another opera house."

"Ha! Which one, sir? If Mr. Pavlov has been unable

to find employment for me, then who can? He has tried, you know. As a personal favor to me, he has contacted every theater and music hall in London. Serious opera isn't nearly as popular as it once was. People want to see comedies now, or plays. Aging sopranos with cracked voices aren't terribly in demand."

"Are you afraid of growing older, then? Is that it? You're afraid of growing old alone?" Cosmo started to tell her that she needn't worry, that he had money enough for them both. But he could hardly reveal his true identity now. Lucinda thought he was a penniless writer, and she must continue to think that until he discovered the spy at the opera.

Besides, he didn't want a woman to love him merely for his money. If her ardor for him depended on the plumpness of his pockets, he didn't want her anyway.

She stared at him, anger flashing in her eyes. "You don't understand, Cosmo! My dream is to open a home for women. I cannot raise sufficient funds for such an endeavor. I need help; I need a backer."

"You need a husband."

"Precisely." With her hands clasped tightly together, she was the picture of pent-up hostility. "Sir Cosmo, I cannot help notice the fine state of affairs you have arranged in your own life. Forgive me for saying so, but your criticizing my love life is as absurd as my criticizing the condition of your finances. It seems to me we're both in arrears and desperately in need of assistance. However, we are the two least qualified people on earth to be making such offers."

"I resent that, Lucinda. You have no need to insult me. I was merely trying to offer some brotherly advice."

"Cosmo, why do we never discuss *your* love life?"

Cosmo raked his hand through his hair. As it so happened, his love life had been quite interesting these past few years, and he had the grey hair to prove it. But he wasn't in the habit of discussing his past loves; in fact, he was uncomfortable talking about anything so personal. Like many of his peers, Sir Cosmo Fairchild would rather have been run through a medieval gauntlet than be forced to talk about his feelings.

"Your point is well taken, Lucinda. Please forgive me. Let me remind you, though, that it is your life that we are writing a book about, not mine. There is no need for me to divulge anything of my past, except as it might naturally be revealed in the course of our friendship. Your life is another matter. Your life—should my publisher be so kind—will soon be an open book."

Tossing her head, Lucinda released a harsh sigh. "I should be in Bedlam for agreeing to this foolishness. You aren't going to publish everything I say, are you?"

"I've been writing down everything, haven't you noticed?"

A look of horror appeared in her eyes. "Cosmo! You wouldn't write all those things! Would you?"

He patted the air with his hands. "Calm down, Lucinda. I promise you, I will not embarrass you by revealing any lurid or unseemly details. Moreover, I will let you review the final manuscript before it goes to my publisher. Is that agreeable?"

She pushed back in her seat, a look of relief spreading across her pretty face. "I knew I could depend upon you, Cosmo."

"Yes, Lucinda. You can depend upon me." Even as Cosmo spoke those words, he felt the emptiness in them. He was the one man she couldn't depend upon. His friendship was based on a falsehood. And he could do nothing but watch as she flew headlong into disaster, marrying a man for all the wrong reasons, a man she couldn't possibly love.

* * *

Shortly after noon, the carriage stopped at the long, winding road that led to Mr. Pugh's country house, aptly titled Milkwood Manor. Sir Cosmo gave the driver strict instructions. He was to continue to the nearest village, then turn around and pick up his passengers at the very spot where he left them. That way, no one at Milkwood Manor would be aware that the shabbily dressed couple seeking employment had been delivered by a rented coach.

To make their ruse more believable, Lucinda and Cosmo held hands as they walked down the curving road toward the manor house. As they approached, they saw through a grove of white birch that Milkwood Manor was a great, rambling estate, with a main house that resembled a sprawling Italian villa. Palladian windows, massive columns and an ornately embellished portico lent the mansion an air of stately elegance.

Boots crunching the pulverized gravel of the drive, Lucinda surveyed the estate where she might live if she married Mr. Lawrence Pugh. It was huge, to be certain, with outbuildings, barns, sheds and milking galleries spreading out behind the main house.

"Are you certain Mr. Pugh will not be here today, Lucinda?"

"He always goes to London for the day on Wednesdays. The man is as reliable as the night crier in that respect. Trust me, Cosmo, Mr. Pugh will not be in Twickenham until early tomorrow morning."

She had thought the dairy farm would be removed from the main house, out of sight perhaps, but apparently Mr. Pugh preferred to live in close proximity to his livelihood. Well, a man could not be blamed for that, Lucinda thought. Ivan Pavlov practically lived in the opera house. It was important that a man be passionate about his work, she supposed. Perhaps that was a sign of Mr. Pugh's good character.

Nearing the front steps, Lucinda's pace began to slow. Up close, Milkwood Manor was in desperate need of repair.

"Rather grand, isn't it?" Cosmo asked, clearly in a facetious tone.

They had stopped and were standing on the wide marble front porch, staring at the great brass knockers on the mahogany double doors. Cosmo squeezed her hand.

Swallowing her disappointment, for she didn't want to admit that she was shocked by the state of dilapidation Milkwood Manor was in, Lucinda forced a small smile. "It is quite grand, if you ask me. It needs some work, I agree, but nothing a woman's touch wouldn't cure."

Cosmo arched his brows. "Are you saying that Mr. Pugh is letting his house fall down around his ears because he is unmarried?"

"It is a sad fact that unmarried people are often waiting for their lives to begin."

"An interesting theory, Lucinda. If you are correct, you will have much to do in the way of renovating this house when Mr. Pugh makes you his wife."

"It will keep me occupied," she replied primly.

"For the next century," returned Sir Cosmo. He lifted the heavy knocker and banged the door.

He knocked three times before a butler opened the door. By then, Lucinda was shivering with cold and cursing the incompetence of her potential husband's staff.

"May I assist you?" The servant who greeted them was not overjoyed by the appearance of two peasants on his master's doorstep. "If you're looking for handouts, we have none. Nothing goes to waste here, I'm afraid. We have cows and pigs on the premises, as you must know."

Clapping his hands together to emphasize the frigid temperature of the outdoors, Cosmo said, "We are looking for employment, man. Might we be introduced to the manager of Milkwood Manor. We have heard that he is hiring."

The butler shook his head. "I doubt that very much." Then he started to shut the door.

Cosmo thrust out his hand and held open the door. "Just let us speak to him, then! What harm does it do? For God's sake, man, it's cold out here. My wife is three months gone, and we haven't a bread crumb for our supper. All I'm asking is that you tell the manager there is a young, hardworking couple here that wants work. And is willing to work cheap."

"How cheap?"

Lucinda gasped, as much from the cold as from surprise at the butler's rudeness. "We need to eat," she inserted. "I don't suppose we have much bargaining power, do we?"

With that, the butler directed them to proceed down the road from which they had come, and go about a quarter of a mile farther onto the estate. There they would find a stone cottage where the estate manager lived and conducted his business.

"Be sure to tell him you'll work cheap," the butler said with a knowing smile before he slammed the door in their faces.

Nine

Lucinda and Cosmo hurried toward the overseer's cottage, eager to be invited inside where they might warm themselves before a fire. *A cup of tea would be nice, too,* thought Lucinda, as Cosmo rapped his knuckles on the warped wood of the front door. It was a building with no discernible style whatsoever, thrown up as a purely utilitarian structure, without regard to aesthetics.

It matched its occupant. The man who yanked open the door and frowned out at them appeared in a worse mood than the butler at the main house.

"What do you want?" he growled, casting a mean, bulging eye toward Lucinda's shivering figure.

"We need work." Cosmo wrapped a protective arm around Lucinda. "May we come in, sir? We've traveled quite a distance with nothing to eat, and my wife here is cold."

"Ain't lookin' fer no handouts, I hope. 'Cause we don't have nothing left over here."

"The butler already informed us of such," Cosmo said, practically pushing his way inside, with Lucinda in tow.

"Come in, then, ' the caretaker said grudgingly.

He wore coarse breeches and braces over a dingy work shirt of patched wool. To Lucinda, who adored the feel of silks and satins and creamy linens against her skin, his ensemble looked like something a martyr would wear to do penance. The grime on the man's face even reminded her of ashes.

The inside of the cottage wasn't exactly cozy, but it was warmer than the frigid air outdoors. Lucinda looked around at the small interior, the roughly plastered chinks in the walls, the bare floor and, in the back, a stone hearth where a good fire crackled.

She and Cosmo crossed the room. Snatching off their mittens and stuffing them in pockets, they warmed their hands, then turned around and allowed the heat from the fire to warm their backsides.

"My name is Wat Dinkins, and this is my wife, Mattie," Sir Cosmo said.

"Uh." The caretaker received this news without the slightest bit of interest. Nor did he evidence any inclination to introduce himself. Seated behind a scarred wooden table, he ruffled through a bulging accounts book as if he were entirely alone.

Cosmo and Lucinda exchanged quizzical glances.

"Well, sit down, then. Ye've warmed yer backsides enough," the nameless caretaker said at last.

Still clutching her cloak tightly about her shoulders, Lucinda sat in the rickety chair indicated. Beside her sat Cosmo, grimacing in obvious discomfort. She had noticed of late that when he sat for extended periods, he walked stiffly afterward. Had he injured his leg as a boy, fox hunting, perhaps? She wanted to ask him, but he didn't seem inclined to discuss his past at all.

That he was willing to undergo such inconvenience on her account caused Lucinda to experience a moment of guilt. She hadn't done a thing to reciprocate Sir Cosmo's kindness. And she knew that his agreeing to investigate her suitors had nothing to do with his book.

Even if he thought any of her romantic escapades were noteworthy, as interesting anecdotes to punctuate an otherwise dry account of a diva's life, she wouldn't allow him to publish such scurrilous material. By the time his book was published, she would be married, after all. It wouldn't do for her new husband, whomever he was, to read all about her efforts to entrap him.

"Well, what sort of employment is available at Milkwood Manor?" Cosmo inquired, an edge of impatience in his voice.

The caretaker closed his journal. "I haven't got any work that ye can do and keep yer hands clean. It's all nasty stuff here on Mr. Pugh's farm."

"We're hard workers," Cosmo said.

"Uh. We'll see about that. Can you milk a cow, gel?"

Having prepared for precisely that question, Lucinda nodded.

The caretaker looked at Cosmo. "Ever slaughtered one?"

Lucinda thought Cosmo paled a bit, but he gave a firm nod and expounded on his credentials, mentioning a charnel house in Hertfordshire where he claimed to have got his start in the livestock business.

"Uh." The caretaker studied Cosmo intently. "Ye don't look the sort who fancies blood under his nails."

Cosmo's features hardened, and his gaze darkened, reminding Lucinda how little she really knew about him. For a man who grew up in the lap of luxury, then forsook his birthright in order to pursue the romantic life of a writer, he appeared to her a rather rugged-looking man. Surely, she had never thought of him as a milksop. Yet the caretaker scrutinized him as if he were unfit for manual labor.

"What's that cane fer?"

"Fell off a horse. Accident happened years ago, when I was young and foolish enough to think I could outrun the wind."

So that's what happened, thought Lucinda. *He hurt his leg in a horse race.*

"Ye ain't a drinkin' man, are ye? Mr. Pugh don't allow no drinkin' on the premises."

Lucinda spoke up. "We're God-fearin' Christians, sir. We do not indulge in the consumption of alcohol."

After another few minutes of questions and answers, the caretaker announced that they were hired. "If yer willin' to work fer the wages Mr. Pugh offers."

"And what is that?" Cosmo asked.

"A shilling a week."

"A shilling a week?" Lucinda and Cosmo cried in unison.

"Uh. That's what Mr. Pugh offers, and that's all he pays."

"Good God, man," Cosmo said, in keeping with the character he was playing. "That's highway robbery. A man can't support a wife and child on wages such as those. Even two shillings a week will barely keep us alive."

"A shilling fer ye both!" A mean grin spread over the caretaker's face. "Ye didna' think he was gonna pay ye each a shilling, did ye? Well, then, ye don't know a thing about Mr. Pugh."

Lucinda gasped. "But I thought he was a rich man," she blurted, unthinkingly.

The caretaker's gaze shot to her. "How didja think he got that way? Take it, or get off the premises immediately."

"We'll take it," Cosmo said.

An hour later, Lucinda was sitting on a low stool in a drafty barn, her fingers wrapped around the warm udders of a cow. Behind her, in the adjoining stall, was another young woman whose milking skills were obviously far more advanced than hers. Though a high wooden partition separated them, Lucinda could see her neighbor through a gap caused by a missing board.

She was a ruddy-faced, toothsome girl with thick, curly red hair tied negligently in a knot at her nape. As her nimble fingers moved beneath her cow, jets of milk squirted into the tin bucket between her feet.

Looking up, the redheaded girl met Lucinda's gaze through the ramshackle partition dividing the stalls. "You'd better do better than that, lass."

"Oh, I'm just a little rusty, is all." By pure luck, a stream of milk began to pour from the cow's udders. Steam rose from the hot liquid as the bucket slowly filled. "My name's Mattie. What's yours?"

"Bonnie." The girl moved her bucket and placed another one beneath the cow's teats. "What on earth are ya doin' here, if ya don't mind me askin'?"

"My husband and I have been out of work for some time, and there's a babe on the way. So, is Mr. Pugh so bad to work for?"

The girl pressed her shoulder against the cow's side. Though she laughed heartily, her expression held a grimness that sent a chill up Lucinda's spine. "Is he so bad? Well, not iffin ya don't mind goin' without food fer days at a time. And not iffin ya don't mind working eighteen hours a day with hardly a moment to eat yer dinner."

Lucinda's fingers stilled. "He sounds like an ogre. I thought he was a nice man. Someone told me that, someone in the last village my husband and I passed through."

"Well, that someone must have been pullin' yer leg, lass. 'Cause Mr. Lawrence Pugh is one a the meanest men on earth. To his servants, that is. Believes that he's doin' us a favor just by givin' us the opportunity to work. And fer those of us who can't find employment elsewhere, I s'pose he is. But it's his way of thinkin' that if he can get cheap labor, why pay anythin' more fer it?"

"Why do you stand for it, then? Why don't you work for someone else?"

Bonnie chuckled again, this time with considerably less gusto. "Me father lives in Twickenham. He's old and feeble. There's no one else to care for him, so's I must work within walkin' distance of me home. Believe me, when he's not livin' no more, I'll be on me way. Goin' to London, I am. I hear they's lots of good jobs there fer young lasses willin' to work hard."

Lucinda's heart squeezed. "And have you ever met Mr. Pugh, personally? Exchanged a word with him perhaps?"

"He don't talk with the likes of me." Bonnie brushed a stray curl from her forehead. "Gave a pair of calves to me mother, though, when she could no longer work here, after the accident."

"The accident?"

"Slipped on the floor of the barn," Bonnie said. "In the middle of the night, when Mr. Pugh had called her to come and help birth a calf. Nearly split her head in two on a rock jutting from the earth, but the local doctor stitched her up and sent her on her way. Never mind, though, Ma was never the same after that. Couldn't work a lick, even after her hair grew back and the scar was covered up."

"Did Mr. Pugh do anything to help your mother after the accident?"

"Like I said, gave her the calves. Had her come in and sign a piece of paper, all legal like. The caretaker witnessed the signatures, and Ma took the calves home. She lived for two more years after that, and all that while, she and Pa stabled the cows, fed them, doctored them and such."

The girl fell silent. Only the hissing of the cow's milk

streaming into the bucket evidenced her industry. At length, she glanced up, meeting Lucinda's curious gaze.

"A day or two after Ma died, Mr. Pugh's solicitor showed up at our door. Claimin' to want the cows back. Said Mr. Pugh owned them, outright. 'Tweren't nothin' we could do about it."

"How could he own them if he gave them to your mother?"

Bonnie shook her head. Her laugh had faded, and her smile vanished. "The piece of paper Ma signed. Turns out she merely agreed to keep the cows, raise them and pay their expenses. When she died, ownership reverted to Mr. Pugh. That's what the contract said, in black and white. Only problem was, Ma couldn't read. She had no idea she and Pa were merely keepin' Pugh's cows, fattening them up till the day Pugh came and got them again."

Lucinda muttered a word she had never said before. Suddenly, Mr. Lawrence Pugh seemed meaner than she had ever dreamed humanly possible.

Was it conceivable that the shy, unassuming man who courted her could also be the shrewd, conniving businessman that Bonnie described?

It boggled her mind to think that Mr. Lawrence Pugh, opera lover, could be so materialistic, so stingy, so cold-hearted. He had exhibited none of those qualities toward her. On the contrary, he had promised her a life of ease and luxury, an existence befitting a princess.

Were his promises mere lies? Were his protestations of love just carefully crafted representations meant to seduce her into marriage? Had Mr. Lawrence Pugh been offering her Spanish coin when he told her he loved her?

Warm milk spewed through Lucinda's fingers, spilling on the coarse smock she had been provided by the caretaker. She had heard enough. Standing, she knocked over the pail at her feet and sent a puddle of milk pouring onto the hard-packed floor. She ripped off her smock and tossed it over the top of the wooden partition. Before she left, she paused in front of Bonnie's stall.

"Can you keep a secret, Bonnie?"

"Sure I can."

"My name isn't Mattie. It's Lucinda Partridge. If you make it to London, look me up. But don't tell a soul you met me here."

The redheaded girl smiled. "If I make it to London, Mrs. Partridge, promise *me* somethin'."

"What's that?" Lucinda asked.

"Don't tell a soul you met *me* here."

She considered it a minor miracle that she didn't catch a fatal ague or throat malady. The conditions at Milkwood Manor were hardly conducive to a diva's good health. But Lucinda had actually hopped into Sir Cosmo's rented carriage with irrepressible energy. She supposed it was the shock and anger that warmed her blood. It certainly wasn't the shabby clothes she wore, or the thin-soled half boots.

A day later, Clarissa clucked over her like a mother hen. "What if ye'd got a sore throat, traipsing about out there in a drafty old barn?"

The two women strolled down Tottenham Court Road, pausing briefly to peer into the occasional bowed glass window at the displays of glittering silverware, enameled snuffboxes and feathered hats. Though the sun was bright, the air was raw, and they walked arm in arm, huddling together to stay warm.

"This weather isn't doing me any good, either," remarked Lucinda. "But I am not worried about getting sick. Not at all."

Clarissa looked at her questioningly. "That's odd. Ever since I've known ye, ye've fretted over that throat of yers like it was lined with gold. Not speakin' the day of performances, wrapping your neck in scarves just to dash from the door of the opera house to a waiting carriage, drinking honey and tea each night before bedtime. What's gotten into ye, Miss Lucinda?"

The blond soprano hugged her friend's arm more tightly. With a light shrug, she tilted back her head, allowing the sun to warm her upturned face. "I don't know, Clarissa. It is just that I feel stronger than I was before. Like I have acquired a new power . . . the power to shape my destiny perhaps."

"Bloody hell, have ye gone and got religious all the sudden?"

"Clarissa, watch your tongue! If you are going to improve your status in life, you must stop speaking like a sailor." Lucinda's frown soon smoothed into an easy smile, however. "Oh, I know, old habits die hard. Good heavens, I am just learning that myself."

"I am sorry me rough language offends." The women walked in silence a moment before Clarissa continued. "But, if ye don't mind me saying so, ye are not making a whit of sense. What sort of power have ye acquired? Where did ye get it from? And does it have anythin' to do with this Sir Cosmo that ye haven't quit talking about since ye got out of bed this mornin'?"

"Oh, I suppose it has everything to do with Sir Cosmo. And yet it is a power that comes from within." Halting, Lucinda tapped one gloved finger on Clarissa's heart. "You see, Cosmo has taught me that I don't just have to sit and wait for things to happen to me. I can actually make things happen."

Clarissa's brows shot together. "Ye ain't . . . I mean, ye are not going to become one of those radical suffragettes, are ye?"

"I am not talking about the power to vote, though I believe I am as capable of helping to choose this country's leaders as anyone else. No, I am talking about the passive role women play in their own lives, Clarissa. Women *wait* for men to court them; they *wait* for men to propose marriage. They have no affirmative say in such matters that govern their entire existence!"

"Do men have it so much better?" Clarissa plucked at a hole in the finger of her mittens. " 'Tis the men who must do the askin' and the courtin', always riskin' gettin' rejected or humiliated. Then, when they have won a lady's hand, 'tis the men who must earn the money, or at least manage it if they was born into a good family. I don't think I would want that responsibility."

"But wouldn't you, just once, want to feel like you were in command of the decisions that shaped your future?" Lucinda's pulse raced. She didn't know why, but her visit to Milkwood Manor had imbued her with a sense of control over her destiny. "Had I not gone with Sir Cosmo to see Mr. Pugh's dairy farm, I never would have known what sort of man he was."

"So, yer feeling all powerful-like because you sneaked into Mr. Pugh's milkin' operation and discovered he was a weasel."

Cold was seeping into Lucinda's bones. Hearing the skepticism in Clarissa's voice, she increased the briskness of their gait. After all, they were on a mission. It wouldn't do to dawdle in front of shop windows all day.

"All right, Clarissa, maybe I am being foolish. But I'm in a jolly mood; don't try and put me out of it."

"Mrs. Partridge, they ain't nothin' makes me happier than to see ye smile." Clarissa gently placed an elbow in her companion's side. "Now, here it is, the shop I was telling ye about. Are ye certain ye want to do this?

Meself, I think it's a chancy proposition. Madame Conte isn't likely to take kindly to being investigated."

"Neither would Mr. Pugh, if he knew that he was." Lucinda looked up at the wooden placard hanging above the small shop's door. "But, I'm feeling very confident in my ability to effect an important change today."

A handsomely dressed woman, accompanied by her maid, exited the shop to a tinkling of bells. Before the door swung shut, Lucinda crossed the threshold, Clarissa on her heels.

The interior of the establishment, or at least the front room, was suffocatingly small. A large refectory table against the wall was laden with stacks of pattern books, fashion plates and periodicals. On shelves lining the opposite wall were bolts of fabrics and laces. In the rear of the shop was a countertop behind which stood a young woman wearing a dark blue woolen gown and thick spectacles.

Behind this incongruously studious-looking woman was a curtained area, where from Lucinda's experience, patrons of the store could be measured for gowns and fitted with the finished products. Behind that was undoubtedly Madame Conte's workroom or sweatshop, where her girls would sew the designer's dresses by hand, perhaps by candlelight, or the occasional dim gas lamp.

One of those girls was Clarissa's cousin, Millie Binder; that was until Millie had become desperately ill a few weeks earlier.

Lucinda moved to the countertop and offered the girl there a false smile. "Is Madame Conte in, please?"

"And who should I say is calling?"

Lucinda thought the young woman was exceedingly uppity to be so plain. Though she had never been in Madame Conte's shop, she had been in many others quite similar. As a rule, she refused to patronize modistes who were so snobby they made Lucinda feel like an urchin. There seemed to be a strange notion among shop-keepers that snobbiness was directly related to the exclusivity of the clientele and the quality of the goods. Lucinda eschewed that theory.

"Tell your mistress that Mrs. Lucinda Partridge is here. I should like to order a complete wardrobe. And I am prepared to pay extra if she can furnish it to me within a week."

The girl's brows shot up. "A week? Why, that is impossible."

"My dear girl, nothing is impossible. Fetch your mistress. Now."

Whirling on her heel, the girl shot through the curtained partition. In a matter of minutes, the velvet drapes parted, and a tall, dark-haired woman emerged.

"Bonjour." Madame Conte's nod was stiff and grudging. Her long, pale hands were clasped tightly at her middle. Her hair, sleek and black, was parted in the middle and knotted tightly at the back of her neck. Her teeth were perfectly straight, with a slight gap between the two front ones. Her dark blue gown, austere but impeccably tailored, was accented by white lawn cuffs and a high white collar.

Lucinda thought Madame Conte was perhaps the most symmetrical individual on earth. Suppressing a shiver, she thought the woman probably scared little children and horses as she walked down the street.

"Thank you for seeing me," Lucinda began. "I need an entire new wardrobe, and you were highly recommended to me."

"By whom?" Madame Conte's huge gypsy eyes flashed.

Without hesitation, Lucinda replied, "The Dowager Duchess of Darthaven. A dear friend of mine."

Millie had mentioned that the duchess recently ordered a trousseau for her daughter, demanding that the entire collection be completed within a week. Despite the fact her daughter had been properly engaged the requisite length of time, all the customs associated with a society engagement had been followed, and a wedding date had been set months in advance, the daughter had put the cart before the horse a bit by getting herself pregnant.

When the duchess realized the trousseau she had ordered six months earlier didn't fit her daughter's blossoming figure, she had ordered another one—one especially designed to hide the young girl's increasing girth.

"I was quite impressed with the gowns you made up for the duchess's daughter," Lucinda said.

Madame Conte's lips compressed. She wasn't about to reveal her client's confidences, but it was clear she wondered whether Lucinda admired the first trousseau or the second one.

"Your use of aprons and pinafores was ingenious," Lucinda continued. "And the empress waistlines giving way to pleated skirts and puffy pantaloons. An absolutely inspired creation!"

Madame Conte allowed herself a small smile. "I see. You want me to create the same sort of collection for you. An ensemble designed to disguise an, er, delicate condition."

Lucinda lifted one brow. "Delicate condition? You're not suggesting that the duchess's daughter . . ."

The modiste frowned. "Of course not! I suggest nothing of the sort!"

Turning to Clarissa, Lucinda made a moue of mock surprise. "Well! Wait till the Almack's patrons hear about this! And we've heard it from a very good source, too!"

"You misunderstood," Madame Conte inserted smoothly, but with a tone of voice that clearly betrayed her annoyance. Though her lips curved in a smile, her gaze was as chilly as a Frost Fair.

"Oh, do I? Well, perhaps so. I shall not quote you, then, madame. Now, may we discuss my new wardrobe?"

Three hours later, Lucinda had seen every pattern and every swatch of fabric in the shop. Excusing herself, Clarissa disappeared while Lucinda stood in a fitting room in her small clothes, shivering while Madame Conte measured her waist, her bust and every other conceivable part of her body. After filling several pages in her worn leather journal with notes, figures and sketches, the modiste returned to the front of the shop with her new customer.

Clarissa materialized through the velvet drapes just as Lucinda was opening her reticule.

Madame Conte, scratching figures on a piece of paper, glanced up. "Where have you been, miss?"

Coloring, Clarissa stood beside Lucinda on the opposite side of the glass countertop. "I'm afraid I'm not feeling well today, madame. Your bookkeeper was kind enough to furnish me with a place to rest and a cup of tea."

Madame Conte said nothing; but her features hardened, and she returned to her figuring. At length, she quoted Lucinda a price, a very high one, for the cost of furnishing her an entire new wardrobe, complete with riding habit, morning dresses with fashionable peasant-style aprons, walking suits with jackets, and ball gowns done up in fluffy fabrics that would hide nearly any flaw in a woman's figure.

"That is quite a tidy sum." From her purse, Lucinda extracted a wad of paper currency.

"Yes, but I understand your need for discretion. And I assure you no one will be the wiser."

Unless they stumble in here and you tell them yourself, you old gossipmonger, thought Lucinda.

But gossiping wasn't Madame Conte's biggest sin. Clarissa squeezed Lucinda's hand, whispering that what the two women had suspected was very true.

"I'd like the entire ensemble completed within a week."

"Impossible."

Lucinda laid her money on the countertop. "Nothing is impossible. Not when a person is willing to pay for it."

"My girls work fourteen hours a day as it is." Madame Conte lifted her chin and stared down her long, narrow nose. "I am in fashion now. I have more business than I can handle."

"Who wouldn't want more business? Who wouldn't want more money?" Lucinda reached in her reticule and pulled out another wad of currency.

Madame Conte's nostrils flared. "A week . . . that would be very difficult. I would be forced to work my girls round the clock, seven days straight."

"But you could do that, couldn't you, if I paid you a sufficient sum?"

"I don't like to work them that hard. They are a lazy bunch, and they get restless and unpleasant when they are asked to work on special orders such as this."

Lucinda clucked her tongue. "Lazy trollops! Oh, that wasn't kind of me, was it? I suppose it does no good to speak ill of such creatures. They're hardly human, after all, are they? Not much better than animals."

Madame Conte's eyes softened in a conspiratorial expression. Here was a woman who understood her own point of view. She relaxed her posture a bit; here was a woman willing to pay for what she wanted. A demanding and discriminating woman, one like Madame Conte herself. Not one of those bleeding heart liberal reformists who thought those lazy girls in back were entitled to decent wages and work hours, a warm workplace and safe working conditions.

"All right, then, I'll have your wardrobe finished by next week."

"Are you certain your girls can do it?"

"They'll do it. If it kills them."

Madame Conte gathered up the money spread on her counter, smiling tightly. Without so much as a nod toward Clarissa, she bade Lucinda a warm farewell. "It is a pleasure conducting business with you, Mrs. Partridge," she said as the two women exited her shop.

On the street, Lucinda turned to Clarissa. "We'll see if she thinks it is such a pleasure when we return with the police."

A night off. A small fire in the costume department necessitated closing the Orange Street Opera House for the evening, much to the chagrin of the patrons who queued up to see the performance. But Ivan Pavlov was adamant. According to him, the opera could not be performed properly without the costumes and props that had been destroyed. Moreover, the source of the fire had not been discovered, and he feared a recurrence would result in great tragedy.

"When the seamstresses and stage workers have repaired the costumes, props and drapes, I will reopen the theater," he told Lucinda and Madame Bartoli backstage. "Not a moment before then."

Madame Bartoli, standing in the threshold of Lucinda's dressing room, propped her hands on her hips. "There have been many strange happenings here, of late, Ivan. Who do you think wishes the opera company harm?"

"What in God's name are you talking about?" Ivan was short-tempered and irritated, understandable given that he would have to explain to the owners and backers of the theater why he had decided to cancel tonight's performance.

The Italian diva tossed her head. "Do not think I am blind. I see what is going on. The stage workers gossip, too. A near fatal stabbing occurred in one of the boxes a few days ago. Now, an unexplained fire. This is too much coincidence, if you ask me."

"No one asked you," growled Ivan. "Now get out of here!"

Fire flashed in the brunette's dark eyes. Wheeling, she left the tiny dressing room and stomped next door to her own. When she slammed the door, the toiletries on Lucinda's dressing table rattled.

Ivan gently closed Lucinda's door and stood for a moment in the center of the room. Staring at the tips of his shoes, shoulders sagging, he stroked his chin. An uncomfortable silence stretched between him and Lucinda.

She spoke at last, bored with his pensive retreat. "Ivan, if you have nothing to say to me, perhaps you should see about your business."

His gaze shot up. "Have you given any thought to my proposal, babushka?"

"I have hardly thought of anything but that." Seated at her dressing table, Lucinda turned from him and picked up her hair brush. Studiously avoiding Ivan's stare reflected in her mirror, she brushed a long strand of flaxen hair till it gleamed like gold in the candlelight.

His breathing reverberated through the room. "Have you reached a decision?"

"No."

After a pause, he said, "Is there anything I can say to influence your judgment? Anything at all?"

Lucinda's hands froze. It occurred to her that if she was going to marry a man for his money, she might as well make certain he would give it to her once they were betrothed. Heaven forbid, she should marry Ivan Pavlov and he should turn out to be as tight-fisted with his money as Lawrence Pugh.

"Ivan, if I were to accept your proposal—"

"Yes, yes—"

"Would you be the sort of husband who doled out the pennies to me, one by one? Would you control every aspect of my existence, monitoring my comings and goings, directing my interests and hobbies? Or would you be generous and kind, allowing me to do as I pleased and pursue whatever passions I pleased?"

She dared glance at him in her mirror.

His fists clenched, and his posture stiffened. "Mrs. Ivan Pavlov would be a lady who exercised her free will, who traveled without restraint and who pursued whatever interests brought her pleasure."

"I should like to open a women's shelter in London." Lucinda warmed to the subject, explaining to Ivan her vision of a house that was sanctuary to all sorts of poor women, women who were down on their luck, or were seeking refuge from abusive spouses. She told him of her friendship with Clarissa and her efforts to assist the girl in leaving her life of prostitution.

"Lucinda! You should not fraternize with such women!" Ivan kneeled beside her, removed the brush from her hands and clasped her fingers. "My love, it is not safe. I want nothing but your happiness, but I must insist that you give up this endeavor!"

"No, Ivan. That is my life's dream. I will not be content until I have at least attempted to achieve my aspirations."

"What about your voice, babushka? What about the opera?"

"I haven't helped a soul by singing, Ivan. I've only helped myself by earning money, and the adulation of a small populace of opera lovers. And it hasn't even been much money. I'm a failure as an artist, Ivan. You might as well face it; I have. Even you haven't been able to secure me another contract after my present one expires."

Color rose to his cheeks. "But you needn't earn a penny when you are Mrs. Ivan Pavlov. I will see to it that your every need is provided for."

"What I need is sufficient funds to open my shelter," Lucinda replied. "If I cannot be assured that you will assist me, I should like to know now."

His expression implored her; his voice was raw with emotion. "Oh, Lucinda! My heart is breaking. I cannot in good conscience allow the woman I love to endanger herself. Money is not the issue. I have enough money for the both of us. I promise you a life of leisure and luxury."

"I've had that. Now I want to do something for someone else."

"Be my wife. Make me happy. Isn't taking care of Ivan Pavlov rewarding enough to keep you happy?"

Lucinda chuckled, and withdrew her hands from Ivan's. "My, but you men do think highly of yourselves! I've never thought a wife's domestic duties were sufficiently noble pursuits to qualify a woman for sainthood. However, I suppose that with some men . . ."

"Do not make light of my entreaty, Lucinda. I love you." He gripped her hand again, then rose and planted a kiss on her lips.

Lucinda gasped. She had been alone in her dressing room many times with Ivan Pavlov; he was the theater manager after all, and it wasn't unusual for him to visit her unescorted. He was just as often in Madame Bartoli's room, a circumstance that had never made Lucinda jealous or raised a single eyebrow from anyone else, for that matter.

His kiss put their relationship on a different footing. Suddenly, Lucinda was apprehensive and eager for him to leave. He was handsome to be sure, and his personality—all fire and passion—appealed to her artistic senses. He had made it clear he would be generous financially, and Lucinda pictured a life with Ivan as one of physical ease and intellectual stimulation.

But he had exhibited one trait that Lucinda distrusted severely. He would control her. He would smother her. He would rein her in when she went, by his estimation, too far beyond the pale for her own good.

The last thing Lucinda needed was a man telling her what to do. She hadn't got this far in life, hadn't survived two disastrous marriages, only to bind herself to a man who refused to let her take a risk on her shelter. Ivan Pavlov might be a progressive artist, but as a social thinker, he was hardly a reformist.

"Ivan, you should go now," she whispered, snatching her fingers from his.

He retreated a step, his heels clicking together as if he were executing a military salute. "I should be a most kind husband, Lucinda. Please reconsider this wild notion about helping trollops and fancy women."

"Perhaps you should reconsider your attitude, Ivan." Their gazes locked.

Ivan lifted one brow and said, "I will not give up so easily. If you insist on building a women's shelter, then I shall not forbid you. I shall . . . how do you say . . . be your partner in the project. Do you see now, Lucinda? I shall do whatever I must to win your hand!" With that, he turned abruptly and crossed the room.

Silence descended like a final curtain. But the door was closed behind Ivan for a scant five minutes when a knock shattered Lucinda's quiet and unhappy interlude.

Ten

Sir Cosmo Fairchild's voice sounded from the empty corridor outside Lucinda's dressing room. "May I come in?"

An unbidden wave of relief swept over her. She had not seen him since the day before—was it a mere twenty-four hours since they had visited Mr. Pugh's dairy farm?—and his appearance soothed her jangled nerves.

Cosmo struck her as a man always in control. His unruffled attitude and calm demeanor were strong, masculine traits that she admired. Having him as her ally strengthened her, too. For the first time in her life, Lucinda wasn't letting herself be pushed around; she was flexing her muscles, and she liked the way it felt.

And Cosmo was there, waiting in the wings, encouraging her and pressing her to do braver things. She didn't have to sit back and wait for one of her suitors to propose. Two of them already had! Now it was up to her to decide which man she would marry. This was her decision—*hers alone*.

What a heady feeling. Cosmo's friendship was like a ready arsenal of ammunition, fortifying her own depleted supply of self-confidence and worth. This new-found source of strength was completely novel. In fact, it was almost too heavenly a feeling for Lucinda to accept. For an instant, she wondered what Cosmo wanted from her in exchange for his friendship. After all, Lucinda's past was filled with people who had *wanted* something from her.

She had never met a man who just wanted to be her friend.

He crossed the room, beaver hat in hand. His silver hair sparkled in the candlelight, and his skin, reddened from the blistering cold outside, looked as smooth as marble. Black fire shone in his eyes, igniting a warmth that spread quickly through Lucinda's body.

He stood before her, a roguish grin curving his handsome lips. Bending low, he took her hand and gently kissed Lucinda's knuckles.

A slow smile spread across her face. It was a smile not for the stage, but for Cosmo, a smile that started at her toes and streamed all the way to her tingling scalp.

Lucinda was a woman who had practiced smiling in the mirror so much that she knew every nuance of every expression she wore. Her features were her vanity, her expressions her wardrobe. Much like fashionable ladies who studied themselves until they knew which dress style, color, gesture, flick of the wrist and bat of the lashes flattered and which ones didn't, Lucinda knew what looked good on her.

That wide grin she was grinning made her all teeth and crunchy eyes, bobbing cheeks and mottled neck. Yet, she couldn't stop the smile from happening. And with a sickening premonition, she realized that with Cosmo, her acting skills were useless. He was the only man she had smiled for with such lack of pretense, and he was the only man who had ever brought to her eyes and lips such a pure, unadulterated display of emotion.

Damn him! The last thing in the world Lucinda Partridge wanted was to fall in love with Sir Cosmo Fairchild. He was not for her. He had nothing to offer her. And, besides that, he was getting to know her entirely too well. A man who knew her every foible, flaw and secret yearning was not marriage material!

Yet the sensation of his lips on her skin was unbearably arousing. Her wintry heart thawed, and a rosebud of desire blossomed within her.

Somehow, she managed to withdraw her fingers from his lips. Inside, her blood burned. But the cool exterior she portrayed was pure theater.

Cosmo's heart clenched. Had he gone and made a fool of himself again? Lucinda's smile faded, and with it, his hopes that she did truly care for him. He thought he had seen a spark of desire in her gaze when he entered the room. He thought he had detected an unalloyed joy in her expression. He thought, just for a moment, that she felt what he did.

Clearly, he had been wrong. Staring at her profile as she calmly ran a brush through her glistening hair, Cosmo knew that Lucinda Partridge was interested in one thing: she needed a husband for financial reasons, and she was going to get one.

The thought made him shudder. A woman willing to marry for money was a woman he didn't want to love. His mother, Monique, even Horsey Hilda who had agreed to marry him, were of the same ilk. Feminine mountebanks. Tricksters. Unfeeling mercenaries. The blood flowing through their veins was colder than the English Channel.

Then, why couldn't he get Lucinda out of his mind? Each time he had his emotions under control, he saw her and committed another silly blunder. Bloody Hell! He would have to learn to suppress his desire for her. Because that's all it was. Pure, physical desire. There was simply no way he could allow himself to love Lucinda Partridge.

"I suppose you know that the evening's performance is canceled." She gazed at herself in the mirror.

He watched her as she pinned up her hair, one long, blond braid at a time, until it was coiled in a loose knot on the top of her head. "I heard there was a fire. Was anyone seriously injured?"

"No, it was put out rather quickly. We are all thankful the fire didn't begin when no one was backstage. As it was, the stage workers had it snuffed out within moments. But not before it burned a rack of costumes, and a canvas backdrop. Ivan was quite put out, I can tell you."

"I suppose he was." Cosmo wondered if the fire had anything to do with the spy ring operating at the opera house. "Were you here when the fire began?"

"I was right here, in my dressing room."

"Alone?"

Lucinda glanced at his reflection. "Madame Bartoli was with me. We were discussing tonight's performance, wondering if Ivan would tinker with the libretto again. She hates it as much as I do, Ivan's constant rewrites. It is as if he cannot quite get the words right. Such a perfectionist."

"And where was he when the fire started?"

"I haven't the faintest notion." With her arms raised above her head, Lucinda anchored her chignon with a long, ebony hairpin. The effect was fashionably Oriental. "He came into my dressing room and addressed both of us. Shortly after the fire, that is. He told Madame and me that tonight's performance would not go on."

"How long after the fire started was that?"

"Just minutes. But it was obvious to Ivan that there was substantial damage. My toga went up in flames, I was told! And the opera was scheduled to begin in less than half an hour. There were already people in their seats. Really, the cancellation caused quite a commotion!"

Cosmo ran his hand through his hair. Perhaps the fire

was a coincidence, but how could he be certain? "Was Mr. Pugh here tonight?"

"If he was, I haven't seen him."

"Doesn't he always come backstage to visit you when he attends a performance?"

"Not always." Lucinda shrugged. "He visits on Wednesday evenings, you know. Mr. Pugh is on quite an inflexible schedule."

Their eyes met in the mirror, and they exchanged a conspiratorial smile. They had laughed uproariously about Mr. Pugh's stinginess half the way back to London from Milkwood Manor. At first it had seemed insanely funny that Lucinda's most ardent admirer had turned out to be such an odd character.

About halfway back to London, however, Lucinda's tears emanated not from laughter, but from sadness. For two hours, she had leaned her head on Cosmo's shoulder and sobbed. He hadn't understood precisely why she was so heartbroken. Was it because Mr. Pugh's affections toward her were suddenly cheapened by his lack of generosity, or was it because she realized he would likely never give her a guinea, much less the kind of riches she was counting on from her potential husband?

"Do you mean to say that Mr. Pugh is often in the audience even when he does not visit backstage?"

She sighed, as if she were tiring of this conversation. "Yes, that is what I am saying, Cosmo."

"What about Lord Wynne-Ascott? Have you seen him this evening?"

The door to Mrs. Partridge's dressing room swung open, revealing Nathaniel Upton, Lord Wynne-Ascott. "Did I hear my name mentioned?" he asked smugly.

Cosmo's trained eye swept the man's tall, elegantly dressed figure. His dark green coat fitted snugly at the waist, suggesting the use of corsets. A high collar and stiff cravat thrust his head forward at an odd angle, creating the preferred posture assumed by London swells, an affectation that Cosmo considered unattractive and uncomfortable. And, of course, the man carried a walking stick, but unlike Cosmo's cane, this accouterment was meant to complement Lord Wynne-Ascott's ensemble.

"I wondered whether you planned to attend the opera this evening," Cosmo replied smoothly. He was unable to hide his disregard for the lordling, however, and didn't really care that the man disliked him, too.

"I have just discovered the performance is canceled." Lucinda turned in her chair, facing Lord Wynne-Ascott. "I am sorry, my lord, that you have been inconvenienced. Perhaps I will see you another time."

Despite her chilly tone, the lord made an exquisite leg, bowing so low his nose almost touched the floor. "I hope you are not still angry with me, songbird. I have come to make amends with you."

She turned back to her mirror. "My lord, I am having a conversation with Sir Cosmo. We are engaged in a business enterprise, as you know, and haven't time to visit with you now. I regret not being able to entertain your company. Another time, perhaps."

Undaunted, the aristocratic man straightened. "What a pity. Lady Sapho Drummond is having a party this evening, and I should like for you to attend with me."

"I will not be going anywhere with you, unescorted," replied Lucinda. "I dare say, you wouldn't expect me to if I were a member of the *ton.*"

Lord Wynne-Ascott sighed.

Sir Cosmo had the distinct impression he had missed a vital element of this conversation. Had the rogue made an improper advance toward Lucinda when they were alone? It wouldn't surprise him.

It worried Cosmo that Lucinda gave such little thought to the social conventions—not because he cared about the rules of decorum, or thought less of any woman who flouted them, but because he knew what other men thought about women who did. Lucinda was accustomed to living alone and taking care of herself, but men like Lord Wynne-Ascott would view her independence as an invitation of sorts.

"Thank you," Lucinda said, "but I am not of the mind to attend a party this evening."

"Too bad." Lord Wynne-Ascott's gaze shot to Cosmo. "Lady Drummond asked me to be sure to invite your friend as well. I believe she rather took a shine to him the other night."

Revulsion roiled in Cosmo's gut. If there was anything he loathed, it was a fraud. And Nathaniel Upton reeked of pretension and fakery.

If there was anything he loved, however, it was the concept of duty and honor. His duty at the moment was to reveal the spy at the opera house. Instinct told him that Lord Wynne-Ascott was not what he appeared to be. Therefore, it would be negligent of Cosmo to refuse to attend Lady Drummond's party.

"Perhaps," said Cosmo, "you would reconsider Lord Wynne-Ascott's invitation." Cosmo met Lucinda's startled gaze in the mirror. "I, for one, believe that we have conducted entirely too much business for one day. Let us have some diversion, what do you say?"

"You want to go to the party, Cosmo?"

"Yes," he lied. He wanted to go home and drink a bottle of whiskey, then fall into bed and try to relieve himself of his infatuation with Lucinda Partridge. But that was not an option. He told the truth when he said, "I should not enjoy going without you, though."

A grudging smile played at her lips. "Well, then, we shall attend Lady Drummond's party. Thank you very much, my lord. Sir Cosmo and I will arrive within the hour."

"You are more than welcome to accompany me in my carriage," the lord replied. "I will wait out front. Take as long as you need. Sir Cosmo and I will have a chat while you finish dressing."

Cosmo welcomed the opportunity. "Excellent idea. Mrs. Partridge, I will see you in a little while."

Her face registered surprise and apprehension. But she said nothing as the two men exited her dressing room.

Following Lord Wynne-Ascott through the nearly empty corridors of the opera house, Cosmo felt a surge of anxiety. If he was, in fact, closing in on the nefarious spy at the opera house, then he was also drawing Lucinda Partridge closer to the center of the deception—and into a world of danger.

Not surprisingly, Lord Wynne-Ascott's equipage represented the very height of fashion and the finest craftsmanship. Even in the dark, the rig's body shone glossy black. A lamp affixed to the carriage illuminated the door and the nattily dressed tiger who stood waiting to assist the passengers.

Cosmo sat opposite Lord Wynne-Ascott on a plush leather squab.

"What do you think of my rig?" the lord asked, tossing Cosmo a lap blanket.

"I don't think my living quarters are this well appointed," answered Cosmo. "The latest thing, I take it."

"All the crack, and worth a fortune." Wynne-Ascott obviously wasn't one to understate his wealth or the quality of his possessions. "By the way, where do you live, Sir Cosmo?"

"In rented quarters near Soho Square."

Wynne-Ascott cast him such a look of sympathy that Cosmo felt compelled to add, "I've been unmarried for so long, I have lost interest in owning a town house. So much upkeep, you know."

"Ah, yes. And having a household filled with servants can give one the megrims. There's always one underfoot, popping up in one's bedchamber to dust the furniture when you're trying to take a hot bath. Barging into the parlor to light the lamps when you're trying to seduce a bit of baggage."

"Christ on a raft, I detest that! Which is precisely the reason I prefer living in smaller quarters. Get a little minx up to your apartment, and there's no one there to interrupt the proceedings if you know what I mean."

"I know exactly what you mean. But, what about a butler? And a valet? Bloody hell, what do you do when you want a hot bath drawn? And how do you tie your cravat in the morning?"

Cosmo would have liked to shock Wynne-Ascott with the truth. The arrogant lord would be dumbfounded by the notion that a man could tie his own necktie, or step into his pantaloons without assistance. But Cosmo needed to establish a rapport with the man before he told him what an ass he was.

"I have a cleaning lady come in several times a week," Cosmo said. That was true enough. "And a gentleman's gentleman who sees to it that my clothes are clean and pressed. Mr. Finchwick appears in the morning and attends to my bath and breakfast. After I am dressed, which is usually about noon, he assists me with my correspondence and does whatever shopping is necessary. I do not have him living under my roof, however. As you said, I prefer my privacy."

Wynne-Ascott was aghast at Cosmo's Spartan living conditions. "Are you quite poor then, man? Have you lost all your money at the gambling tables?"

Cosmo's laughter was deep and hearty. In fact, he

laughed so long that Wynne-Ascott joined him, though
the lord had no idea Cosmo was laughing at him.

At length, Cosmo said, "You don't mince words, do
you, my lord?"

"You don't look poor. Indeed, your coat is very well
cut, and from an expensive if not conservative piece of
wool. I've an eye for such things, Cosmo. And your boots
are as fine as the pair I am wearing."

Which is the hallmark of good taste, Cosmo inferred.

Suddenly, Wynne-Ascott's features hardened, and the
frivolity escaped his voice. "Who, then, are you trying
to fool?"

"I beg your pardon?" Cosmo asked coolly. How in the
devil had Wynne-Ascott discovered he was spying for the
British Home Office?

"You're not what you appear to be, sir. A penniless
scribbler?" The viscount snorted derisively. "I think not.
Not with those clothes, those boots, that stiff-rumped demeanor of yours. You were to the manor born, Cosmo,
and don't think I can't see it."

"Takes one to know one, I s'pose," Cosmo replied,
stalling for time.

*Would he have to kill Wynne-Ascott right here in the carriage,
in front of the opera house? What if Lucinda happened along
at just the wrong moment?*

A thousand thoughts swirled through his head, but he
delayed acting on any of them; he had to find out who
had betrayed him before he did away with Wynne-Ascott.

"And precisely who do you think I am?" Cosmo asked
quietly.

"I don't know who you are, but I know what you are."

Beneath the fringe of grey hair that fell over Cosmo's
forehead, a black bushy brow arched. "You're quite well
informed, Wynne-Ascott. And playing a pretty deep
game of it, if I must say so."

"There is much at stake, Cosmo."

"Indeed."

"I have no intention of allowing you to bluster your way into my territory and destroy everything I have spent the last few years working for. I've been patient. I've bided my time. And I am soon to reap my reward."

"Doesn't pay to be greedy, old man."

"To the victor goes the spoils."

"Boney has bit off more than he can chew, my lord. Perhaps you should retreat while you still have your head."

Wynne-Ascott stiffened. "Is that a challenge? Calling me out, are you? Why, you imbecilic paperscull! Don't you know, you haven't a chance with Lucinda? You think that she's going to fall in love with you because you're a romantic figure."

"What the hell are you talking about?" Cosmo's muscles were tensed, his nerves as taut as coiled springs.

"Do you fancy that you are playing Lord Byron to her Lady Caroline Lamb?" The venom in Wynne-Ascott's voice filled the compartment with a poisonous vapor.

Lord Byron and Lady Caroline? Cosmo's pulse spiked. The conversation had taken an odd tilt, indeed. Was Viscount Wynne-Ascott accusing Cosmo of being a government operative? Or, was he indicting him for something entirely different?

"You've made some rather egregious misassumptions," he said slowly.

"Have I?" Wynne-Ascott seethed, his anger a red-hot ember in the frigid darkness. "Lucinda was warming to my advances; she was coming around, I'm sure of it. Until you came onto the scene. Suddenly, she's got some pretty toplofty ideas in her head about wantin' to be treated like a lady of the *ton!* She never acted like that before, insisting on chaperones, worrying about the indecorousness of being alone with me!"

"What makes you think she is *acting?*" countered

Cosmo. "And why shouldn't she be treated like a lady? She is one, as far as I am concerned."

"She's an opera singer," spat Wynne-Ascott. "A step above a burlesque girl, if you ask me, or a circus performer. Two steps above a demirep."

"Is that what you think of our Mrs. Partridge? Good God, then why are you pursuing her?" Cosmo's blood boiled. He would have leapt across the compartment and strangled Wynne-Ascott with the slightest bit more provocation. But the relief he felt at realizing he hadn't been exposed as a spy himself brought clarity to his thinking. His job was to learn whether Wynne-Ascott was a spy, not to murder the man for maligning Lucinda's reputation.

"I might ask you the same question, sir. Why are you pursuing Mrs. Partridge? And why are you going to all the trouble of assuming the identity of a starving writer?"

"Well, you haven't had much success in buying the affections of Mrs. Partridge, have you?" replied Cosmo. "I thought I would take a different tactic. She is the type of woman who likes brooding artist types."

"I knew it! You are masquerading as an artist to appeal to her sensitive nature! How underhanded! How despicable! How incredibly . . . brilliant!"

In the blink of an eye, Wynne-Ascott's mood changed. He was no longer angry with his competition. Now he was showing grudging admiration for a worthy adversary.

"What a good sport you are!" cried Cosmo.

"I figured it all out," the viscount said. "You might be able to fool Lucinda, but you can't pull the wool over my eyes. A hungry writer doesn't wear a bespoke suit or carry such a fine walking stick as that!"

"You saw through my disguise. Clever bastard!"

"At first, I thought you were some sort of spy . . . perhaps hired by the theater manager to monitor ticket sales, something like that. I mean, you look so out of place in the opera house. And then, it dawned upon me. You're just like me. You are me."

"Am I?" The thought made Cosmo feel dirty.

"But you want to be something else. You want to be someone who is more than the sum total of his bank account."

"Doesn't everyone?"

Wynne-Ascott spoke rapidly, excitedly, as if he were impatient with himself for having been so slow to identify Cosmo's game. "Oh, I don't blame you for modeling your character after Lord Byron! If I had thought of it first, I might have done the same! A woman like Lucinda Partridge doesn't care for jewels, money or fine houses. No, she wants to be wooed, and cherished and swept off her feet."

"How very romantic."

"Exactly! She wants a brooding cripple like Lord Byron!"

Cosmo's voice turned hard as ice. "A brooding cripple?"

"You cannot get more romantic than that, can you? Bloody hell, what a clever ruse!" Wynne-Ascott leaned forward and slapped Cosmo's knee. "I should hate you, old man, but I can't help admiring you. Still, I must tell you, I have no intention of giving up on Lucinda. I saw her first. And I intend to have her."

"And what will you use to lure her into your snare, now that you have determined money cannot buy her affections?"

Wynne-Ascott leaned back and, with a heavy sigh, rubbed his chin. "Now, there's a puzzle. I don't know, sir. I don't know." His eyes gleamed yellow in the dark. "But I shall figure it out. For, by God, I do love nothing better than a good horse race!"

Never had Cosmo hated a man more in his life.

Reaching out, he grasped Wynne-Ascott's extended hand and shook it. Through clenched teeth, he answered, "Well, then, may the best man win."

A short time later, the carriage rumbled to a stop in front of Lady Sapho Drummond's Curzon Street town house. Despite the severe cold, ground-floor windows were thrown open, releasing the heat of the crush inside, along with the gentle strains of a small orchestra.

Stepping to the cobbled street, Lucinda gathered her cloak about her shoulders. In this fashionable area of London, gas lamps lit the polished stone facades of Georgian architecture and gleaming lacquered doors. Her breath frosted the air, but she warmed to Cosmo's touch as he guided her toward Lady Drummond's house. Lit by the golden spill of a hundred candles and the twinkling canopy of stars above, the night shone with promise.

Her heart thudded against her ribcage. Certainly, Lucinda had met members of the *ton* before. As patrons of the opera house, they frequently wanted to meet the lead soprano after a performance. But it was the *noblemen* who most often took a lasting interest in Lucinda, and it was an interest that played out in her dressing room—never in a public assembly room or a private parlor. This was the first time Lucinda Partridge had been the personal guest of such an esteemed personage as Lady Sapho Drummond.

She was moving up in the world; she could feel it. She supposed her newfound confidence showed. That was why she had been suddenly thrust into the spotlight, suddenly invited to the home of a person she had never before dreamed of socializing with. *If you consider yourself worthy,* Lucinda thought, *then others will assume you are, too.*

She silently gloated over her new self-discovery. It was a sort of magic. If you acted like you were somebody, others would believe it, too. And when others believed it, you really were somebody. The transformation from dreamworld to reality, then, was all a matter of willpower and determination and belief in one's self. How incredible! It was truly like magic! A magic that Lucinda suddenly controlled.

Crossing the threshold, Lucinda felt as if she had entered a wonderland. It was a magnificent house, with black-and-white-checkered floors in a foyer graced by a curving, black-marble staircase. Walls painted pale blue were capped by a domed ceiling that sported painted angels cavorting among the clouds. In the center of the entry hall was a grand burled-walnut table, ornamented with golden claw feet, and laden with a basalt vase sprouting hothouse roses of red and white. Gasping with astonishment, Lucinda was only half aware that a liveried servant had taken her cloak and hat.

Cosmo's breath was warm on her neck. "Come inside, Mrs. Partridge, and we will have a drink of punch. Champagne, if you prefer."

Lord Wynne-Ascott took her opposite elbow, and Lucinda entered the huge drawing room flanked by two handsome men. Not a few heads turned to scrutinize the three from head to toe, and if Lucinda hadn't been accustomed to a life on the stage, she would have blushed with embarrassment.

But there was a fair number of approving nods among the men who scanned her form from head to toe, and the looks cast by the women could fairly be called inquisitive, rather than disdainful. Lucinda lifted her chin a notch and smiled at a few of the more curious tabbies. Having no cause to be rude, the ladies could only smile in return. Which gave the further appearance that Lucinda had as much right to be there as they.

And in her newly discovered fantasy, appearances were everything.

From the corner of her eye, Lucinda caught sight of a great white wave swelling up and rolling in her direction. Turning, she faced head-on the approach of a tall, bosomy woman whose shoulders were as broad as Cosmo's.

The woman stopped in front of Lucinda and extended a fat arm encased in white kid, elbow-length gloves. Atop the gloves sparkled jewels of every sort: ruby rings, diamond bracelets, gold cuffs, and even a huge Egyptian scarab that was affixed to her middle finger like a tenacious, blood-sucking beetle. A fake mole winked at the corner of one eye, and the crepey skin of her décolletage glowed with tiny flecks of powdered gilt.

Lucinda shook the woman's hand while Lord Wynne-Ascott made introductions all around.

"How very charming that you were able to attend," said Lady Sapho Drummond, from deep in her wattled throat. "I have followed your career these past few years with great interest. You have a beautiful voice, dear."

"Thank you." Lucinda hardly knew what to say to this imposing figure of a woman. "I hope you won't take offense, but you have an unusually deep and melodious voice. You're a natural contralto, I would estimate. Quite rare for a woman."

Lady Drummond's thick makeup creased when she smiled. Patting her silvery hair, she purred, "I take that as a great compliment, *ma petite*. Now, if you will excuse me, I must see to the comforts of my other guests. Nathaniel, do take the girl for a spin around the dance floor! And, Cosmo!" She waggled her ivory fan at him. "Don't you dare leave this party without saving at least one waltz for me!

"With that, Lady Sapho Drummond swept away in a cloud of perfume and glitter.

Lucinda exchanged an amused look with Sir Cosmo. He had turned a shade paler at the thought of waltzing with Lady Drummond.

Lord Wynne-Ascott slapped him on the back. "Sir Cosmo, you dashing devil you! She has taken a fancy to you, old boy! My God, she's got a husband rich as Croesus, too! I wouldn't let her out of my sight if I were you."

"Oh, I intend to keep an eye out for her," replied Cosmo, gripping his cane tightly. "You've no cause to doubt that."

Lucinda thought for once he was probably lucky to have an excuse not to dance. But a wave of regret washed over her as soon as she realized she would not be dancing with him, either.

Eleven

"Why didn't you tell me?" Cosmo whispered, when Wynne-Ascott had crossed the room to visit an old acquaintance he spied.

Lucinda stood at the edge of the dance floor, studying the intricate steps of a country reel. If someone asked her to dance, she was certain she could participate without embarrassing herself.

Facing Cosmo, she said, "Tell you what, sir?"

"That he had proposed to you."

"But, I did."

"Pugh has proposed, I know, and so has Pavlov."

"Yes."

Cosmo's brow furrowed. "And the viscount? Has he not declared his intentions toward you?"

Her face reddened. For a moment, she met Cosmo's gaze; then she turned her attention to the gaiety on the dance floor. Cosmo's heart clenched. She was a woman of lusty appetites and genteel manners, a woman who needed to be squeezed and loved and respected. Yet, he couldn't hold her in his arms because he hadn't the nerve to tell her who he was and what he was. And he couldn't dance with her because of his lame leg.

Self-disgust struck him like a hammer. Lucinda's expression had lit from within the moment she entered Lady Drummond's house. The grand furnishings, the elegant gowns and flowing laughter—it was new to her, and so exciting. Everything in the world sparkled when Cosmo saw it through Lucinda's eyes. Oh, if he could only show the world to her, share the physical pleasures of just being alive with *her.* She deserved so much more than she was settling for, and he wanted to give it to her. His heart ached to give it to her.

But he could not.

A tear glistened at the corner of her eye.

Cosmo touched her face, his gloved finger absorbing the warm liquid drop. "Wynne-Ascott didn't offer marriage, did he?"

Lucinda's shoulders squared. "No."

Not an ounce of self-pity, Cosmo thought. *How unlike me!*

"Did he injure your feelings terribly?" he asked, his lips close to her neck.

She stiffened, but made no move to step away from him. Despite the crush of the party, the heat of too many bodies pressed together and the noisy jostle of the dancing, they were, for that moment, totally alone in the Drummond drawing room. No one was listening; no one was paying them a bit of attention.

Cosmo's breath was warm on her neck. Lucinda withdrew a small ivory fan from her reticule and, with a flick of her wrist, unfurled it. The small breeze she created was ineffective in curbing the heat wave that threatened to engulf her, but at least it gave her hands something to do.

"I did not tell you, sir, because I did not seriously consider Lord Wynne-Ascott's proposal. There was no use discussing it."

"You are not suggesting he made the offer in jest?"

"No." Lucinda hid her embarrassment behind a mask of indifference. "I suppose he was quite serious when he offered me *carte blanche.*"

After a long pause, Cosmo said softly, "He is a very wealthy man, Lucinda."

"I am well aware of that."

"He is capable of fulfilling your every need and wish."

"My every *material* need and wish, that is."

Cosmo leaned so close that Lucinda's arm nudged his middle each time she flicked her fan. "To tell the truth, dear lady, I have never heard you express any needs other than material ones."

His remark, uttered in the most intimate of tones, was a direct insult to her character. A flood of anger roiled in Lucinda's stomach, and her chest ached with repressed violence. Refusing to look at Cosmo, she watched a particularly festive couple move about the dance floor.

"How dare you," she whispered through clenched teeth. "You have challenged my honor, Sir Cosmo. I should never speak to you again."

From the corner of her eye, she noted the upward tug at his lips.

"The truth hurts, I suppose. Don't take offense, though. Truly, I have nothing but the highest degree of respect for you. After all, you've never misrepresented yourself. You're not like other women I've known. You've never pretended you were in love. You've made it quite clear what you want, and you are willing to sacrifice everything in order to get it. You are not unlike me in that respect."

"I want to build a women's shelter." Lucinda bit out the words as if they were vile-tasting. "To that end, I will do most anything, even marry a man I don't love. That is not such a great sacrifice to a woman who doesn't believe in everlasting romantic love, is it?"

"Are you such a cynic, Mrs. Partridge?" Cosmo clucked his tongue.

"Don't mock me." She shot him a warning glance, then returned her gaze to the dance floor. "I am quite certain romantic love is possible for many women, but I am not one of those women."

Lucinda didn't tell Cosmo that if it weren't for her lofty goal of building a women's shelter, she might find love . . . with him. For one thing, he wouldn't believe it, and he would most likely fall down laughing. For another thing, he had done nothing to indicate he was in the market for a wife; on the contrary, he seemed quite content with his bachelor status. And thirdly, she had ruled him out as marriage material the instant he said he was a starving writer.

Cosmo would never do as a husband. Marrying him would be tantamount to throwing away all her hopes and dreams for helping the less fortunate women of London.

He stood with his head cocked and his hands behind his back. Daring a look, Lucinda saw that his eyes were lambent with an unidentifiable emotion. He stared too intensely at her to be mocking her, and yet there was a trace of amusement in his expression.

"What can you possibly be thinking?" she finally blurted.

He seemed to consider his answer for a long while. Then he ran his fingers through his shaggy grey hair, and replied, "I am wondering if you are the most noble female I have ever met, or the most stupid."

Gasping, she snapped shut her fan. "Are you calling me stupid now? 'Struth, I don't know whether to laugh or cry—or punch you in the nose! You are a most unusual man, Cosmo. You ply me with compliments, then question my integrity. You flatter my vanity by telling me my voice is beautiful; then you disparage my character by suggesting I am a cunning fortune hunter. You study me as if I were the oddest creature you have ever seen. Yet, you appear to have some degree of affection for me. Tell me, are you ordinarily this ornery?"

"Ornery?" He laughed. "And I thought I was on my best behavior. Mrs. Partridge, I hate to tell you this, but most of the time, I am the veriest boor, deep in my doldrums and as contrary as a two-year-old with a tooth-ache."

"La, how can anyone stand to be around you? More importantly, how can you stand to be around yourself?"

"Ah, now there is the question! Perhaps that is why I am so often alone. I seem to have had some difficulty in the area of conducting a romance. Perhaps you have named the reason why."

"Poppycock! You are so very handsome that I won't even attempt to rebut that silly remark. You must know that women find you attractive. How could you not?"

He shot his cuffs, grinning. "All right, I admit it. Compared to me, Brummel's a slob, and Sir Byron's a clumsy fop."

"Don't overdo it, Cosmo."

"But you haven't noticed any women chasing after me, have you? You haven't seen any women dressing up as pages and chasing me through the streets, or jumping naked out of cakes at parties?"

Lucinda stifled a giggle. "Did she really do that? I had thought the rumors of Lady Caroline's behavior were exaggerated."

"Exaggerated or no, she is hot after the man. No matter what he does to discourage her, she pursues him. She loves him, you see. And that is an emotion I do not seem to arouse in women."

"You give off the air that you don't want to be loved," Lucinda noted.

His expression tightened. Cosmo looked away, his gaze fastened on the dancers, but Lucinda knew he wasn't really interested in them.

"Well, I like you, Cosmo. For what it's worth."

He turned and met her gaze. A rueful smile smoothed

the sharp angles of his face. The wrinkles at the corners of his eyes seemed more deeply etched than Lucinda had remembered, and for a moment, she saw a frightening depth of experience and pain in his eyes.

"Thank you, Mrs. Partridge. You do seem to have an amazingly high tolerance for me. For that, I am grateful. Not many women would put up with my incessant questions and my constant moralizing. 'Twas rude what I just did to you, challenging your values and questioning your character. I deserve to be slapped in the face."

A twinge of pity for this unhappy, brooding, mercurial man softened Lucinda's ire. The Sir Cosmo whom Lucinda had come to know had the tenderest feelings, she was sure. It was his harsh exterior that put others off. But she was coming to realize that he purposefully put people at arm's length because of his discontent. He was a man who couldn't love himself, and therefore couldn't love anyone else.

Unable to resist a small smile, she touched his arm— and wondered how it was that she was now attempting to console the man who had just insulted her. Either he was a master at manipulating her emotions, or she truly was papersculled. Either way, Lucinda couldn't tamp down her emotions. She just barely managed to restrain herself from wrapping him in her embrace and pressing his face to her breast.

Lord Wynne-Ascott's reappearance called a halt to her mental debate.

"My, are the two of you still here? Whatever can you be discussing so seriously? Good Lord, you're at a party! And a very exclusive one at that! You'll offend Lady Drummond if you don't appear to be having a good time."

Cosmo restrained himself from planting a fist in the arrogant aristocrat's nose. Lord Wynne-Ascott was simply too happy a man for him to have anything in common with. "You're all too correct, my lord. I should be ashamed of myself and I am. Lucinda, would you care to dance?"

Lucinda's eyes sparkled. Slipping her fan into her reticule, she said, "Yes, Sir Cosmo. I should be delighted to dance with you. But, your leg . . ." She looked uncertainly at his cane.

Cosmo tossed it to Wynne-Ascott. "Hold my cane, will you, old man?"

Lord Wynne-Ascott's eyes widened, and he caught the walking stick with such an expression of distaste, one would have thought he had swiped a viper from midair.

Cosmo mocked him with a deferential nod, then took Lucinda's proffered hand. They joined the couples moving about the dance floor just as a lively reel ended, and the orchestra began a new set. The music slowed to a three-count trickle.

"A waltz, Cosmo? But how very wicked of you!"

"I'm afraid it is the only dance I can perform," he answered, taking her hand in his.

Though their bodies did not touch, a wave of heat shimmered between them. Cosmo moved without the grace he had once owned, but Lucinda was an expert partner. She followed his lead without clumsiness or hesitation, adjusting her stride to his.

An astute observer might have noticed that the pair moved more slowly and covered less ground than the other dancing couples, but Cosmo didn't care. Holding Lucinda's hand, he felt he was walking on air. The pain in his leg vanished, and his heart felt young again. Her eyes sparkled, and her fingers tightened around his, vanquishing any doubts he had had about the wisdom of taking to the dance floor.

"You are a very good dancer, Cosmo."

He chuckled. "Oh, dear lady, you flatter me. 'Tis you who are the expert. Though I am hardly surprised to find that you dance like an angel. After all, you sing like one, too."

Her smile gave Cosmo immeasurable pride. He had made her happy, if only for a moment. He considered that happy expression on Lucinda's face his greatest accomplishment ever.

"Is your leg hurting you?" she asked him.

"Not at all, really."

"Are you ever going to tell me how you hurt it?"

At length, he said quietly, "No."

He was grateful that she didn't press him. Cosmo wanted to pull her close to him, to feel her body pressed against his. But the waltz, even when the dancers weren't touching, was scandalous. The youngest girls had been cleared from the floor by their fretting mamas, leaving those young ladies who cared not a fig for their reputations or whose virtues were so soundly established that a waltz couldn't hurt anything.

Cosmo didn't dare risk further injury to Lucinda's image by embracing her. But her gaze was full of promise, and her lips invited a kiss. She followed his movements like a lover, and Cosmo couldn't resist thinking what a bountiful lover she would be.

Such thoughts made his legs grow heavy and his muscles ache with repressed desire. Unable to stop himself, he drew her hand to his lips and kissed her gloved knuckles.

A throaty chuckle escaped her lips. "Cosmo, you are a bad boy!"

"Do you think anyone saw me?"

"I think everyone saw you. Including Lady Drummond. She is wearing a frown that would make Othello's death scene look like a carnival."

Cosmo followed Lucinda's gaze and saw that her description of Lady Drummond was apt. "I suppose we are being quite rude, then. Do you care, Mrs. Partridge?"

"Not as long as I am with you, Cosmo."

Her words startled him, but when he gazed into her lush blue eyes, it was her expression that shocked him. Cosmo's heart leapt at what he saw there, or what he thought he saw. The woman in his arms stared at him with naked hunger in her eyes. He wasn't fooling himself, was he?

Turning, he found himself staring straight at Lady Drummond. She smiled, but Cosmo thought it was as fraudulent as his career as a writer. Smiling in return, he was surprised to see a familiar face materialize behind Lady Drummond's shoulder.

"Ho, there, is that our friend Mr. Pavlov?"

"What? Ivan at a fancy ball?" Lucinda glanced over her shoulder. "Good heavens, you are right. And he is speaking to Lady Drummond as if they are old friends. But, then, Lord Wynne-Ascott did mention that she loves opera above all else. Which is why I was invited to attend, I'm certain."

"Do not undervalue yourself, Lucinda. You are the most beautiful woman in this room, and by far, the most charming."

Blushing, Lucinda replied softly, "You are all that is kind, sir. But an opera singer is considered beneath the salt to people of Lady Drummond's ilk."

"That is ridiculous. Wynne-Ascott, who no doubt knows the lineage of every personage in London, told me that Sir Drummond was Wellesley's barber! He received his title because he cured the viscount of a stomachache! A malady which, I am willing to venture, he would have survived without Drummond's ministrations. B'gads, he might have recovered sooner! At any rate, the Drummonds are parvenus of the highest order, dear. You have no cause to feel inferior to them. Or to anyone else, for that matter."

Frowning, Lucinda said, "If they are parvenus, then why is Wynne-Ascott so enamored of them?"

"Because they are fashionable," replied Sir Cosmo, a bit more crisply than he intended.

"Let me see if I understand this." She chuckled. "The social climbers toady to the *ton*, and the *ton* amuse themselves with the *nouveau riche*, is that it?"

"And judging by the rapt expression on Lady Drummond's face—"

"Oh, my, she does appear to be mesmerized by him. But, I am not surprised. He can be so intense when he is discussing his art."

"I'd say that the *nouveau riche* surround themselves with artists in an attempt to appear cultured, up to snuff, and all the crack."

"And whom do the starving writers pursue, Cosmo? Don't tell me that you are looking for an eligible heiress. I think I should give up my lunch if you told me that. Or a rich and fashionable eccentric like Caroline."

Cosmo gave a mock shudder. "Hardly. I have no objection to women treading the boards, Mrs. Partridge. In fact, I like nothing better than to see you on stage, adored by a theater full of people. But, when you are off stage, I flatter myself that you are not acting. Caroline does nothing that is not calculated to draw attention to her, or provoke a certain reaction from poor Byron."

"Rest assured, Cosmo, I never act when I am with you."

Her sweet smile and throaty voice so terrified Cosmo that he could do nothing but frown. He hadn't wanted to feel such tenderness toward Lucinda, and each time she displayed even the smallest measure of affection for him, it unraveled his composure.

Her flush told Cosmo that she was as flustered as he was by the web of emotions connecting them.

They danced in silence, enveloped by this new aware-ness. Words seemed unnecessary. Besides, Cosmo didn't have the vocabulary to express what he felt—yearning, confusion and desire, but something else, too. Some-thing akin to regret, but more painful. *Something black and bottomless and too terrible to confront. Something in Cosmo's heart that prevented him from loving a woman whom he wanted desperately to be in love with.*

The room spun around him, and the heat beneath his collar was suffocating. But the waltz continued, and, though Cosmo's throat was parched, his fingers held tightly to Lucinda's. Her lips parted; she whispered some-thing, and Cosmo inclined his head.

"What did you say, Lucinda?"

She shook her head. "Where have you gone, dear?" she asked on a sigh. "Sometimes you seem so far away."

He couldn't answer her. The sound of his own inner turmoil deafened him.

He did not love her. He could not. Silently, he tried to convince himself of that simple truth. He had long ago concluded that Lucinda was not the type of woman he wanted to fall in love with. She was a fortune hunter of the highest order. An admitted one, at that!

On top of everything, he had come to the realization that he could not make her happy. She required more than he could give.

Oh, but he would if he could!

His conscience assailed him. If he had a pocket full of gold and his family's money backing him, he could have her. If he were rich, he would propose to her with-out hesitation. But he had forsaken wealth in favor of a life that he could be proud of. He had chosen honor over riches. He had chosen pride over happiness. *Bloody Hell,* he screamed silently. *He'd chosen loneliness over love!*

Suddenly, Cosmo wondered exactly what he had been thinking when he told his mother she could spend his inheritance on slippers, stockings and smocks, for all he cared.

Perhaps he *should* have cared. Perhaps he should have remained true to his birthright, and simply finessed his way out of marrying his cousin—instead of asking for a strong drink the moment he laid eyes on her! He could have had his cake and eaten it, too. Then his mother would be happy because he would still be tied to her apron strings, he would be happy because he could afford to marry Lucinda Partridge, and Lucinda would be happy because she would have all the blunt she ever needed.

Of course, the holes in Cosmo's logic were so gaping that even he dismissed this line of thought as treasonous to his own integrity. He had lived his life to date as a man should, with courage and honesty. No going back now. But, dear God, how he craved to hold Lucinda in his arms. And how he longed to tell her she didn't have to marry one of those three odious men who were courting her. If Cosmo could have solved Lucinda's problems that instant by endowing her with every penny he owned, he would have.

"Here's your cane, old man," Wynne-Ascott said, poking the stick in Cosmo's kidney.

Jarred back to the present, Cosmo drew a deep breath. He didn't know if his feelings for Lucinda came from a strength in his character or a weakness. He only knew that he wanted her so badly it pained him.

The rest of the evening passed in a blur. Within the blink of an eye, Lucinda had lost Cosmo's attention. He appeared distracted, disinterested, and entirely disengaged from her.

Was it because she had questioned him about his leg? Or was it because Lady Drummond had tracked their progress about the dance floor like a hound on the scent of a fox?

A wintry morning brought little solace. Marching down Tottenham Court Road, Lucinda slipped her arm in Clarissa's. Blinking back a wall of hot tears, she cried, "Oh, fudge! Do you suppose he was angry because of Lord Wynne-Ascott's rudeness?"

The redheaded woman's eyes were swollen, her nose as bulbous and red as a beet. She had cried all the way from Lucinda's lodgings to Town, where the women had disembarked their rented hack at Charing Cross and set out on foot.

"I can't rightly say, Miz Partridge. Men are odd creatures, they are. I'm startin' to b'lieve they's just as odd when they's Quality."

"Why wouldn't they be? They're all the same, rich or poor." Glancing at her friend, Lucinda felt a pang of guilt. "Oh, Clarissa, listen to me. Blathering on like a heartless idiot while you're crying your eyes out! I am sorry, dear!"

"It's quite aw right, Miz Partridge. Ye listened to me blubberin' half the night, and ye was so exhausted ye couldn't hold yer head up."

Lucinda couldn't argue with that. She had been dead on her feet by the time she returned home from Lady Drummond's assembly. But Clarissa had been sprawled on the bed, sobbing so violently she could hardly breathe. Sleep hadn't even been a consideration once Lucinda heard that Millie Binder had died. Weakened by the horrible working conditions in Madame Conte's sweatshop, and denied rest or proper medical care, the girl had finally succumbed to an infection in her chest. It was an inglorious, undignified and all too early death. The women had spent most of the night talking and plotting their revenge on Madame Conte.

In the morning, they had visited Bow Street and told

their story to a magistrate. Luckily, they encountered a sympathetic ear, and a warrant was issued forthwith for Madame Conte's arrest. Lucinda and Clarissa would leave nothing to chance, however. When they learned the runner would appear at the seamstress's shop at ten o'clock, they determined they would meet him there.

"Don't worry, Clarissa, Millie's death will not be in vain. Once word of Madame Conte's arrest spreads throughout London, the other modistes will be too afraid to work their girls to death."

With a brave gulp, Clarissa swiped a tear from her ruddy cheek. "Yer right, Miz Partridge. Can't bring Millie back now. Best thing to do is move on and try to save the other girls' lives, if we can."

In front of Madame Conte's shop, they stopped and looked around. At precisely ten o'clock, there was no Bow Street runner in sight.

"Do you think he has forgotten?" Clarissa asked.

Lucinda shook her head. "More likely he was delayed conducting other business. After all, there are not enough runners to go around, considering all the crime that is committed in London."

The women stood arm in arm, their teeth chattering against the cold. Huddled close to the building, they attempted to stay away from Madame Conte's window and out of her line of sight.

Traffic on Tottenham Court Road was brisk, and the streets were crowded with horses and carriages. Passing shoppers, with their curious stares, exhibited clear opinions on the prudence of standing in the cold when the warmth of a shop was only steps away. Lucinda kept her eyes trained on the door of Madame Conte's shop, worried stiff that her quarry would slip out before the Bow Street runner arrived.

A half hour passed before a battered hack drew up in front of the dressmaker's. A burly-looking man wearing a dark blue uniform with shiny brass buttons emerged. With his surly expression, he appeared formidable and extremely capable of routing Madame Conte. Lucinda's breast surged with optimism. This was not a man to be trifled with. Millie's murderer would soon be apprehended, and justice would prevail.

Beneath his dark blue woolen cap were brows as oily and black as beetles. Gripping a thick wooden truncheon, the runner stood in front of Lucinda and Clarissa. "G'morning, ladies. Are we ready to go inside?"

"Wh-what took you so long?" Clarissa asked.

The man skewered her with his grape shot gaze. "Had a bit of business to take care of near the docks, ma'am. Sorry to make you wait."

His tone suggested he was anything but sorry, but Lucinda could forgive the man his rudeness if he was willing to put Madame Conte out of business. As he pushed into the store, she followed—and was buffeted by an even icier wave of cold air immediately upon stepping inside.

Clarissa was at her side, whispering, "Lor, where is everybody?"

Indeed, the cacophony that had once emanated from the sewing shop in the rear was replaced by silence. The place was as quiet as a cemetery.

Lucinda's heart thumped like a rabbit's foot. "She has gone."

The runner shrugged his massive shoulders. " 'Pears that Madame Conte has flown the coop, ladies."

"Closed shop," whispered Lucinda, her chest aching. "But why?"

"And why now?" whined Clarissa.

"Happens sometimes," the runner said matter-of-factly. "Probably heard yer friend turned up her toes. Reckoned she'd be up to her neck in hot water. Closed down before the authorities had a chance to nab her."

"There is something very havey-cavey about this," Lucinda said.

"Like I said, ma'am," the runner repeated. "This sort of thing happens all the time. Conte will open up somewhere else, just give her time. Then you can come back and swear out another complaint. We'll nab her then. I promise you."

Lucinda stared at the man in complete amazement. Perhaps he was right; perhaps Madame Conte realized she would be in trouble with the law when Millie Binder died. But somehow Lucinda couldn't believe that the woman she had met just a day earlier, the woman who was so eager to sew up an expensive trousseau that she promised to work her girls overtime even if it killed them, would shut down just because she heard Millie Binder had met her maker.

As the shop door shut behind the runner, Lucinda and Clarissa clung to one another, shivering and stunned. Never in her life had Lucinda felt so desolate or so ineffective. Her resolve to open a women's shelter, a place where girls like Millie Binder could escape the kinds of conditions that Madame Conte had imposed on her, hardened. She knew now that she would let nothing deter her from her goal.

That meant she had to marry one of her suitors, quickly. It also meant she had to force Sir Cosmo Fairchild, and the way he made her feel, out of her mind, *completely*.

Outside, on the opposite side of Tottenham Court Road, Sir Cosmo Fairchild sat in a rented carriage, watching the front door of Madame Conte's shop, waiting for Lucinda and Clarissa to emerge.

Twelve

Cosmo leapt from the hack with as much agility as his leg would allow him. He crossed the street just as Lucinda and Clarissa emerged from the shop.

Lucinda looked up as he approached, and all three stood outside Madame Conte's bow-shaped window.

Touching the brim of his beaver hat, Cosmo smiled. "Good day, Mrs. Partridge and—"

"Clarissa MacDougal," replied the red-haired woman. Despite her coarse appearance, she had a sweet voice and kind eyes.

"Might I offer you ladies a lift? It is frightfully cold, and I see you haven't a carriage waiting."

"What on earth are you doing here, Cosmo?" Lucinda asked.

"Would you believe that I just happened down the road when I spied you coming out of—" Cosmo glanced theatrically at the wooden placard hanging by a chain above the modiste's door. "Ah, Madame Conte's."

"No, I would not believe it for a moment." Lucinda clutched her companion's arm and said tightly, "You were following me, Cosmo. How dare you?"

"Do not forget, dear lady, that I am writing a book about your life as a diva. Everything you do is of interest to me. Everywhere you go is pertinent and material to my book. Everyone you meet, especially your suitors, is relevant to my investigation."

"Investigation?"

"Excuse me. A better word would have been *research.*"

She bristled, her angry breath misting in the cold. Beside her, Clarissa MacDougal, obviously a very loyal friend, bristled, too.

"Cosmo, I agreed to allow you free reign in investigating my suitors. You are doing me a great kindness in that regard, since I am going to marry one of them and the more I know about their respective characters, the better decision I can make. But, I did not, sir, agree that you should dog my heels constantly. Where I go when I am not at the opera house is none of your business."

She told the truth, as she knew it. But, then, she didn't know that Cosmo was a spy. And that his principal job was to spy on her. He had spent most of the night outside Lucinda's apartment, watching everyone who passed her door. After all, if one of her suitors visited her, he wanted to know about it.

As it happened, no one ventured near Lucinda's door. In the morning, he had watched her emerge with this shabbily dressed redhead, and his curiosity had been piqued. Following Lucinda had been perfectly natural. Explaining that to Lucinda was slightly more tricky.

"You are correct," he said, bowing slightly. "I had no reason at all to follow you. But I drove past your apartment this morning just as you and your friend stepped into a hackney cab. I was unable to attract your attention before the carriage took off, so I told my driver to follow you."

"Why, pray tell, were you visiting me at such an ungentlemanly hour?"

Her arch manner unnerved Cosmo. The night before, she had shown a great deal of warmth toward him. Today, she appeared to be extremely put out with him. "I was going to invite you to share nuncheon with me."

"You know that I am rarely up before noon."

"I was going to slip a note beneath your door. Upon rising, you would find my invitation, and therefore have plenty of time to dress before my return. Excuse me, Mrs. Partridge, but I thought I was showing you a kindness. The last thing I wanted was to offend you."

She seemed suspicious of Cosmo's explanation, but then, it was a bit queer, he admitted to himself.

"How long have you been out here?" she asked pointedly.

"My driver lost you in traffic at the corner of Charing Cross Road. 'Struth, I didn't expect you to walk three blocks on foot—not in this cold! Anyhow, some dandy in a high-sprung phaeton cut me off at the intersection. Almost turned himself over. Caused a devil of a jam, that scoundrel did! When we got through, my man drove slowly in the direction we had last seen you walking. I pulled to a stop when I saw you exiting—" Cosmo looked up again. "Madame Conte's."

"Oh." Lucinda frowned.

Clarissa smiled. "I think that's awfully nice, Sir—"

"Cosmo." He grinned. "Cosmo Fairchild."

"Now, there's a nice name, for ye." Clarissa nudged Lucinda. "Come on, Miz Partridge, don't be too hard on the man. He was just tryin' to show ye a kindness."

Pursing her lips, Lucinda remained silent.

"She don't like ta talk much on days when she's singin' at the opera," explained Clarissa.

"Yes, I know." Cosmo gestured toward his hack. "Well, what do you say, ladies? Shall we adjourn to my carriage, or shall we stand about on the street all day and freeze?"

Grudgingly, Lucinda accepted Cosmo's offer, and the party of three piled into the hackney cab parked on the opposite side of the road.

"You will accompany me to nuncheon, now that I have you captive in my vehicle, won't you, Mrs. Partridge?" Cosmo tossed both ladies lap blankets, then sat opposite them on the hard leather squabs.

"I think I had better return home—"

"Oh, Miz Partridge," Clarissa cried, "I think you should go."

"You are also invited," Cosmo said.

The ruddy-faced woman gasped. "Oh, no, but I couldn't dine with a pair as fine as ye two. 'Twouldn't be proper. Why, there ain't even an establishment that would allow me on its premises lookin' the way I do." She gazed down at her shabby coat. "Lor, I ain't no better dressed than a climbin' boy."

"I think you look fine," Cosmo replied. "And I should be honored to dine with you. What do you say, Mrs. Partridge, you won't deprive Clarissa and me the fun of eating at a fancy hotel dining room, will you?"

The look on Lucinda's face was undoubtedly one she had never worn on stage. Yet it conveyed every emotion she felt as clearly as if words had been stamped on her face. If she said no, Clarissa would be denied an experience that for the obviously underprivileged woman would truly be memorable. Glaring at Cosmo, Lucinda had no alternative but to say, "All right, then. We shall join you for a light nuncheon."

With his cane, he rapped the trapdoor above his head and gave the driver instructions to proceed south to Number Seven Albemarle Street. The women were quiet as the carriage rumbled southward through Charing Cross, westerly down Shaftsbury and then on to Piccadilly. When the horses halted in front of Grillon's Hotel, Clarissa broke the silence.

Peering out of the window, she cried, "Zounds, we ain't eatin' here, are we?"

"Why not?" Cosmo exited first, and offered the gaping redhead his hand. "Do you have an objection to the food here?"

She jumped inelegantly from the carriage, her eyes as round as copper gaming chips. "No, sir! I mean, I ain't never eaten at so fine a place. I thought we'd go to a chophouse or a good tavern, and that would 'ave been a rare treat fer me!"

Emerging behind Clarissa, Lucinda smoothed her skirts and pulled her woolen cloak tightly about her body. "Really, Cosmo," was all she said.

He ushered the ladies up the steps and into the warmth of the hotel's lobby. A well-known figure at Grillon's, Cosmo was quickly met by an efficient-looking man in a liveried uniform.

"Sir Cosmo, so pleased to see you." The hotel steward's gaze glanced off Clarissa. "May I be of service to you?"

"Table for three, please. And tell the chef we are very hungry."

The steward looked more pointedly at Clarissa. "Three, sir?"

A large sum of money discreetly changed hands.

"A table for three, it is." The steward stiffened his back, squared his shoulders, and led the party to the dining room. Pulling up the rear, Cosmo was amused at the expressions his small procession invoked. Heads turned, brows shot up and lips puckered disapprovingly.

Meeting the gaze of one particularly rude matron, Clarissa paused tableside, and said, "How do you do, madame? I see the turbot is very good; you've left hardly a morsel on your plate!"

"Of all the impertinent—" The perfectly groomed woman stared in astonishment, first at Clarissa, then at her companion. "Edith, can you believe it?" Finally, she leveled her gaze at Sir Cosmo. "What sort of funny business is this, sir, bringing a woman of such low character into an establishment such as this?"

"I was about to ask the same question of your friend Edith," Cosmo drawled.

At a cozy table in the rear of the room, he held out a chair as Clarissa settled into it. The steward assisted Lucinda and gathered the ladies' cloaks and hats. "Have a nice dinner, sir. Please let me know if there is anything else I can do for you, and your lovely companions."

A waiter, equipped with menus and a wine list, materialized. Cosmo ordered a feast and an excellent bottle of Bordeaux. Then he turned his attention toward his guests.

"Tell me, Mrs. Partridge, is Madame Conte a very good seamstress?" The art of simple conversation often led to revealing tidbits of information.

"I wouldn't know," Lucinda replied.

"Then, why were you visiting her?"

The beautiful soprano seemed flustered. After a beat, she answered, "I, er, I was recommended to her by Madame Bartoli. She has many of her own gowns sewn up by Madame Conte. It seems that Conte is becoming quite fashionable these days."

"I see. Did you place a large order?"

Coloring, Lucinda said, "I suppose I did."

"Good. A woman with a new wardrobe must surely want to be seen in it. Which I am all in favor of. I do hope you will enlist me in assisting you, Mrs. Partridge. I promise to take you to as many balls, assemblies, parties, and outings as it takes in order to show off your pretty new gowns."

"How loverly," Clarissa gushed.

But Lucinda shook her head. "Thank you, Cosmo, but I don't think that will be necessary. You have been far too attentive to me, as of late. I can not continue taking up so much of your time. Aren't you falling behind in your book writing?"

Cosmo's chest squeezed. Unable to account for Lucinda's coldness, he tucked away his own feelings of warmth for her and became merely a spy once more. A spy who was very suspicious of Lucinda Partridge's morning excursion, and her sudden defensiveness about it.

"As I have said, Mrs. Partridge, everything you do is of interest to me. Extensive research is always done prior to sitting down with pen and paper. Please do not trouble yourself that I am taking too much time getting to know you and your daily routine."

She nodded. "How much longer do you expect to spend researching me, sir?"

"Not much longer, I hope. There is the matter of investigating your suitors, of course."

"That shouldn't take too long. I have ruled out the possibility of marrying Lord Wynne-Ascott. Mr. Pugh is in second place, but we already know the drawbacks to marrying him. So, there is only Mr. Pavlov left to investigate, and he never goes anywhere except the opera house."

"And to Lady Drummond's assemblies."

Lucinda said nothing.

Cosmo's chosen bottle of wine was presented, opened and poured. As Clarissa consumed the expensive Bordeaux, swallowing her first glass without pausing to breathe, Cosmo focused his attention on Mrs. Partridge.

"You still haven't told me why you were at Madame Conte's this morning."

"I did tell you. To buy dresses."

"That has an odd ring about it. You have told me repeatedly that your pockets are to let, Mrs. Partridge. Why would a woman about to lose her only source of income commission a new wardrobe?"

Her mouth opened and closed. For a long moment,

their gazes locked. Clarissa emptied her second glass of wine and was stretching across the table for the bottle when the waiter intervened and poured another round.

"Didna' know wine could feel like velvet slidin' down yer throat," the redhead cooed.

"You are quite welcome, madame," replied the well-trained server, who, for his quick movements as well as his politeness, received a wad of notes in his white-gloved hand.

"Well?" Cosmo asked.

"I commissioned my trousseau," replied Lucinda, lifting her chin a notch.

Her trousseau. The words rang in Cosmo's ears, deafening him to Clarissa's patter. The reality of Lucinda's marriage struck him like a thunderbolt. Picturing her in the arms of another man brought his blood to a boil.

But, why? Hadn't he just the night before concluded that Lucinda Partridge was not meant for him?

The meal continued in a series of exotic and perfectly cooked meats, fishes and fowls. Bowls of turtle soup appeared, followed by plates laden with turbot, smelts and roasted turnips.

Clarissa ate heartily, expressing her gustatory enjoyment with sighs and dreamy smiles. Lucinda picked at her food. And Cosmo simply stared at the magnificent delicacies, including the smoked Lapland reindeer tongues, Russian caviar and curried vegetables that passed beneath his eyes.

"Ain't ye goin' to eat that, sir?"

"No, you may have it," he said as Clarissa stabbed a slab of venison on his plate during the fourth course that was served to them.

At length, after summoning another bottle of wine, and allowing his glass to be refilled, Cosmo said, "So, you are planning your wedding before you have even chosen a husband, Mrs. Partridge. Isn't that a bit like putting the cart before the horse?"

"There is no use putting off till tomorrow what can be done today."

Cosmo didn't like Lucinda's toplofty attitude. Moreover, he found her practicality unsettling to the extreme. "Tell me, Mrs. Partridge, in your calculations regarding a marriage partner, has affection ever been a factor?"

Her expression turned to stone. "I have married twice, sir, the first time, because I thought I was in love, and the second time, because I thought my husband was in love with me."

"You were wrong both times." Cosmo knew he was being cruel, yet he couldn't help himself. That Lucinda was willing to wed a man she didn't love offended and angered him. Unable to comprehend her reasoning, he could only attribute to her the most unseemly motives. Motives that were at odds with the instinctual affection he felt for her.

"Yes, I was wrong." With a sigh, Lucinda traded plates with Clarissa. "Are you taking pleasure in reminding me of my past mistakes? Or is this part of your precious research, too?"

Cosmo was as gratified to see Miss MacDougal enjoying her meal as he was relieved by her diffidence. She didn't seem at all interested in the conversation going on between him and Lucinda; indeed, she seemed oblivious to everything except what was on her plate.

He couldn't tear his gaze from Lucinda. Her expression had softened, and her eyes held a sort of defiant sadness. "Do you regret your actions?" he asked.

Her throat constricted, emotion threatening to spill out in the most heartfelt of confessions. But Lucinda was determined not to expose her true self, or the level of her desperation. Of course, Cosmo thought her a fortune hunter; she knew that. He considered her a shallow and buffle-headed woman who had set her cap for a rich husband with no regard to whether she loved that man at all.

Well, perhaps he was right, she thought, her chest tightening with frustration. She had charted a deliberate course for marriage because it was the only vehicle she knew of that would enable her to achieve her dreams.

And didn't the end justify the means?

He cleared his throat and tossed his napkin on the table. "I did not intend my words to be offensive, Mrs. Partridge."

"Are you not a wordsmith by trade, Sir Cosmo? If that is the case, I find it difficult to believe that your insult was the result of a negligent employment of your vocabulary. I think you said exactly what you meant, and that you meant precisely what you said."

"Perhaps I did. It is just that I do not understand why a woman such as you would marry a man she did not love."

"I need money, Sir Cosmo."

"There are other ways to get it, Mrs. Partridge."

"Name one, Sir Cosmo."

He hesitated. "You could continue on the stage."

"But you know how few opera houses there are remaining in London," she argued. "And I can't do burlesque or comedies. I am an opera singer, sir, trained in the classical style."

"Perhaps you can get an extension on your contract at the opera house," he suggested.

"Ivan has interceded with the owners on my behalf. Numerous times. He has assured me that there is no chance that my contract will be renewed."

"Has he? Are you quite certain that your case has been adequately presented to the owners?"

Lucinda rankled at Cosmo's judgmental tone. "You are suggesting that I have not tried to find other employment, that I am lazy, or spoiled! I resent that, Cosmo. The truth is that a diva's career is short-lived. Once her voice begins to crack, she is finished. Stage work is for young women. I must find another way in the world for myself."

"And the only other course you can think of is to marry a rich man."

Leaning forward, Lucinda spoke through clenched jaws. "Can you think of a better way to raise the blunt to finance my women's shelter?"

Clarissa, thank God, was so involved with her food that she wouldn't have noticed if Boney himself sauntered through the dining room.

Pushing back in his chair, Cosmo assumed a languid air, and such a posture of moral righteousness that Lucinda had to restrain herself from throwing the saltcellar at his head. "You could, dear lady, find another line of employment."

The only other line of employment that Lucinda felt she was suited for was the one she was trying to get Clarissa and countless other women out of. Given the precariousness of the opera scene and the scarcity of employment opportunities therein, Lucinda had, on many occasions in the past, thought herself fortunate to have escaped that awful fate.

"How dare you suggest that I sell myself," she seethed.

His eyes rounded. "Mrs. Partridge, I did not mean—"

"Oh, I know precisely what you meant. Do not mince words with me any longer. You would have me on my back with a never ending succession of strangers rather than married to a respectable man who can provide me with a roof over my head, and sufficient funds to continue my charitable work!"

"On the contrary!" He leaned forward, his gaze earnest. "I meant that perhaps you could find another position, outside the opera world, one that might make use of your many talents. I have not known you for very long, Mrs. Partridge, but I am certain that you are the type of woman who can do anything once she sets her mind to it!"

"Well, I have set my mind to marry, sir. And that is what I shall do."

"If you marry Mr. Pugh, you'd better figure out a way to convince him your women's shelter will be profitable."

With a shudder, for she had already made up her mind that life with Lawrence Pugh would be insupportable, Lucinda said, *"Profitable?* How can you place a value on a woman's life?"

With a dark chuckle, Cosmo replied, "I wouldn't know, but our gentleman dairyman will want to know what sort of return he can expect from his investment."

She fell silent. Mr. Pugh was nothing if not a businessman, that was true. Her mind slowly turned that thought. If he thought of her women's shelter as an *investment,* he might be willing to underwrite her venture.

Then she flashed on the image of his chubby fingers and beefy lips, and a shudder gripped her shoulders. "There seems to be a chill in here all of a sudden."

"Yes." Cosmo turned his attention on Clarissa. "Miss MacDougal, how are you faring?"

His question startled her. Eyes widening, she mumbled around the chicken leg in her mouth. "Thif if vewwy goot!"

"Clarissa, dear," said Lucinda, "you shouldn't talk with your mouth full of food."

The woman swallowed. "This is very good," she repeated. "Lor, 'tis the choicest food ever passed me blasted lips. 'Scuse me language. Can't thank ye enough, Sir Cosmo. And ye, too, Mrs. Partridge. Fer allowin' me to come here with ye. Got a few of the nabobs overset, it did, when I came traipsin' through the room. But ye didn't care, neither one of ye. Shows what sorta good folk ye are."

"You are very welcome, Clarissa." Lucinda's anger faded. Seeing Clarissa happy gave her immeasurable pleasure. If only she could do for the other poor wretched girls of London's mean streets what she had been able to do for Clarissa.

Well, she would. And she wouldn't let Cosmo, or his righteous moralizing, hinder her.

He could preach about true love, and the sanctity of marriage, all day long if he wanted to. He could sit on his high horse and judge her till the cows came home. Or until the cow farmer built her a women's shelter, for that matter. But he couldn't make her ashamed of what she was going to do, that is, marry for money. And he couldn't convince her that her goal of building a shelter was out of her reach.

Because she knew how many women there were in London who needed help, and she intended to help them.

Even if it meant marrying a man she didn't love.

Even if it meant ignoring the increasingly disturbing feelings she felt for Cosmo Fairchild.

It might have been a prelude to the drama on the stage. In the marbled lobby of the opera house, Lady Drummond promised to plunge a dagger into her ample breast if Cosmo refused her invitation.

Which he *did* decline. In fact, he defended himself against the determined woman's entreaties for a good ten minutes before she launched her final offensive, a nearly hysterical display of wounded feelings and injured sensibilities that resulted in Cosmo's at last being forced to admit he didn't mean to be rude, and would, upon reflection, be honored to share her private box.

Anything less than such a maudlin and public exhibition of temper would never have resulted in Cosmo's being wedged between Nathaniel Upton, Lord Wynne-Ascott, and the overbearing, well-cushioned figure of Mrs. Sapho Drummond. He edged forward in his seat, propping his arms along the edge of the box. Not so much to get a better view of the stage, as to put some distance between himself and Lady Drummond's overflowing hips.

As usual, he found himself totally absorbed by the opera. He loved the story, as much for Cleopatra's strength as for Caesar's bravery and determination. In her Roman toga, Lucinda made a particularly plucky Caesar. The audience showed their affection with numerous spontaneous outbursts of applause, their clapping thunderous whenever Lucinda performed an aria. Her voice may have weakened, but her popularity was apparently as strong as ever.

It struck Cosmo as odd that the management of the Orange Street was so keen to cancel her contract.

Watching her move across the stage, he felt the stirrings of desire. Lucinda, even with her complicated whalebone stays, simply could not conceal her ample feminine form beneath the shapeless white gown of the Roman emperor. Reminded of her womanly charms, an uncomfortable edginess assailed Sir Cosmo. Truly, she was the most alluring creature he had ever seen. Even garbed as a man, she radiated a beauty that he could not resist.

God knew he had tried. Since he met her, Cosmo had regarded Lucinda in the most critical light, had purposely put the worst construction on everything she said and did, had deliberately put her at arm's length from himself.

He had almost succeeded in convincing himself that he didn't love her, that she was, in fact, unworthy of his love. When the truth of the matter was that he was unworthy of her.

Behind him, Lord Wynne-Ascott and Lady Drummond shared a sniff of snuff. When the hefty woman erupted in a predictable fit of sneezing, Cosmo scooted closer to the edge of the box and rested his chin on his forearms. Annoyed that anyone could be distracted while Lucinda was on the stage, he continued to stare at her, and though she refused to meet his gaze, Cosmo knew she was aware of him. There was no pretense between them now. A strong, irresistible force surrounded them, drawing them together, yet somehow compelling them apart. Lucinda could not deny that she felt it. What remained to be seen was whether she would marry someone else in spite of it.

He watched as Cleopatra, played by Madame Bartoli, defied her brother Ptolemy and prayed for Caesar's safe return. The younger soprano had a lovely form and figure, and her performance was loud and flawless, if not particularly inspired. But she never aroused the audience the way Lucinda Partridge did.

Lucinda's voice lacked its usual volume, its ear-popping strength, its youth. But what her singing lacked in raw endurance was made up for by the *emotion* Lucinda managed to convey. Her voice, Cosmo noted, had taken on a more mature quality, and, unlike the much younger Madame Bartoli, who hit every high note in her arias without fail, Lucinda's voice was nuanced with a much vaster range of human experience. She sang not like a dove, but like a woman whose heart had been broken.

In the second scene of the final act, Lucinda turned and met Cosmo's gaze. She sang,

Beloved! I hold you in my arms;
Our destiny has changed its course

The words echoed in his mind; his body tensed with frustration and longing. Had his and Lucinda's destinies become one? And, had it changed course?

At last, he admitted to himself that he loved her, loved her irrevocably and without redemption. There was nothing about her he didn't adore, even her weaknesses, even her foibles. She was willing to marry for money, yes, but her motivation was selfless. He had always known that. She wanted to help women less fortunate than she, and to that end, she was prepared to sacrifice her own happiness.

Watching her, Cosmo felt a swell of admiration. Character, rather than volume, range, or strength, was what made Lucinda's voice so awe inspiring. Textured and complicated, her range was in her emotions and experience; her talent was in her ability to draw out her listeners' emotions. As tears slid down Cosmo's face, he paid silent homage to the only woman who had ever provoked him to cry. He didn't care. It felt good to give in to this emotion; he hadn't felt so alive in years.

At length, Cosmo removed a handkerchief from his inside coat pocket and dabbed his face. Behind him, Lord Wynne-Ascott chuckled at his sentimentality. Lady Drummond sneezed, and Cosmo, looking over his shoulder, passed her his linen.

When he turned back toward the stage, his gaze snagged on a familiar face in the audience. It was an upturned face staring straight at him. But when Cosmo focused on the crowd below, the man had turned away from him. Cosmo peered downward and, in the golden haze of the overhead chandelier, searched the audience. That face was imprinted on his mind, but his brain refused to summon up a name. Who was that man who had been staring at him? Where was he now?

Whoever it was, he did not look back toward Cosmo. Cosmo scanned the audience, then leaned even farther over the edge of the box, attempting to pick out the familiar features. One by one, he studied each person in every row of the lower audience.

Then Cosmo saw him. The man's name was Henri LeFlaive. He was well known in Paris as a French operative who had worked extensively in Britain. It was said that he had the ear of one of Wellington's top men, and that he had supplied his superiors with much information about the viscount's battle strategies as well as England's military capabilities.

Henri LeFlaive. There was his spy. The man wasn't at the Orange Street Opera House to hear Mrs. Partridge sing Julius Caesar, of that Cosmo was certain. Perhaps Cosmo should arrest the little Frog right now, and put an end to this nefarious spy ring. But the information that Sir Milburn's operatives had furnished indicated that one of Lucinda's suitors was involved, also. So, LeFlaive had a conspirator. And Cosmo had no intention of capturing one little rat while allowing the other to go free.

His exhilaration at having spotted LeFlaive in the audience deafened him to the roar of the crowd. The curtain descended, and the opera was over. But Cosmo couldn't take his gaze off LeFlaive.

The French spy had made a terrible mistake, and Cosmo was closing in on his quarry. His heart raced with excitement.

The bullet that passed his ear ruffled his hair, but Cosmo didn't realize he had been shot at till Lady Drummond screamed.

Thirteen

"Bloody hell, the bastard's shot me!"

It wasn't the sort of language customarily heard from a woman. In fact, Lady Drummond's unladylike outburst drew a brief smile to Cosmo's lips, despite the seriousness of her pronouncement.

Whirling, he saw with relief that she wasn't shot. Her hands fluttered up in a futile effort to defend herself against the bullet that flew past her nose and embedded itself into the wall behind her. She tumbled out of her chair and hugged the floor as if she were dodging a fusillade. Cosmo stifled a laugh. All of Lady Drummond's maneuvers had been conducted subsequent to the offending bullet having planted itself in the plaster behind her. Still, she quivered like a mountain of aspic.

Lord Wynne-Ascott, crouching beside her, appeared no less the coward than she. "Zounds! Who's the blasted bugger who's shooting at me, Cosmo? Can you see who it was? For God's sake, man, do something!"

Below them, the audience continued its applause, oblivious to the near fatal shot that had been fired at the threesome in the upper box. Their clapping had drowned out the crack of gunfire that accompanied the rogue shot. And their sudden exodus was giving cover and opportunity to whoever had fired his pistol inside the opera house.

"And what would you have me do?" drawled Cosmo, having ascertained that Lady Drummond was unharmed. He turned and scanned the audience, but the mass was commingling in an indistinguishable crowd of beaver hats and feathered headdresses. Monsieur LeFlaive was nowhere to be seen.

Of course, LeFlaive could not have fired the shot that nearly had bobbed Cosmo's ear. Cosmo had been staring straight down at the man's squirrelly profile when the bullet was discharged.

Someone else, one of Lucinda's suitors, no doubt had noticed Cosmo's interest in Henri LeFlaive. So, he was getting very near the viper's nest. So near that LeFlaive's conspirator had taken the reckless step of firing his pistol in the opera house and risking exposure.

Well, at least Cosmo could rule out Lord Wynne-Ascott. Considering the location where the bullet lodged, that august gentleman couldn't have fired the shot.

"Come, my lord," Cosmo said, "I shall assist you in getting Lady Drummond upright."

"Oh, God help me!" The woman had rolled to her back, hands crossed over her chest in a pose that suggested a quiet, permanent period of rest. Her round and bulging eyes, however, very much betrayed her lividity. "Someone tried to kill me! Nathaniel, who could have done such a thing?"

As literal-minded a nabob there never had been, thought Cosmo, as the aristocrat straightened and gave Lady Drummond's inquiry some very deep thought.

"Have you given anyone the cut direct, lately, Lady Drummond?" Lord Wynne-Ascott scratched his chin. "You know how awfully riled an up-and-coming out-and-outer can get when snubbed by new money! Perhaps you omitted some highly esteemed personage from the guest list of your most recent assembly. I've known of duels to be had over such lapses in protocol! Or perhaps it had something to do with that salacious little *on dit* concerning Lady Stanton that you unwittingly negotiated to her husband, before you learned who he was, of course."

"*New money!* Nathaniel, you stiff-rumped idiot! Help me up, boy, before I vow never to speak to you again!"

Wynne-Ascott left off on attempting to divine a motive for Lady Drummond's attacker. Bending down, he took hold of Lady Drummond's shoulders, while Cosmo grasped her legs as best he could, decorum permitting. With a great deal of straining, the men managed to get their cargo seated on a chair, where she remained, fanning herself, when Cosmo departed the box.

Proceeding directly to Mrs. Partridge's dressing room, he rapped his cane on her door. When it opened, he was staring into Ivan Pavlov's face.

"Am I interrupting something?" Cosmo said, crossing the threshold. His shoulder brushed the Russian's as he strode into the room.

Lucinda sat at her dressing table, watching the tableau behind her in the reflection of her mirror. "Ivan was just leaving," she said, her tone wary.

The man gave Cosmo a long, menacing look before nodding curtly and exiting the tiny room.

As the door slammed shut, Cosmo closed the distance between himself and Lucinda. Leaning his cane against the wall, he grasped her shoulders and drew her to stand against him. Through the thin silk of her dressing gown, her round body was lush and comforting. A flood of desire roiled through him as Cosmo cupped her pretty face in his hands and lowered his lips to hers.

He loved her. He had known it for a long time, but now that he felt the warmth of her kiss, experienced the sweet, secret taste of her mouth, he knew he couldn't live without her.

"Marry me." The words escaped his lips before he even knew he had said them.

She drew back, her body stiffening. Eyes wide, Lucinda simply stared open-mouthed at him. Without so much as breathing a word, she told him loud and clear that she was not receptive to his affections.

He wrenched himself away from her. "I am a fool! Forgive me, Lucinda, for my momentary insanity! You are bound to marry a rich man. How could I forget?"

"Cosmo, you don't understand! To marry for love— oh, would that I possessed that luxury!"

"Luxury?" Cosmo turned and faced her. "Since when is love a luxury?"

Her gaze dropped to the floor. For a long time, she was silent. When Lucinda looked up, her eyes shimmered behind a veil of tears. "Love has never served me well, Cosmo. Whenever I have followed my heart, I have been disappointed. I'm too old to take another chance such as that."

"So you have given up? You have decided to wallow in your unhappiness? How pathetic, Lucinda! How terribly sad!"

"I'm not asking for your pity, Cosmo. I know you can not understand my reasoning. But don't believe for a moment I can't be happy without love in my life. I have my work. I have my calling!"

"I thought your calling was here, in the opera house."

Her eyes flashed. "To hell with the opera house. I am going to build a women's shelter in London, a place where people like Clarissa can come and find sanctuary. Did you know that one of her customers beat her black-and-blue a few weeks ago, Cosmo? And yet, she continues to ply her trade because she thinks so little of herself and has such little confidence in her ability to do anything to help herself."

"I could say the same of someone else I know, Lucinda."

"Are you calling me a—"

"No, dammit," Cosmo growled. "I am suggesting you are responsible for your own happiness, and no one else's. Quit trying to save the world, Lucinda, and worry about your own future for a change."

"Open your eyes, Cosmo. You are a romantic to your very core, and so naive it pains me. Perhaps you can be happy living like a pauper because you are following your own dream, that of being a penniless writer. But being penniless holds no charm for me. *I need money.*"

He couldn't help but chuckle. "I like a woman who knows her mind. Trouble is, Mrs. Partridge, I don't think you know yours at all."

"Laugh at me if you will. But I have a plan."

Sighing, he replied, "It is the most ridiculous plan I have ever heard."

Her tears having evaporated, Mrs. Partridge stared at him with cold, angry eyes. "Mr. Pugh has increased his offer."

"Was he in the audience tonight?"

"Yes, of course."

"And did he visit you backstage after the performance?" Running his hand through his hair, an idea popped into Cosmo's brain. Suddenly, he attached great significance to the dairy farmer's whereabouts during the time period when he and Lord Wynne-Ascott were hoisting Lady Drummond into her chair.

"And that is when he again proposed marriage to you. Well, tell me, Mrs. Partridge, what are the terms of his offer? Are they advantageous to you, or will your heirs be paying back your debts to Mr. Pugh plus interest at three times the rate charged by the Bank of England for the rest of their lives?"

"I'll thank you not to speak so disparagingly of Lawrence. He recognizes the benefits of underwriting my charity. And he is more than willing to back me financially."

Cosmo laughed again. "Pray tell, how did you convince the selfish bastard to do that?"

She pursed her lips, but Cosmo thought he detected a grudging glint of amusement behind her gaze.

"I merely explained to him that if he wanted to run for a seat in the Commons, it would be vastly helpful to have his name on some public institution devoted to the rectification of lost women's souls. I'm not prideful; I don't mind if my shelter is called Pugh House. After all, good works can be very profitable if one wishes to become a politician, sir. I should have thought you knew that."

"Ho! You are a clever minx." Cosmo bowed as low as his lame leg would permit. "My compliments to you, Lucinda. I had no idea that Mr. Pugh harbored political aspirations, but in convincing him that your women's shelter was a good investment, you have proved your unparalleled intelligence."

"Thank you," she replied, primly.

"And so you have decided to accept Mr. Pugh's offer, then?"

"Oh, no! Mr. Pavlov is pressing his offer most strenuously. And I dare say, he has sweetened the pot considerably."

"Have you ever thought of becoming an auctioneer, sweetheart? Or a purveyor of fine goods? Hell, you are a devil of a bargainer. Too bad they don't let women practice law!"

She smiled tightly, despite her obvious pique at Cosmo's flippancy. "Mr. Pavlov has also offered to give me the money necessary to build my women's shelter."

"You told him about Mr. Pugh's offer—"

"Of course."

A frightening suspicion took form in Cosmo's mind. "Pavlov visited you tonight, after Pugh left this dressing room?"

"Yes. Ivan had only been here a few moments before you banged on the door."

"Long enough to promise you great riches if you would marry him."

She waved her hand airily, and sighed. "I am leaning toward accepting Mr. Pavlov's suit."

"What? Without giving Lord Wynne-Ascott an opportunity to enter his bid?"

She looked at Cosmo, her eyes round. "Do you think he will wish to?"

"Why wouldn't he? He's a sporting man, after all."

Lucinda seemed to consider this a moment. "You have made an excellent point. Perhaps I should give Nathaniel a chance to better Mr. Pavlov's and Mr. Pugh's offers. He has the blunt to do so, sure enough."

"You could strike a deal with Wynne-Ascott and retain your independence. After all, he does not wish to marry you."

"Thank you for reminding me, Cosmo."

"You're a practical woman. I'm certain you had thought it yourself."

"You are straining my patience, sir. I hope you don't think me so foolish that I cannot see what you are trying to do. You lampoon my folly in hopes of showing me the error of my ways, but your witty sarcasm is useless. 'Struth, I am weary of being insulted by the likes of you. Perhaps you should go."

"Prudence would seem to dictate that I leave and never speak another word to you. But, for once, Lucinda, I am determined to follow my heart instead of my head. I asked you to marry me. Now I am telling you that I love you."

Shaking her head, she gave a tremulous little laugh. "Oh, Cosmo! How is it that a man who looks older than his years can harbor such silly, romantic notions! Darling, if you intend to pursue a career as a writer, what you need is a rich wife, not a penniless opera singer! What sort of couple would we be, with our ambitious dreams and not a guinea between us!"

Cosmo's arousal emboldened him. Stepping closer to Lucinda, he saw that her cheeks darkened, and her lashes fluttered uncontrollably. She was undoubtedly affected by him; her rapt, apprehensive expression begged him to kiss her. Her sparkling eyes held a world of promise. But she was holding fast to her belief that marriage was a prison sentence. And what Cosmo didn't know was whether his love could liberate her from that unfortunate conviction.

Lowering his head, he covered her lips with his. It was a long, sweet and tender kiss, sending shards of heat through Cosmo's lower body. Grasping Lucinda's shoulders, he drew her against his chest and held her tightly. She fit in his embrace like a glove, her body soft and supple in all the right places, her sweet perfume filling his senses.

His kiss deepened, and Lucinda responded. They clung to one another, their breathing jagged. Cosmo knew in that moment that he would do anything to win Lucinda's love. The idea of her marrying a man she didn't love was out of the question. He intended to have her.

Once, he had deemed himself unlovable, and unsuitable for marriage. But if he could win the love of Lucinda, truly the most virtuous and selfless woman he had ever known, he could win back his self-esteem. If Cosmo could convince Lucinda that his love was real, he might once again believe in his own worth.

She turned her head from him, a tear glistening in her eye. "You are too good for me, sir," she whispered, "I cannot love you."

"Because I have no money?" he growled, clasping her

upper arms. "If I had money, would you feel differently about me?"

She looked at him, her chin wobbling. "If you were the richest man in London, my feelings for you would be the same. The trouble is, Cosmo, my feelings are irrelevant. I am going to marry a rich man. And that is all there is to it."

Releasing her, Cosmo took a step back, his hands coiled at his sides. *"We shall see about that, Mrs. Partridge!"*

When the door slammed shut behind him, Lucinda's tears were unleashed. But her mind was made up, and there was no going back. She was going to marry, and she was going to marry well. What was it her mother said? *It's just as easy to love a rich man as a poor one.*

Not in this case, Lucinda thought, slumping dejectedly in her chair. Loving Sir Cosmo Fairchild was far easier than loving Mr. Pugh, Mr. Pavlov or Lord Wynne-Ascott. Yet, she couldn't afford to love Cosmo! Not only was he poor, but he reveled in it!

Brushing her hair furiously, she tried to think of all the reasons why Cosmo was poor husband material. He was handsome, that was true. But perhaps he was too handsome. Lucinda found it increasingly difficult to resist running her fingers through his shaggy grey hair. And every time he turned his deep chocolate eyes on her, she melted.

That sort of appeal hardly recommended him as a husband! Lucinda would constantly be watching the reactions of other women as they approvingly surveyed Sir Cosmo. With a shiver, she recalled her first husband, a handsome devil who turned the head of every tabby he passed. Unfortunately, he did more than turn their heads. Lucinda didn't want to relive *that* pain and agony! Which was precisely why marrying for money, rather than love, was a prudent move. She could marry any one of her three suitors and feel fairly confident that she could defend her territory.

Pinning up her hair, she thought of another reason why Cosmo was the wrong man to marry. Not only was he poor, but he seemed to revel in it. How he managed to wear such fine clothes, or remain on familiar terms with every maitre d' in Mayfair, she didn't understand. She supposed he was living above his means in a futile effort to impress her. Or perhaps he was banking on the future profits of his book. Either way, the bills would roll in someday, and unless Cosmo's exposé was a brilliant success, Lucinda couldn't comprehend how he would pay his creditors.

He would wind up so deep in dun territory, his head would be below ground. Lucinda certainly didn't need a man who was always dodging bill collectors. The mere thought of it made her stomach turn over.

Oh, he was bad marriage material all right! Lucinda ticked off the reasons. Finally, and most important, was his apparent disinterest in her plan to build a women's shelter. In all the times she had discussed her dreams of helping women less fortunate than she, Cosmo had barely uttered a word in response, much less voiced his approval or encouragement. Had he no compassion for those women? Or did he think Lucinda's idea was mere idle woolgathering?

It was of no moment what he thought. Staring at her reflection, Lucinda laid down her brush. The woman who stared back at her was hopelessly confused. Cosmo's kiss had shaken her to the very core. In his embrace, she had felt a quickening of her pulse and a depth of emotion she had never experienced. Her desire had been so strong, she had trembled with fear. If the world had stopped spinning at the very moment Cosmo said, "I love you," Lucinda would have been happy spending eternity in his arms.

But the world hadn't stopped spinning. Life would continue as it always had for Mrs. Lucinda Partridge. Bills would be incurred, and they would have to be paid. Young women like Clarissa would turn up on her doorstep in need of nourishment and succor. And Lucinda would do everything in her power to help them.

There was one thing Lucinda did intend to change about her life, though. From now on, she was going to rely on her brain, her logic and her power of reasoning to make the single most important decision of her life. Having followed her heart twice before, only to have it stomped on and crushed, she knew better than to place too much faith in a handsome man's whispered, *"I love you."*

She loved Sir Cosmo Fairchild. Hopelessly. But marrying him was strictly out of the question.

The next morning, Cosmo sat in a rented cab, waiting for the fashionable set to tumble from their beds. He was particularly eager that Wynne-Ascott rouse.

When, at the crack of eleven o'clock, the man did emerge from his town house, Cosmo surreptitiously followed him to Town. In his rented cab, he was inconspicuous as long as he remained a respectable distance behind Wynne-Ascott's gleaming coach-and-four. When the elegantly dressed lord entered Rymer's on Bond Street, Cosmo disembarked his rig and followed.

Wynne-Ascott wasted no time in seating himself. Kneeling before him was a small, beak-nosed man, coatless and bespectacled, and struggling in vain to remove the aristocrat's boots.

"I say, be careful, old man, you're bending my ankle in a most unnatural position!"

The toadish-looking man paused, nodded apologetically, then stood and turned his back to Wynne-Ascott.

Without comment, the lord thrust his boot between the other man's legs.

"Having difficulties, my lord?" asked Cosmo, by way of announcing his presence.

Grimacing, Wynne-Ascott glanced up. "Oh, hello, Cosmo. Damn nuisance, this is, having one's boots taken off at such an ungodly hour. Blast, my neck is still stiff from sleep, and I haven't had a bloody thing to eat! How's a man supposed to enjoy having his boots fitted under such appalling circumstances."

Cosmo clucked his tongue, then threw himself into a leather chair next to Wynne-Ascott's. "Hell if I know, man. Damned tragedy, if you ask me, that a man should suffer so to have a pair of boots fit to his feet."

"I'd rather have a tooth pulled!" Wynne-Ascott grunted as his left boot slid off, and the toad who was hanging on to it sailed halfway across the shop. "Good God, don't scrape the leather, man!"

Landing in a crumple, the little man held his customer's boot aloft.

"Thank God," Wynne-Ascott sighed.

His expression wary, the toad returned.

Wynne-Ascott's right foot was either swollen, or it had grown three inches since his last pair of boots had been cut. At any rate, dislodging the gleaming Wellington from his starboard oar proved considerably more challenging a venture than the previous operation. Much grunting, groaning and sweating ensued on the part of both Wynne-Ascott and Toad, but to no avail.

When, after several attempts to separate the lord from his right Wellington, it appeared boot and owner were destined to remain united, the impatient aristocrat propped the heel of his foot on the other man's posterior. He gave a vigorous shove. The boot slid off. Toad looked like he had been fired from a catapult.

"B'gads, now look what the idiot's done!" Wynne-

Ascott sighed, crossed his legs and rubbed his aching right foot. "Hope he hasn't knocked himself senseless. Wouldn't want to go through this ordeal again."

"Can't say as I blame you," murmured Cosmo.

The boot fitter lay on his stomach, head nestled between a row of wooden shoe lasts, unmoving.

After a moment, in which he determined that Wynne-Ascott had no intention of offering aid to the unfortunate boot fitter, Cosmo pushed out of his chair and crossed the floor of the tiny shop. Leaning on his cane, he bent and offered his hand to the prostrate man.

"Are you all right?" he asked.

Blinking, the man replied, *sotto voce,* "I hate him."

Cosmo leaned farther down. "Well, if it is any consolation, I do, too, though for vastly different reasons, I am sure. If I could afford to abandon his company completely and never lay eyes on him again, I should do so happily. But, I cannot. Nor can you, I suspect. So, up it is with you, Mr.—"

"Soleman. Not that *my lord* has ever asked." The little man scrambled to his knees, then lurched to his feet. Dusting himself off, he gave Wynne-Ascott a malicious stare.

"Well, Mr. Soleman. This is your lucky day." Cosmo clapped the man on the back and accompanied him to Wynne-Ascott's chair. "For I do believe that I am also in the market for some boots. Several pair of the finest your firm can produce!"

"Going to buy some boots, old man?" Wynne-Ascott's mouth dropped open. "What will Mrs. Partridge think when she sees how well shod you are? She'll know you've been bammin' her, won't she?"

Cosmo shrugged as he lowered himself into the chair. "Don't suppose it will matter much. By the time she sees these boots on my feet, she'll not be interested in my bank account."

An hour later, the men sat side by side in stocking feet and shirtsleeves. By this time Cosmo had ordered three pair of the most expensive boots a man could buy in London, but the price he would pay was well worth the goodwill his purchase invited.

Wynne-Ascott was in an uncommonly voluble mood after having his feet traced and the bumps on his toes mapped. Relaxing in his leather chair with a glass of sherry, he was happily positioned so that he could see every dandy who pranced down Bond Street. Content with his lot in life, the aristocrat began to chatter.

"Mrs. Sapho Drummond . . ." Cosmo took a pinch of the snuff offered by Wynne-Ascott. "Now there's an interesting woman."

"Interesting, yes, but have you ever seen such a climber! B'gads, sometimes I can practically feel her slippers on my shoulders."

"A user, is she? Why do you allow it, then?"

Wynne-Ascott tapped a small amount of brown powder on his inner wrist, inhaled it, and sneezed. After wiping his nose with Mr. Soleman's pocket square, he said nasally, " 'Tis a mutually convenient arrangement, I assure you, Sir Cosmo. Lady Drummond knows the most interesting people! Surrounds herself with military types, wealthy bankers, actors, singers and the most peculiar foreigners! One never knows whom one will meet in her salon. Hell, I've met some fine little bits of—"

"What's her husband like?" Cosmo asked.

"Rarely at home. On the road with Wellington, you know. Now there's a parvenu if I've ever seen one. But, a man of letters, from what I understand. And a prodigious letter writer. Sapho always has a ready supply of witty anecdotes about the viscount's personal habits, told with the greatest respect and affection, I assure you."

Cosmo busily reflected on Wynne-Ascott's description of Sir Drummond and his wife. With practiced nonchalance, he asked, "Lady Drummond ever been to France?"

"Says she spent her early years there, married to a marquis that got his head chopped off during the Terror. But I don't know if I believe it. After all, Sapho's a bit on the theatrical side, if you ask me."

"You aren't suggesting her stories are clankers, are you?" Cosmo laughed. "I wouldn't think she'd last very long among the *ton* if she wove too colorful a background for herself."

Mr. Soleman looked up with plaintive eyes. "Sorry to disturb you, my lord, but I've measured every inch of your foot as you sit at rest. I'm afraid I'll have to ask you to stand. Some feet spread out considerably when bearing weight. And I want your boots to fit perfectly."

Grumbling, Wynne-Ascott stood on the parchment form that Mr. Soleman laid on the floor. For a moment, conversation ceased while the boot fitter held a tape measure to the arch of Wynne-Ascott's flattened foot.

"Thank you," the little man said when he was finished.

Wynne-Ascott sat down. "Can't imagine how men wear ready-made boots, can you, Cosmo? I mean, how do they endure it?"

Exchanging looks with Mr. Soleman, Cosmo said, "Don't know, old man. Must be dreadfully boring to be poor."

"Or even worse—*a member of the merchant class!*"

Cosmo shuddered. "Too horrible to discuss. Let us change the subject, shall we?"

"Splendid idea! What do you think of that Pavlov fellow?"

"Thought you'd never ask! Far be it from me to be rude—mighty fine snuff, by the way, where'd you get it?—but Pavlov seems a pretty queer fellow to me. What do you think?"

"Got the snuff at Mr. Jake's in Cork Street, and Pavlov is more than rude, old man, he's a damned poor sport! Never takes a bet, never laughs at a good joke, and never gets in his cups! What do you think about that?"

"Rudeness personified," murmured Cosmo. Now that he had gained Wynne-Ascott's confidence, he thought to provoke the man's baser instincts. "I suppose Mrs. Partridge was correct when she characterized him as a brooding intellectual. According to her, he's a genius! Hell, she thinks he is one of the most talented musical conductors and librettists London has ever seen. I think she rather fancies him. What do you think about that?"

"Fancies him? Ivan Pavlov? That skinny little Frog?"

"*Frog?*"

"Speaks French all the time with Sapho! Drives me dotty. They think I can't understand!"

"Can you?"

"No!" cried Wynne-Ascott, jerking his foot so violently that Mr. Soleman fell over backward. "Damned rude, if you ask me, to speak a foreign language in my presence."

"But, I thought Pavlov was Russian."

Wynne-Ascott waved his hand. "I only know what I am telling you. I asked Sapho once where she met the blasted fribble and she only giggled. Thought for a while she was having a *romance* with him, if you know what I mean."

"I think I do," replied Cosmo. "Have you changed your mind, then? Do you still think they are conducting an alliance?"

Wynne-Ascott, lips swelled, shrugged his shoulders. "So she thinks he's a genius, does she? And you're a penniless romantic! That bounder Pugh has probably got her believing he's kind to dumb animals and generous to children! Damn it to hell, Cosmo, how am I going to convince her that I am the man she should give her affections to?"

"Pugh hasn't got a chance of winning her hand, my lord. And I've all but given up, too. I haven't the patience for this sort of competition. That leaves Pavlov as the only other contender for Lucinda's affection. I'm afraid it's the Russian you'll have to deal with now."

Slamming his fist into his open palm, the aristocrat spit out a stream of profanities. "Nasty little quiz, I'll show him!"

"What will you do?"

"I'll call him out if I have to!"

"On what grounds?" asked Cosmo.

After a pause, Wynne-Ascott answered, "On the grounds he nearly killed Lady Drummond."

Cosmo leaned closer to his new best friend and, in a herculean attempt to conceal his excitement, drawled, "Why, whatever do you mean by that?"

"Shouldn't have said that." Wynne-Ascott, face red, cleared his throat and gestured for Mr. Soleman to disappear. After the little man vanished, the aristocrat propped his elbow on his chair and cupped his hand over his mouth. If his effort was meant to hide his face, or prevent anyone from hearing what he said, it was in vain, for he looked every bit the tattling schoolboy posed to reveal a great secret.

As for himself, Cosmo was sure he looked every bit the spy receiving a bit of vital intelligence.

"Can you keep a secret?" Wynne-Ascott whispered.

"I had better be able to."

"Pavlov was shooting rats that night. The night Lady Drummond nearly took a bullet through her bosom."

"Damme, but I don't see how the Russian could mistake Sapho Drummond for a rat."

The lord gave out a bark of laughter. "Didn't I say he was a missish jackanapes? Can't even fire a pistol without losing control of it! According to Sapho, Pavlov was standing on the opposite side of the theater, behind the curtains. A rat ran across his foot and threatened to scamper out onto the stage. Thinking to prevent such an embarrassment, Pavlov pulled his pistol out and shot at the damned rodent."

Hardly able to suppress his incredulity, and amazed by Wynne-Ascott's gullibility, Cosmo shook his head. "A man would have to be a rather poor shot to aim for a rat and shoot at the upper box on the other side of the theater."

"Pavlov said a stage worker carting a piece of scenery bumped into him, causing his hand to jerk up. The gun discharged, and the bullet pierced the curtain, flew across the theater and embedded itself in the rear wall of Sapho Drummond's box."

"Damn lucky she was," remarked Cosmo. "Did she tell you all of this?"

"She had to. I saw her take Pavlov's pistol from him, and I asked a multitude of questions. Took me the better part of an hour to get the full story from the pair of them."

"And when did this exchange of weaponry take place?" Cosmo's blood was boiling with excitement. A picture of what was happening at the Orange Street Opera House formed in his mind. And it was a picture worthy of a cheap adventure novel. Imagine, a spy ring that included a wealthy socialite, a French spy, and a Russian traitor.

"Just after you left the box that night. You didn't know it, but I followed you to Lucinda's dressing room. Wanted to see for myself whether you were serious in courting my sweetheart. To my utter distress, I saw you go in as Mr. Pavlov left. I hid behind a corner, out of his sight, and watched him ascend the stairs. Went straight to Lady Drummond's box, he did, where he practically fell on his knees apologizing!"

"What else did you hear of their conversation?"

"That's all." Wynne-Ascott leaned back in his chair, obviously tired of sitting bootless and weary of gossiping about Mrs. Drummond, too. "Are you quite certain you've given up on Lucinda's suit?"

Cosmo merely smiled. "You don't think I'd bam you 'bout such a thing, do you?"

"All's fair in love and war," quipped Wynne-Ascott. To the reappearing Mr. Soleman, he added, "Can you add a cuff on those? I hear cuffs are all the crack nowadays."

Nodding, Mr. Soleman assisted the aristocrat in putting on his boots. Fortunately for all parties, the boots went on more easily than they came off. When Cosmo was reshod also, the two men emerged into the wintry afternoon and stood for the briefest of moments in front of Rymer's shop. Wynne-Ascott offered the use of his carriage, but Cosmo's rented cab awaited on the other side of the street. As it was too cold for further conversation, the men shook hands and bid one another *adieu*.

Cosmo headed toward the Home Office building, knowing that he should be pleased with himself for having uncovered a viper's nest of spies and traitors. Despite the satisfaction of having done his job well, an unrelenting ache gnawed at his heart. What was victory without the glory of love? What was life without Lucinda Partridge? And how was he going to convince the cynical lady that their love could last?

Fourteen

"Mr. Pugh. Yes, it will be Mr. Pugh, the dairy farmer." In her dressing room, Lucinda sat before her vanity table, clad in a Roman toga and gold sandals.

Clarissa stood behind her, piling her golden hair into loose coils on the top of her head. "Ye've changed yer mind a hundred times in the last three hours, Miz Partridge. Why don't ye just put their names in a hat and draw one out, fer pity's sake!"

"I can't do that, Clarissa. Can I?" Lucinda buried her face in her hands.

"Now, ye've got ta sit still, madame! How'm I s'posed to fix yer hair with ye squirmin' all over the place."

Lucinda straightened. "I'm sorry, Clarissa. But, how am I to choose which man I should marry."

"Follow yer heart."

A tear threatened to slide down Lucinda's cheek, but she stifled her emotions. It wouldn't do to get a frog in her throat just minutes before her performance. Her last performance, according to Mr. Pavlov, who had visited late that afternoon with the unpleasant news that *Julius Caesar* was being canceled.

"How can that be? The house is packed every night," Lucinda had argued.

But Pavlov was intractable. According to him, the production was losing money, and there was nothing to do but shut it down. Which meant Lucinda was out of employment and as much on the fringes of destitution as Clarissa was. Marrying for money was now an absolute necessity.

"Or perhaps I should marry Mr. Pavlov," Lucinda said, her expression solemn. What was the use in crying? She was a practical girl and had concluded long ago that crying was a frivolous way to spend her emotion. "He was terribly insistent this afternoon."

"A little too pushy fer me own tastes," noted Clarissa.

"What do you mean?"

The redheaded woman shrugged. "I heard most'a what he said. Oh, I know I shouldna' been listenin' at the door, but what was I s'posed to do, ignore me own ears? Anyway, I heard him tellin' ye to make a decision and make it tonight. Don't seem fair to me, that's all."

"He is only concerned for my welfare, Clarissa. And he renewed his promise to finance the women's shelter."

"What about our fancy lord, As-Wincot."

"Wynne-Ascott," Lucinda corrected. "And I don't think I should become his mistress, do you? After all, it wouldn't look right, would it, for the head of a charitable institution for fallen ladies to be one herself?"

Clarissa snorted. "We can cross him off our list, then, can't we?"

"And Mr. Pugh, too, I suppose." Lucinda sighed. "Upon my word, I do not think I could abide his *touching* me."

"Somethin' tells me he would want to, dearie."

"And I can not marry Cosmo because he hasn't any money."

"What difference does that make?" Clarissa stared hard at Lucinda's reflection.

"I wouldn't be able to build my women's shelter without a man to back me."

Clarissa stuck the final pin in Lucinda's hair, then

dropped her arms and stood with her fists on her hips.
"Fergive me fer sayin' so, Miz Partridge, but ye should
think about yer own happiness first. Fergit about buildin'
that shelter if it's Sir Cosmo yer wantin' to wed. He's a
fine-looking swell, and an honorable man, too! What's
more, he loves ye. I can tell by the way he looks at ye,
all cow eyes and hungry-like."

"Yes, I do believe he loves me." Lucinda's chest
ached, and she wondered if she would be able to sing
a note tonight. If she were choosing a husband based
solely on her feelings, it would be Cosmo. She loved him
so dearly that it pained her. Her pulse skittered like a
nervous horse every time he touched her, and her arms
ached to hold him close. When he kissed her, she was
happier than she had ever thought possible.

"Clarissa, I don't believe he even understands why I
want to build the shelter."

"Then, tell him. And tell him that ye love him."

"What good would that do? I cannot marry him!" Lucinda stood and paced her tiny dressing room. She
couldn't cry and she wouldn't. But her stomach was in
a knot from the effort it took to suppress her emotions.

"Do ye love him?" Clarissa asked softly.

Lucinda felt the woman's hands on her arms. Turning,
she sank into Clarissa's soothing embrace. Now this was
a switch, she thought, allowing herself to be comforted
by a woman whose life she had rescued on more than
one occasion. Clarissa was giving *her* advice! And, though
her brain tried to ignore that advice, Lucinda's instincts
listened.

"I do love him, Clarissa," she whispered, cheek nestled against the other woman's shoulder. "I love him
desperately."

"Then, marry him."

Lucinda shook her head. Confusion swirled like a tem-
pest inside her. She didn't know what to do. Should she

put her own happiness ahead of her plans to build a women's shelter? Was it wise to marry a man for love when love had betrayed her twice before? Could she marry a man who didn't share her dreams?

The knock at the door relieved her. Ivan Pavlov poked his head inside her dressing room and said, "There are some changes in tonight's libretto."

"But, Ivan, the translation is perfect. Why must you continue to tinker with it?"

From the dressing room next door, came Madame Bartoli's shrill voice. "I cannot memorize these lines in five minutes, you idiot!"

Ivan sighed his frustration, thrust a sheet of paper toward Lucinda, and said, "Truly, translating this opera from Italian is the most difficult project I have ever undertaken. I always want my libretto to be *perfect*. Please don't be difficult, like Cleopatra. The change in your part is very minor, my love. Indulge me."

"Yes, Ivan." Lucinda felt sorry for the Russian, always trying so hard to get the words just right, always incurring the wrath of the temperamental Madame Bartoli.

She smiled sadly at him as he closed the door and raced to placate the soprano next door.

Sir Milburn Sinclair had been astounded at Cosmo's full report. "This Mrs. Drummond . . . she has masterminded the entire spy ring?"

Cosmo stalked from one side of the richly appointed room to the other, nervous as a caged panther. "I haven't much time, sir. Henri LeFlaive recognized me last night. Chances are that he will have told Pavlov I saw him, too. They know we are closing in."

"Yes." Sinclair sat behind his desk, fingers steepled beneath his chin. "But, tell me, Cosmo, how did they pass along the messages to the Frog, er, I mean the Frenchman in the audience?"

Cosmo turned on his heel, a wicked smile tugging at his lips. "That is the part that is truly ingenious. Pavlov changed the words of the libretto every so often. It was a code, sir. A code that only Pavlov and the French spies understood!"

"Do you mean to tell me that Lucinda has been singing to the enemy all this time?"

"Without knowing it, she's been the conduit by which Pavlov has passed along the information he obtained from Mrs. Drummond."

"Wait till Wellington hears about this!" Sir Milburn stood from behind his desk and met Cosmo in the center of the floor. "There he is in Portugal, with a rat in his midst. If what you say is true—and I have no reason to doubt your deductions, Cosmo—that man is worse than a parvenu."

"He's privy to everything the viscount says and does. Could easily intercept any communication going to or from Wellington's camp. Sends the communiques to his wife in a letter, who passes them to Pavlov."

"Who changes the words to the libretto—"

"And thus sends the messages to the Frenchman in the audience," said Sir Milburn. "A capital scheme, if I must say so myself. You're a damn genius yourself, Cosmo, for cracking this case."

Cosmo felt like anything but a genius. Pounding one fist into his open palm, he cried, "Bloody Hell! The scoundrels should be hung by their toes for what they've done!"

"They very well might be," said Sir Milburn darkly. "If you hadn't apprehended this spy ring, there is no telling what sort of military information Boney may have acquired. As it is, he is slowly moving his troops away from the Iberian Peninsula, and focusing his attention on Russia. Up till now, his actions have seemed completely inexplicable."

"I suppose with the information he possesses, he knows he can't beat Wellington in Portugal."

"And he thinks we aren't prepared to engage him in Russia. That's what *our* spies tell us, anyway."

Cosmo ran his hand through his hair. His leg throbbed and his body ached. But worse than the physical pain he felt from the exertion and fatigue of having spent several nights awake, first watching Lucinda's door and then Wynne-Ascott's, was the soreness in his heart, the longing he felt to hold Lucinda in his arms. As soon as Drummond, Pavlov and LeFlaive were apprehended, he would go to her again and, if he had to, beg her to marry him.

Sir Milburn interrupted his thoughts with a discussion of more practical matters. "I shall send a few brutes over to the Drummond town house immediately. We'll pick her up with as little fanfare as possible, so that Pavlov and LeFlaive are not alerted to our actions before tonight's production."

"Yes. I would like to catch LeFlaive red-handed if possible. Perhaps he will have some incriminating evidence on his person. That will make our case watertight."

"Do you think you can get into Pavlov's office and see if there is any incriminating evidence there?"

Cosmo considered Sir Milburn's request. "It will be difficult. Ivan never leaves the opera house. And if LeFlaive has given him any hint that I recognized him, Pavlov will be waiting for me."

"If he hasn't already flown the coop," Sir Milburn said grimly.

The thought put Cosmo into action. There was no time to waste. LeFlaive might already have told Pavlov that Cosmo recognized him. When Drummond did not appear at the opera, the Russian would undoubtedly flee London as quickly as possible.

"I am off, then," he said to Sir Milburn and, after shaking the other man's hand firmly, strode toward the door.

As he crossed the threshold, the older man called out to him. "Oh, Cosmo. If you don't mind me asking, what do you intend to tell this Mrs. Lucinda Partridge? She is going to have some very pertinent questions herself when that Russian librettist is led away in shackles. We can't have her spilling it all over London that a spy ring was operating out of the opera house, you know. Could be embarrassing to the Crown."

"Don't worry about Lucinda," Cosmo replied, his heart racing at the thought of folding her in his embrace. "I shall not let her out of my sight until I am satisfied that she is a friend of the Home Office."

Sir Milburn's eyes twinkled. "You are a rogue, Cosmo. Damme, but I envy you!"

Inside his hackney cab, Cosmo had an impulsive notion. He rapped his cane on the trapdoor above his head and, when it opened, told the driver, "Old Tottenham Court Road, will you? And make it snappy, man!"

Descending in front of Madame Conte's, he was surprised to see that the shades on the shopfront were drawn. He tried the door, but it was locked. As he turned to leave, thinking that the modiste had closed her establishment due to illness, he heard voices and the bustle of activity from within.

His insistent knock brought nothing but silence, however. Very suspicious. Whoever was inside wanted no visitors.

Cosmo was not in the mood to be put off. He had come to get Lucinda's trousseau and pay for it. She had all but admitted that she couldn't afford to pay for such an expensive, extravagant wardrobe, but she thought it necessary to outfit herself for her new husband. Since Cosmo intended to be that new husband, it was only fitting he pay for her trousseau.

Another vigorous round of knocking elicited a scrabbling on the opposite side of the door. A thin voice from within said, "Who is there?"

"Sir Cosmo Fairchild. I am here on behalf of Mrs. Lucinda Partridge. She ordered up a trousseau and I wish to collect it."

"Never heard of the woman. Go away, we are closed."

"That's devilish odd! I saw her here just the other day! She's a pretty blonde, accompanied by a redheaded woman. You must remember her."

After a hesitation, the voice replied, "Go away, sir! We are closed permanently. I have nothing here that belongs to Mrs. Partridge!"

Thoroughly vexed, Cosmo had no choice but to return to his cab. Settled inside, he glanced out the window just as the carriage was pulling into the stream of traffic. A vaguely familiar figure approached Madame Conte's door. Cosmo's brain flashed on the image of the man he had seen leaving the modiste's shop just moments before Lucinda and Clarissa emerged. It was the same man, a big clod of a fellow with features like potato knobs, wearing a Bow Street runner's uniform! What the devil was he doing there?

Banging on the trapdoor, Cosmo yelled to his driver to halt. The cab jerked to a stop while Cosmo stared at the Bow Street runner knocking on Madame Conte's door. There was something very havey-cavey about this picture.

Upon reflection, Lucinda's behavior when Cosmo confronted her outside Madame Conte's shop had been very odd, too. Was the spy ring more complicated than

Cosmo had thought? Had he stumbled onto another strand of a spider's web much more intricate than he had realized?

He watched the runner look up and down the street. Words were apparently exchanged with the female voice on the other side of the door. Then the door opened a crack, and the big man slid inside.

Cosmo, every nerve in his body alert, scribbled a note to Sir Milburn. This certainly wasn't within the jurisdiction of the Home Office, but Milburn Sinclair knew every law enforcement officer in London. And the old man owed Cosmo a favor.

Passing the note through the trapdoor, Cosmo gave strict instructions to the driver regarding the delivery of his communication. Then he descended from his cab and watched it rumble down Old Tottenham Court. It wasn't in him to let even the smallest mystery go unsolved.

Where was Cosmo? Maintaining her concentration throughout the opera was difficult, especially considering Ivan's last-minute changes to the libretto.

Madame Bartoli's dark eyes flashed angrily as she stumbled through her own lines. In the second scene of the first act, where she usually sang,

> *O stars! You stay here;*
> *I am resolved*
> *to go to Caesar's tents . . .*

Pavlov had changed the words to,

> *O stars! Be silent and hide*
> *While I escape*
> *and return to Caesar's tents . . .*

It was a minor alteration, but Lucinda thought Ivan had tinkered with the libretto too much. Not only had he made Madame Bartoli angry, but the word changes he had instituted were difficult to sing. Moreover, they added nothing to the structure of the opera.

But, he was the opera's producer as well as her manager. Lucinda trusted Ivan Pavlov completely. So, when in the third scene of the second act, Caesar discovered that the woman he believed to be Lydia was actually Cleopatra, instead of singing,

These shores are an evil omen for us, Lucinda sang,
This cosmos poses mortal danger for us.

The words were awkward, and Lucinda had difficulty getting her mouth around them. Her voice cracked twice, causing the audience to stir restlessly. Yet, when her final aria was sung, and the curtain began to descend, her admirers showed their loyalty with a polite round of applause. One truly terrible night could not erase the months of memorable performances she had given them. Someone in the front row yelled, "We love Mrs. Partridge!" and the chant was taken up by the entire crowd.

Flowers and love notes littered the stage as the curtain finally touched the floor. Madame Bartoli, thoroughly disgusted with Pavlov's libretto changes, stomped from the stage. Lucinda hesitated, to sweep up a beautiful bunch of hothouse roses, then headed toward her dressing room.

She couldn't cease wondering where Cosmo was. His absence, more than Ivan's word changes, had ruined her performance. It struck her as odd, funny almost, that in all her years of singing, she had never enjoyed it as much as when she sang to Cosmo. His presence at the opera, his warm, intense gaze on her as she moved about the stage, had inspired her to some of her finest performances. If she never sang again, it would be because he had broken her heart.

Winding her way through the crowded corridors, she realized with a shock that her heart *was* broken. She had told Cosmo she didn't want to marry him, and so she had no right to want him back in her life. She had no business wondering where he was; indeed, he would have been a fool to sit in his box and gaze lovingly at her after she had rejected his suit.

But she couldn't help it. She loved him. It was the most impractical of emotions, but there it was. She hated herself for turning Cosmo away, yet she had done the right thing. She had sacrificed love for a greater good, the opportunity to help underprivileged women rehabilitate themselves. And she should feel good about that. Why, then, did she feel like someone had plunged a knife in her belly?

Stepping into her small dressing room, eyes downcast, she said, "Clarissa, will you put these flowers in water?"

Her question was answered by Ivan Pavlov's voice. "Ah, what pretty flowers, babushka. So becoming to a winter bride."

Lucinda's gaze shot up. Clarissa was nowhere to be seen. "Ivan, what are you doing here?"

"I have come to take you away, but you must change into something warmer before we begin our journey."

"I told you, I have not yet made my decision. Please leave." Lucinda tossed the flowers on a divan and crossed the room to her dressing table.

Quicker than she had ever thought possible, Ivan closed the distance between them. Grasping her arms, he gave her a little shake, then stared at her with a depraved intensity that made her blood run cold.

"There is not time to conduct a leisure *toilette*, Mrs. Partridge. We must hurry away from here. I am taking you to Gretna Green, where you will be married to me.

From there, we will honeymoon in Scotland, under assumed names, of course. Your precious Cosmo will not think to look for us there. No doubt, he will assume I've made haste for Dover and jumped the first ship to Callais."

Horrified, Lucinda gasped. "No, Ivan, I won't go with you!"

He tightened his grip on her arms and chuckled maliciously. "You have no choice, babushka. Try to escape and I shall kill you. Scream and I will strangle your pretty throat. If I cannot have you, no one will! Now, get behind that screen and change! Now!"

With a rough shove, he propelled Lucinda toward the tole screen on the other side of the room. Pulse pounding, she stepped behind it. Her mind reeled. In an instant, her entire world had tilted wildly. Ivan Pavlov wasn't the romantic intellectual she had taken him for. On the contrary, he was a dangerous madman who planned to force her into marriage. With trembling limbs, she began to undress, hoping against hope that someone—*Cosmo preferably*—would miraculously appear and rescue her.

Icy fingers closed around her ankle. Inhaling sharply, Lucinda looked down. Crouched on the floor, amidst a bank of filmy lingerie and plumed headdresses, was Clarissa.

The redheaded woman put her finger to her lips. Stepping out of her toga, Lucinda silently mouthed, "Find Cosmo!" Then she donned a dark-blue cambric morning gown with matching pelisse and hat. When she emerged from behind the screen, she wore a mask of dignity and bravery.

"I am ready," she said, detesting every inch of the man who stared back at her.

Ivan smiled. "Babushka, you look lovely. And I am glad to see you are resigned to your fate. I promise that

I will make you a good husband. Come, our carriage awaits, and we haven't any time to lose."

Lucinda accompanied him out the door, through the winding corridors and into a carriage parked in the rear alleyway. As the rig lurched down the street, picking up speed when it left the City borders, she watched the landscape slide by. Her hopes and dreams seemed as blurry as the bleak and wintry panorama outside her window. If Cosmo couldn't stop Ivan from carrying out his nefarious scheme, she would be Mrs. Ivan Pavlov before morning.

The irony of her predicament coiled like a viper in her gut. Just a few hours earlier, she had told Clarissa she would marry the Russian genius. Now Lucinda hated him. She hated him as much as she loved Cosmo. And that was an immeasurable amount.

She wanted Cosmo. She wanted *only* Cosmo. It all seemed so simple now. She should have agreed to marry him the moment he asked. They were meant for one another; they brought out the best in one another. But Lucinda had been too stubborn to realize it.

Brushing a tear from her eye, she marveled at her own stupidity. Was it too late to rectify her mistakes? Now that she was in the clutches of the evil Pavlov, Lucinda realized that being married to a man she didn't love would amount to hell on earth. How had she ever thought she could endure such a marriage? How had she ever thought she could live without Cosmo Fairchild?

She didn't even care if he was a penniless writer. She didn't mind if his book was a flop and he lived out his days a total failure. She didn't care if she had to take a position as a charwoman to support them both. Suddenly, Cosmo was her only salvation, her only prospect for happiness.

She only hoped Clarissa could find him in time to save her.

* * *

One of Sir Morton's men was kind enough to lend Cosmo his coach and driver. Pressing a wad of pound notes into the driver's hand, Cosmo barked his orders. "To the Orange Street Opera House, man, and be as quick as you can."

The driver did his best, practically running over drays and carts that impeded his rig. Cosmo counted every minute, fearful for Lucinda's safety. After all, if LeFlaive had already told Pavlov they were in trouble, there was no telling what desperate measures the men would take.

His experience at Madame Conte's had been a revelation. When Sir Morton's men arrived, they stormed the shop. The scene they discovered there was damning in the extreme. Young girls carrying heavy bolts of fabric out the back door and loading them into a wagon. Underfed women packing boxes of patterns and sewing implements. Clearly, Madame Conte was fleeing her shop. Her illegal sweatshop was moving to a new location.

The Bow Street runner was as corrupt as they came. By the time Cosmo had finished interrogating him, threatening all sorts of inhumane punishment if the man didn't tell the truth, he had pieced together the mystery.

Lucinda hadn't furnished her name to the runner, but he knew her by description. The burly man had responded to a complaint she made to the magistrate after Madame Conte literally worked one of her girls to death. But he had made a backdoor visit to Madame Conte before Lucinda and Clarissa arrived.

Conte had paid him well for his tip. By the time Lucinda gained access to the shop, the modiste and her girls were gone. They would come back later for their inventory, but they would never answer to Lucinda's charges.

Or so Madame Conte had thought.

Cosmo hadn't thought it possible, but he loved Lucinda Partridge even more than he did before. At last, he understood her need to open a women's shelter. He had seen the faces of those young girls when Madame Conte was led away in shackles. His heart had ached at the resignation in their expressions, the despair in their weary gazes. He had fought the urge to take every one of them home, feed them, and properly clothe them.

But Lucinda's way was better. She had thought it through. She would build a place where women could find refuge and rehabilitate themselves. She would help these unfortunate women help themselves.

And he would do everything in his power to help her.

The carriage jolted to a stop in front of the opera house. A streak of pain shot up Cosmo's right leg as he leapt to the ground, but he made his way to Lucinda's dressing room with surprising speed. Now he could honestly say he shared Lucinda's hopes and dreams. Now he knew what it would take to win her heart.

Clarissa scrambled to her feet just as the dressing room door shut behind Lucinda and Ivan Pavlov. It was sheer luck that she had been behind the screen, bending to pick up Lucinda's fallen stockings, when Pavlov entered. Watching him through the cracks in the tole panels, Clarissa had recognized the evil look on his face. Instinct told her to conceal her presence.

Her quick thinking had paid off. Clarissa knew exactly what to tell Cosmo, if she could locate him. Gasping with pain, she scuttled across the room. After huddling behind that screen for nearly an hour, she could hardly walk. But sore muscles and scraped shins wouldn't prevent her from searching all of London if that was what it took to find Cosmo Fairchild. She grabbed her coat, prepared to set out into the blistering cold night.

As it turned out, she didn't have to cross the floor before Lucinda's door burst open, and Cosmo strode into the room.

"Where is Lucinda?"

His eyes were black as black could be. Clarissa shook with fright, knowing that his rage would flare when he learned what Ivan Pavlov had done.

Indeed, when he heard her speech, Cosmo's anger was unfathomable. But instead of bursting with violence, he became oddly and menacingly quiet. Then he shot through the door as if the devil were behind him.

Clarissa sat in Lucinda's chair and stared at herself in the mirror. She was happy knowing that Lucinda would be rescued by the man she loved. Maybe now the beautiful soprano would come to her senses and marry the right man.

Fifteen

Lucinda sat opposite Ivan Pavlov on the hard squabs of his carriage. She gripped the seat beneath her thighs as the rig rocked precariously along the pitted roads leading north from London. Her captor had hired an extremely fast coach and professional postilions who would get their passengers to Gretna Green as quickly as possible, then serve as witnesses to their marriage.

At length, partly from boredom, partly from curiosity, she broke the silence. "How long have you been planning this little caper?"

Pavlov's face, lit by the ghostly glow of the outer lanterns, split in a cadaverous grin that filled Lucinda with loathing and dread. But she refused to let the dastardly man know how frightened she was.

"I'm afraid it was your friend Sir Cosmo who precipitated this hasty development, Mrs. Partridge. You see, when he recognized Mr. LeFlaive in the audience, I knew I hadn't much time."

Puzzled, Lucinda waited silently for Ivan to continue. Like most criminals whose evil deeds had been discovered, he had a compulsion to explain his motives.

"I am not a bad man, babushka. In time I hope you will realize that. But I pledged my allegiance to France many years ago. It was a heady time, during the early years of the Revolution. Many of us who wore the cockade then still support Bonaparte with all our heart, you know."

Shivering from cold, Lucinda managed to nod.

His gaze took on a dreamy look. "Ah, we were so idealistic then. I thought opera should be sung only in Italian! Imagine my humiliation when I was forced to take employment in an English opera house where the owners insisted the librettos be translated to English!"

"You always told me you wanted to translate the words into English so that a wider audience could enjoy the music. Besides, I thought you were rich, Ivan. Why were you forced to seek employment anywhere?"

"I am rich now, yes. But I was poor when I arrived in London. Selling English military secrets is how I earned my wealth. And I could not have done it without you, Mrs. Partridge. When you become my wife, you will share in the spoils of our endeavors!"

Gasping, she pulled her lap blanket more tightly around her. "You're selling English military secrets to the French?"

"I am no more despicable than your precious friend, Cosmo Fairchild, who spies for his country."

"Cosmo, a spy?" Lucinda's head ached, but the more she thought about it, the more she believed it.

Pavlov relished her confusion and shock. "You were an integral part of Sapho Drummond's network, Mrs. Partridge. Without your assistance—"

"Lady Drummond is a spy, too?" After a beat, Lucinda said, "But, I never assisted you!"

"You sang to the spies in the audience, babushka. Each time I revised the libretto, I changed the message sent to my fellow Frenchmen. It was all in code, very complicated! Tonight, for example, you told Mr. LeFlaive to leave London. You didn't know it, but you were the prettiest messenger the French spies have ever employed."

It took a moment for that bit of intelligence to sink into Lucinda's brain. She had been an unwitting dupe. Shaking her head, Lucinda murmured, "Why didn't you just pass written notes to people like Mr. LeFlaive. Wouldn't that have been easier?"

"On most occasions, I didn't know the identity of my conspirators. That is the beauty of the network Lady Drummond devised. None of us were to know the names and faces of the others; it is safer that way. LeFlaive made himself known to me only when he recognized Cosmo in the opera box with Lady Drummond."

"And you didn't know Cosmo was a spy till then?"

"Oh, Lady Drummond had her suspicions. She has friends in the Home Office, you know." Pavlov stroked his beard. " 'Twas she who decided he should be removed from the picture. Precisely the way I got rid of Clappford, that other British agent who fancied he was on to me. When I realized Fairchild was courting you, and that you were silly enough to return his affections, I quite agreed with Sapho. Getting rid of Fairchild was like killing two birds with one stone, as far as I was concerned."

"Why didn't you leave London earlier? When you first suspected the British Home Office was on to you?"

"Cosmo did not know who the spies were until he saw Mr. LeFlaive and followed the proper trail. Until then, he was simply nosing around. Just before tonight's performance, I received word that Lady Drummond had been arrested. I knew then that my time had run out. That is why I had to warn LeFlaive and get out of town immediately. I only hope that waiting for you, Mrs. Partridge, won't mean the end of me."

Lucinda wasn't certain whether it was the motion of the carriage, or the staggering impact of Ivan's confession, that made her stomach feel like it was free-falling. She could hardly believe her ears.

But everything Ivan said made sense, didn't it? Cosmo had never intended to write a book about her; he had appeared at the opera for quite another reason. Stunned, she thought of his expensive suits and extravagant spending habits. So, he wasn't a penniless writer, after all. She didn't know whether to be angry because he had misrepresented himself, or pleased because he wasn't destitute after all.

If he wasn't destitute, she might yet marry him.

But, if he wasn't destitute, then why had he never offered to help finance her women's shelter?

Hundreds of questions swirled in Lucinda's mind. More than anything, she wanted to see Cosmo for herself and ask him what *his* motivation was. Ivan's state of mind should be the least of her concerns.

Still, the man seemed intent on baring his soul. For a half hour, as the carriage tore down the road at breakneck speed, he described how he met Lady Drummond in Paris, and how he befriended her and a loose-knit group of French sympathizers who were willing to spy for Boney when he became emperor.

In London, Pavlov joined the Orange Street Opera House because he knew he could revise and alter the librettos to his heart's content without interference from the owners. A more serious opera management company would have objected to his constant switching of the lyrics.

"So, did you actually try to get my contract extended?" Lucinda wondered.

He laughed. "Mrs. Partridge, you could have sung at the opera as long as you liked! It took a lot of effort to get you out of your contract!"

Her anger resurfaced. "But, why—"

"Because I wanted you to marry me. If you had no money, you would be more inclined to consider my suit. I didn't need you at the opera house as much as I wanted you in my bed. Madame Bartoli could sing my messages as well as you!"

Swallowing her hatred of the man, Lucinda remained silent. With each revolution of the carriage wheels, however, her hopes of being rescued sank. Feeling quite a bit sorry for herself, she struggled not to cry. She would not marry Ivan Pavlov if he were the last man on earth. And if she had to kill him to prevent that from happening, she would.

"We are traveling at a mighty fast pace, Ivan. Do you think you should instruct the driver to slow down? This is terribly dangerous."

Ivan swayed with the carriage. "It is best we get to Scotland as quickly as possible."

Outside the night was pitch-black, relieved only by a crescent-shaped sliver of moon. The cattle gobbled up the ground, skimming over potholes, leaning into dangerous curves like race horses. Even if Clarissa did find Cosmo before the night was over, there was simply no way he would be able to overtake Pavlov's swift equipage.

Amazingly, the Russian drifted to sleep, chin on chest. Lucinda remained awake, alert and fearful, desperately trying to devise a way to escape.

She could open the door and throw herself out.

For a long time, she stared at the brass handle and considered her options. The horses had barely slowed since leaving London. A leap into the night might result in a broken neck. But marriage to Ivan would be a *slow death,* a fate far worse than anything Lucinda could imagine. If she was going to die, she would rather it be quickly.

Slowly, she edged down the length of the squabs. In his sleep, Ivan snorted. His body jerked. Lucinda nearly jumped out of her skin. It was another moment before her breathing and heart rate normalized. Then, peering out the window, she reached for the handle. A strip of pockmarked road was visible; beyond the glow of the lanterns there was only blackness.

Suddenly, beneath the thunder of the horses' hooves, and the rumble of the carriage wheels, she heard something else. Her ears pricked, and she leaned closer to the door. Ivan remained asleep, oblivious to the sound of cattle and carriage coming up behind them.

Lucinda's pulse skipped like a happy child. Holding her breath, she prayed Ivan would remain asleep and that the carriage behind would soon overtake them. *Oh, dear God, please let it be Cosmo!* she screamed silently.

But her hopes were quickly dashed. Overhead, she heard the driver curse, then lash his horses to a faster speed. The carriage rocked wildly, startling Ivan. Shaking himself awake, he realized at once what was happening. Lifting the trapdoor above him, he called to the driver, "Faster man! Let that bastard overtake us, and I'll shoot you and every one of your crippled nags!"

"God's teeth, I'm whippin' the beasts as 'ard as I can widdout killin' 'em!"

"Well, whip them harder!" Ivan yelled, landing in his seat with a thud as the carriage skidded over a deep trough.

But the carriage behind closed the distance quickly, its horses having the advantage of a forward light to guide their way. As Ivan cursed and threatened, the thunder of hooves and wheels grew to a din.

"He is on our tail!" At last, the Russian, unwilling to accept defeat, withdrew a small pistol from his inside coat pocket.

"So, you are the one who fired at Cosmo the night he took me to dinner!" Lucinda hoped to get him talking again.

His eyes glowed like a Bedlamite's. "Your Cosmo has proved a difficult target, but I shall kill him this time.

Just like I killed that other little English spy who stumbled onto Drummond's network!"

"You are an evil man, Ivan, and you shall pay for your misdeeds!"

"Hush, woman. If that idiot Englishman runs us off the road, we will all be killed."

At that moment, the carriage hit a stretch of deeply pitted road. The wheels crashed onto the hard earth, then bounced. For an instant, the body of the rig was suspended in air while, inside the compartment, Ivan and Lucinda floated weightless, their bodies disconnected from the squabs, their feet quite unglued from the floor. Unable to suppress her fear, Lucinda screamed. When the carriage wheels hit ground again, she found herself in Ivan's lap.

His bearded face nuzzled the crook of her neck.

"Don't you touch me!" Lucinda squirmed violently, batting at Ivan with her fists and kicking as hard as she could.

His strength was surprising. "You might as well give in. Eventually, you will grow accustomed to my embrace, and, in days to come, I venture to say you will even enjoy my touch."

The carriage jolted again, and Lucinda's head nearly touched the ceiling. Somehow, Ivan's arms remained fastened firmly about her waist. Despite her struggles, she could not free herself.

"I will never enjoy your touch!" Lucinda managed to turn and slap Ivan full in the face. "Release me, you pig!"

Stunned at first, Ivan then burst into laughter. "You seem to like it rough, babushka! How delightful!"

Before she knew what was happening, Ivan tossed her to the opposite squab and threw himself on her. As he did, a loud thud was heard on the roof of the carriage.

Footsteps pounded above them.

"Thank God, it is Cosmo!" Lucinda whispered.

The Russian's body went still. Then, as the trapdoor slid open, he looked up.

Cosmo stared down into the compartment, while over his shoulder, the crescent moon shone.

"How in the hell—" Ivan gulped.

"You are a dead man," replied Cosmo quietly.

Something like astonishment widened the features of Lucinda's attacker. Rolling off her, he fumbled for his pistol, but in his lust, he had left it on the other seat cushion. His gaze fastened on the weapon just as Cosmo slid through the open aperture.

Ivan lunged for his gun. Cosmo, landing heavily on his bad leg, stumbled against the side of the compartment. The Russian's fingers closed around his pistol, and turning, he leveled it at Cosmo. A shot rang out, and the glass window beside Cosmo's head exploded.

"You are one damned lousy shot," Cosmo said, smoothly drawing his own pistol from inside his coat. Firing once, he shot Ivan Pavlov in the heart. The man slumped over, quite dead, and aside from Cosmo catching her in his arms as she fainted, that was the last Lucinda remembered about that fateful night.

Epilogue

Much of what happened following Lucinda's rescue was told to her later, when she regained consciousness.

After dispatching Pavlov to his Maker, Cosmo quickly commandeered the carriage and instructed the driver to stop at Carlisle, a tiny village just ten miles from Gretna Green. There, he rented separate quarters for himself and Lucinda. With the help of an innkeeper's wife, he tucked the insensate soprano into bed. Shock and fatigue had taken their toll; it would be morning before Lucinda awakened.

While she slept, Cosmo made arrangements for Pavlov's body to be returned to England. Then he rented a fresh coach, a driver and professional witnesses. Only after he had made the necessary arrangements for transportation to Gretna Green did he knock on the door of Lucinda's room.

At the sound of his gentle rapping, she called, "Come in!"

Wrapped in a woolen gown three sizes too big, Lucinda lay against a bank of fluffy pillows. A tattered patchwork quilt and a vigorous fire in the hearth had warmed her bones and put a little color in her cheeks. Cosmo thought she looked angelic, her blond hair spread across the pillow, her blue eyes sparkling.

Carefully, he sat on the side of her bed and took her hand in his. "Are you all right, Mrs. Partridge?"

The sound of his voice soothed her. Lucinda reached for him and, unable to satisfy her need to touch him everywhere, contented herself with running her fingers through his shaggy grey hair. With a sigh, she laid her palm on his bristly cheek.

"I should have known, Cosmo." Filled with emotion, her voice cracked.

"Should have known what, love?"

Staring into his black eyes, Lucinda saw the world of hurt that remained there. For an instant, she wondered if she could ever furnish Cosmo with enough love to heal those wounds. Perhaps not, she thought. But she would spend her life trying. "I should have known that it was you who loved me."

He nodded. "I tried not to."

"Why, Cosmo?"

A long moment passed before he answered. When Cosmo finally spoke, his voice was thick with suppressed emotion. "Once before, I thought I was in love, Lucinda. Well, I suppose I *was* in love—"

His pained expression was almost more than Lucinda could bear. "You don't have to tell me," she whispered.

Clutching her fingers tightly, he bowed his head. "But I must tell you. You see, I felt as though I had never been loved simply for myself. Truly loved, that is. I thought if you knew the truth about me, that I wasn't a penniless writer, you would cease caring about my friendship and begin seeing me as a, well, as a sort of—"

Lucinda's gaze lowered; a sense of guilt and shame washed over her. She had been heartless, and if Cosmo accused her of being a fortune hunter, she could hardly blame him.

"Ivan told me that you are not a penniless writer. He told me many things about you, Cosmo. None of them

altered my true feelings toward you because I loved you
from the beginning, I think. As a friend at first, that's
true. But I couldn't help comparing you to my other
suitors. The thought of marrying any one of them was
dreadfully frightening when I considered how dearly I
wanted to be with you. I don't think I realized how
empty a loveless marriage would be until I met you, and
loved you."

"If you had known from the beginning that I wasn't
poor, Lucinda . . ." Cosmo's voice trailed, but his pierc-
ing gaze looked deep into Lucinda's soul.

She answered as candidly as she could. "I suppose I
would have considered you a potential husband long before now. But, if you tell me this minute, Cosmo, that
you are destitute, I won't leave you. I mean that. I love
you, and I don't care what you are, or what you've done
in the past. I suppose I have learned much these past
few weeks. Needing you has made me a better person,
Cosmo."

"You are the finest woman I have ever met, Lucinda."

"You didn't always think so." She gently squeezed his
hand.

"No, I thought you would turn out to be like someone
else I once knew. There was another woman, Lucinda,
before you." He hesitated, unsure how to proceed. After
a harsh, rueful laugh, he sighed. " 'Twas unfair of me
to be angry with you for what she did. And I was a fool
to judge you based on my previous tragic love affair."

"Neither of us is without fault, Cosmo. But our per-
ceptions of one another are filtered through our past
experiences. We mustn't be too hard on ourselves."

"Can you forgive me for betraying you, Lucinda?"

"For using me to draw out a spy, you mean? Well . . ."

He drew her fingertips to his lips. "I love you more
than my own life, Lucinda. I couldn't bear it if you sent
me away. But, I would understand."

"Can you forgive me, Cosmo, for being so blind? For continuing on my silly husband hunt when the most wonderful man in the world was right beneath my nose?" Lucinda looked as deeply inside him as the man would permit.

The mystery behind his gaze drew a frown to her lips. "What is it? Come now, you must tell me. If I am going to be your husband, we cannot have any secrets between us."

"Something tells me you will always be full of secrets, Cosmo."

His rather sad smile did not deny it.

At length, Lucinda said, "If we are to be married, we must also understand one another's dreams, Cosmo. Since I have known you, I have talked about nothing but building a women's shelter. Still, you have yet to utter a word of encouragement regarding the matter."

"That was before I met Madame Conte."

Lucinda listened in amazement as Cosmo told of the wicked modiste's arrest. When he was finished, she clapped her hands and cried, "Oh, Cosmo, you are truly my hero!"

"No, Lucinda, you are *my* hero. Like Caesar, you came, you saw and you conquered . . . *my heart, that is.*" Leaning forward, he wrapped her in his embrace and kissed her.

"Will you ever tell me how you hurt your leg?" she whispered against his ear.

Hellish memories of his battlefield experiences rushed back to Cosmo. "I was shot in Spain . . ." he began. And as his story unfolded, Lucinda held him more tightly in her arms.

When he had finished, Cosmo was amazed to find that while the pain of his memories remained, the black despair in his soul had somehow dwindled. It was as if

Lucinda had absorbed some of his grief, and in doing so, lessened his anguish.

Later that afternoon, Lucinda and Cosmo traveled to Gretna Green and were married at a typical blacksmith's establishment. Returning to London as a married couple, they set up house in St. Alban's Street.

Without Pavlov's interference, Lucinda quickly renewed her contract at the opera house where *Julius Caesar* ran for another year. By that time, the soprano and the spy had saved enough money to open the Fairchild-Partridge Shelter for Women.

And while Lucinda ran the daily operations of the charitable organization, Cosmo supported his wife and young daughter with his earnings as high-ranking administrator in the British Home Office.

For the rest of their lives, and after, Cosmo and Lucinda never ceased loving one another.